The Trials and Tribulations of a Confederate Soldier

The Trials and Tribulations
of a Confederate Soldier

Richard G. Zevitz
Michael C. Braswell

RESOURCE *Publications* · Eugene, Oregon

Resource Publications
A division of Wipf and Stock Publishers
199 W 8th Ave, Suite 3
Eugene, OR 97401

The Trials and Tribulations of a Confederate Soldier
By Zevitz, Richard G. and Braswell, Michael
Copyright © 2012 by Zevitz, Richard G. All rights reserved.
Softcover ISBN-13: 978-1-6667-7596-9
Hardcover ISBN-13: 978-1-6667-7597-6
eBook ISBN-13: 978-1-6667-7598-3
Publication date 11/10/2023
Previously published by Branden Books, 2012

This edition is a scanned facsimile of the original edition published in 2012.

Dedicated to the thousands of prisoners
on both sides who lost their lives during
the American Civil War, 1861-1865.

CONTENTS

FOREWORD

One of the most overlooked military campaigns of the American Civil War was a two month long siege waged by the North at Madrid Bend, a tristate area of vast strategic importance located on the Mississippi River. It was the setting for an important struggle between the North and the South for control of that vital waterway and the upper Mississippi Valley. Overshadowed by Union Brigadier General Ulysses S. Grant's hard-fought victories at Forts Henry and Donelson and by the bloodbath that was Shiloh, what transpired at Madrid Bend in March and April of 1862 was of keen interest to the American public on both sides of the conflict.

Although largely ignored by historians, the military events that took place during the river wars – culminated with the Confederate losses of Memphis, New Orleans, and Vicksburg, exposing the South's heartland to the North's armies.

The combined Federal army and navy operations at Madrid Bend extended from New Madrid, Missouri all the way to Island No. 10—so named because it was the tenth island below the mouth of the Ohio River where that river joined with the Mississippi at Cairo, Illinois. Island No. 10 was regarded as among the most formidable fortresses faced by any army during the Civil War. When it was finally wrested from Confederate control, 4400 Southerners were captured and transported to prison camps in the North. One such prison was Camp Randall in Madison, Wisconsin.

A dark chapter in the four year Civil War saga was the mistreatment of prisoners held by both sides during the war. In sheer numbers alone, the great suffering and senseless loss of life endured by thousands of captured soldiers detained in enemy military prisons provide a striking example of man's inhumanity to his fellow man. In the prison camp at Andersonville in southwest Georgia, nearly one in three Union army prisoners perished. At Camp Douglas in Chicago, so many Rebel prisoners died there that a nearby graveyard soon became the largest Confederate burial site outside of the South. Camp Randall was not much better and in some respects even worse.

In searching for the causes of the inhumane conditions that led to its early closing by the U.S. War Department, historical research has revealed a cast of interesting lesser known characters who fought in the Civil War. The Spears brothers, Confederate soldiers from Choctaw County, Alabama, lived and died at Camp Randall. They were captured when Island No. 10 fell. This is their story and the story of an unlikely bond of friendship between one of the brothers, Corporal George Spears, and Lieutenant Eli Forrest, nephew of Nathan Bedford Forrest that brings this book of fiction to life.

This book is presented as a work of fiction. Names, characters, places and incidents, although set during the American Civil War and based in many instances on historical figures who lived and played a role in events of that war, are to be taken by readers as the products of the authors' imagination.

THE FALL OF FORT HENRY

War clouds gathered along the rivers bordering the western front of the Confederacy. There is something about the look and flow of a river. It moves as it will, sometimes in a meandering dance of pastoral seduction on a lazy summer afternoon. Just as quickly, it can turn about into a relentless torrent of wind and rain, reclaiming fertile fields and lives of strangers.

Fort Henry on the Tennessee River and Fort Donelson on the Cumberland protected the mighty Mississippi and the rebel fortress on Island Number Ten from the blue flood that was gathering upstream. The Mississippi was as the Native Americans had named it—the father of waters—for it represented in many ways, the lifeblood that kept the heart of the Confederacy beating. New Orleans, Memphis, Vicksburg and other port towns and cities fed the arteries that nourished Southern armies and civilians alike. The men in gray defended it from the men in blue who wanted it, but the men in blue had a plan. Like an enormous, magical snake, the "Anaconda Plan" would move through the Tennessee and Cumberland rivers into the Mississippi, slowly strangling the Confederacy by blockading and capturing rebel forts and ports of call that fell in its path.

On the morning of February 6, 1862, a combined force of armored Union gunboats and 15,000 Union troops under the command of Brigadier General Ulysses S. Grant was coiled and ready to strike. The first target was a point where the Cumberland and Tennessee Rivers closed to within ten miles of each other, just below the Kentucky state line, but within the territory of secessionist Tennessee. From here, the two rivers flowed northward in parallel courses until they fed into the Ohio River. Fort Henry guarded the Tennessee River, while Fort Donelson controlled the Cumberland River eight miles to the east. Resting on the fate of these two rebel fortresses was the question of whether or not Confederate forces would succeed in planting their northern line on the Ohio River. The South's military leaders knew that failure to halt a Federal advance along the two rivers would expose the flank of the Confederate army in West Tennessee. Would they be able to hold back the blue flood? The question was about to be answered.

The rider pulled his rain-soaked, exhausted horse to a halt in front of the headquarters of Major General Albert Sidney Johnston, Commander of the Confederate Western Department. Covered with mud, the bleary-eyed courier handed a leather pouch to a confederate officer who hurried inside.

"Damn it all to hell!" bellowed Johnston, shaking the rolled up communiqué at his general staff. "We've lost Fort Henry which means the Kentucky line has been broken."

General Johnston slammed his fist on the desk in front of him. "It may be too late to re-establish the line, but by God, we've got to plug the hole."

Hardee put his coffee cup down. "Just last week, Tilghman assured us he had the situation in hand. With 17 guns and almost 3000 men, he should have been able to hold out longer—at least until we could get him some reinforcements."

"What were the Union numbers?" Colonel Munford asked. "Any ironclads involved?"

General Johnston stared at the rain falling steadily outside, his hands clasped behind his back. "There were four ironclads. Grant started landing troops just north of the fort. Several days later, the ironclads showed up."

"Still, with more than a dozen artillery batteries...," Colonel Munford continued.

General Hardee interrupted the Colonel, "The report two weeks ago indicated that because of flooding, the six lower batteries were under water. So General Tilghman only had 11 guns in working order."

Munford persisted. "That may be the case, but it's hard to believe Tilghman didn't have enough fight in him to even hold out for a day."

"That's enough, gentlemen. What's done is done. The only good news coming out of this mess is that most of the garrison evaded capture." Albert Sidney Johnston's jaw was set in a way his general staff was familiar with.

"We've got to make the best of a bad turn of affairs and we have to do it quickly. The more troops we can get to Fort Donelson, the better chance we have to stop that infernal Grant."

Turning to his adjutant, the Commanding General pointed to the map in front of him. "Get a dispatch to Gideon Pillow at Clarksville. I want him to move his 8000 troops near Fort Donelson and begin preparing a defensive position for a land-based attack."

Pointing to Colonel Munford, General Johnston continued. "Edward, arrange for a detachment of Starkweather's Cavalry and some supply wagons to make contact with the troops coming from Fort Henry and hurry them along to the Donelson staging area."

When the last assignment had been given, General Johnston ran his right hand through his thinning hair and looked at his officers. "Gentlemen, time is short. We have a long night ahead of us. Let's make the most of it."

Private George W. Spears had found himself at Camp Duncan in Clarksville in late January of 1862. He was one of 8,000 Confederate soldiers ordered to reinforce Fort Donelson. Spears was a long way from his home in Alabama and the unit he had enlisted with. When he came down with a bad case of the grippe, he had become too sick to travel with his Alabama regiment so he had been left behind in a military hospital to recuperate. Now Private Spears was without his comrades, assigned instead to a local Tennessee regiment under a colonel he didn't know. Still, he was glad to be out of the hospital, sitting on a tree stump and breathing the brisk morning air.

"You got any tobacco?"

George Spears stood and turned to face a smiling Confederate officer. Standing close to six feet tall, the man Spears observed had a tanned face with dark, deep-set eyes which seemed to be full of mischief. His hair was black and collar-length and like many of the officers at Clarksville, he wore a short, well-trimmed beard.

"I reckon I got a twist of chewing tobacco left in my knapsack."

"Might you be willing to spare a small plug for a man in great need of a chew?" the officer continued.

"Reckon so," George replied, rising to his feet while foraging through his knapsack.

George handed the twist to the officer. "Here you go."

Cutting off a modest chew with his pocket knife, the officer returned what remained of the twist to the private. "Name's Elijah Forrest—my friends call me Eli," the officer said, extending his hand to Spears. "I'm a lieutenant in this here regiment. Used to be a captain—now I'm a lieutenant. Much obliged for the tobacco."

George shook Forrest's outstretched hand. "Well, then, you're welcome Lieutenant."

"What's your name, private and where you from?"

"George Spears, Sir. I hail from Alabama. Just outside a small town 'bout a day's ride north of Mobile."

The lieutenant spit a stream of tobacco juice. "That so? I was in Mobile once. Still remember the smell of salt, sea air. Myself, I was born in Mississippi. Before the war, I lived in Memphis."

"Tell you what, George. I happen to be in possession of a fine bottle of good Kentucky bourbon. After supper, why don't you meet me down by the creek next to the sentry station for an evening sip before we turn in. Tomorrow's gonna be a long day so a little refreshment seems to be in order."

George stammered, "I don't know, Sir. I mean…you know. You bein' an officer and all—a lieutenant and me bein' a private."

Eli Forrest laughed, "Well then, that's an order, Private. And another thing, don't ever call me 'Sir' again, unless we're in the presence of other officers. Like I said, I used to be a captain. Actually rode with 'Jeb' Stuart's cavalry in Virginia and now I'm a lieutenant in the infantry in Tennessee. At the rate I'm going, I'm likely to end up being a private before this war's over."

Still laughing, Forrest sauntered off toward the officer's mess. "See you after supper."

George Spears shook his head in disbelief. He had never met an officer like Eli Forrest. The call for morning drill went out. He headed back to retrieve his musket.

A full moon did little to take the chill off a late January night. Spears and Forrest were both bundled up as they stood on the bank of Shepherd's Creek.

George Spears looked at the man standing across from him, uncorking a bottle of whiskey.

"Sir, I don't really drink that much. I mean…"

Eli Forrest looked at Spears. "What's my name?"

"Lieutenant…I mean, Eli."

"That's better. I'm Eli and you're George."

Eli turned the bottle of whiskey up and took a long drink. "I know you're wondering why an officer is fraternizing with an enlisted, especially one he has just met."

Wiping his mouth with the back of his hand, he handed the bottle to George.

"Truth is, I tend to like enlisted men more than most officers. They're less pretentious, more down-to-earth. I may be an officer, but that doesn't necessarily make me a gentleman—by birth, choice or position."

Eli laughed at the thought of it.

George held the bottle of whiskey with both hands. "Lieutenant, I mean Eli, I don't really drink that much."

Eli chuckled, "Well, I'll be damned my new friend. Tell you what, you take a sip when it's your turn and I'll make up the difference, when it's mine."

George took a sip of the bourbon and coughed. It burned all the way down. He took another sip and handed the bottle back to Eli. Within short order, the bottle was passed back and forth with increasing frequency. The sips George had taken over the course of the last hour had warmed his gullet and loosened his tongue. Leaning against a boulder next to the creek, he handed the half-empty bottle back to Eli.

"Mind me asking you a question?"

"Not at all, George. Sharing a bottle entitles you to ask anything you want to."

"Back when we met earlier today, you said something about being busted from Captain in 'Jeb' Stuart's Cavalry to Lieutenant in our regiment. That's quite a fall. I was kind of wondering how that came to be?"

Eli rubbed the stubble on his chin. "Well, George, the reason is as old as the first time a man set eyes on a beautiful woman. I had a fling with a certain southern belle by the name of Kate MaGruder. Trouble was, she thought I was a proper suitor, someone who planned to stay. Truth is, I was just passing through."

Eli offered the nearly empty bottle to George who declined.

"So you had a fling with a pretty girl."

Eli turned the bottle and finished off what was left of the whiskey.

"Kate wasn't just any southern belle, she was Major General John Bankhead MaGruder's middle daughter. Seems General MaGruder was also a personal friend of President Jefferson Davis. When Princess isn't happy, neither is Daddy and if Daddy happens to be a general with prominent friends, somebody's gonna pay. I happened to be that somebody. The best General Stuart could do was get me transferred to this fine regiment as a lieutenant. So my friend, the long and short of it is that now I'm walking instead of riding—the price I paid for a woman's affection."

"I don't feel so good," George said, rubbing his head.

"I don't expect you do," Eli replied with a smile. "You'll feel even worse in the morning. The good news is you will survive."

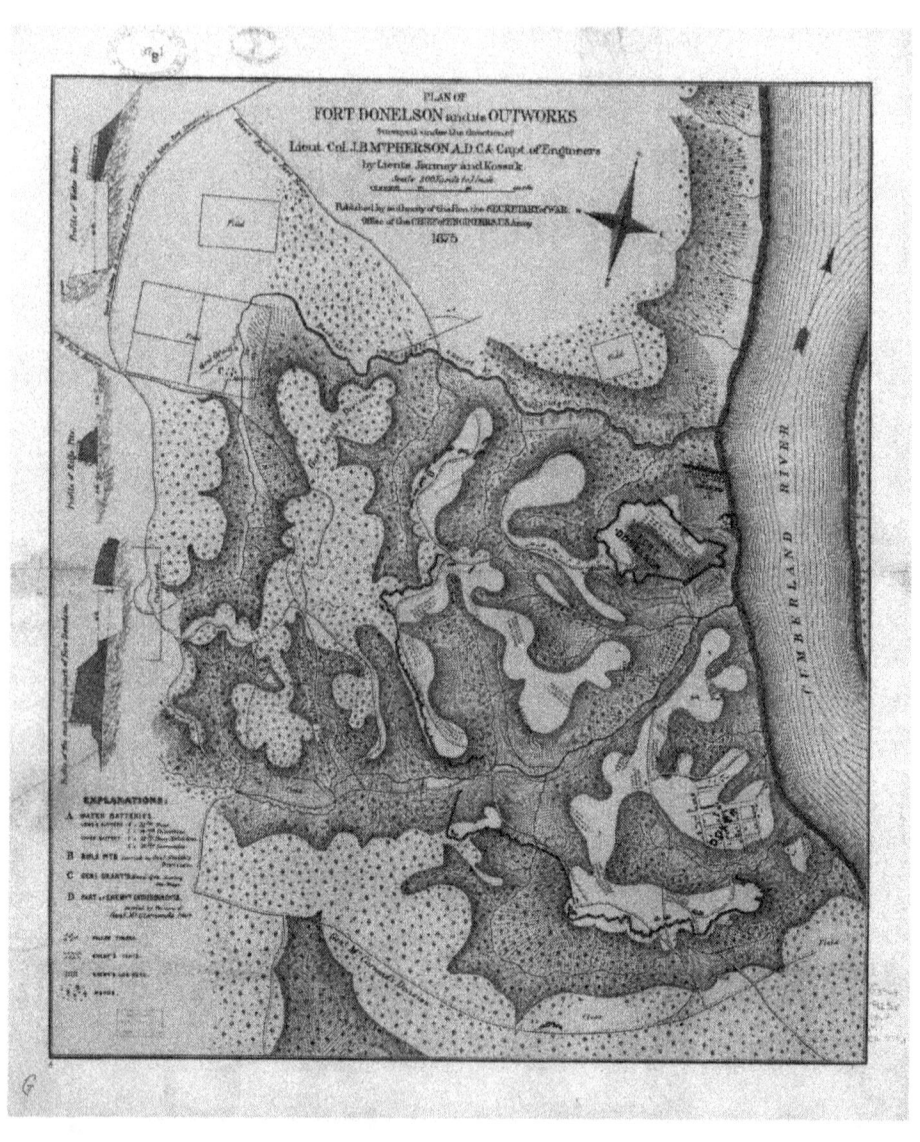

MAP I. FORT DONELSON, FEBRUARY 12-16, 1862.
J.B. MCPHERSON (LIBRARY OF CONGRESS)

THE BATTLE FOR FORT DONELSON

From Clarksville, George Spears, Eli Forrest and the rest of the Tennessee regiment moved down the Cumberland River by steamer. By the time they pulled into Fort Donelson on the afternoon of February 13th, the fighting had already begun. George Spears was about to get his first taste of combat. Like the other green troops, he was both nervous and excited. The men were led directly off the boats, up a steep road, and marched double time nearly three miles to a wooded ridge where another Tennessee infantry regiment there was being hard pressed by the enemy.

The smoke was thick from cannon, rifle and musket shot and the air was filled with the sounds of battle. Explosions and screams of wounded and dying soldiers were mixed in with rebel yells and shouts from officers. "Hold fast" was the mantra of Confederate officers while Union officers shouted "Forward, let's go" and other expletive-laced epithets as they tried to take the ridge. Spears felt weak-kneed both from the three mile, double-time march and the desperate action he was engaged in. Fire and reload. Hold the line. He did as he was commanded, shooting into the smoke, sometimes seeing the enemy, sometimes not.

While reloading, he once caught a brief glimpse of Eli Forrest, walking up and down the line, waving his sword and shouting encouragement to the beleaguered troops. Firing off another round, Spears noted how quickly Eli could change from an irreverent, carefree lieutenant to a serious and seasoned veteran.

After the final charge of Union troops was repelled, George leaned on his musket to catch his breath. The soldier on his left pointed to a ravine below their rifle pits and shouted, "Fire!"

Artillery shells had ignited dry leaves and brush. The whole area was ablaze and rapidly overtook wounded Union soldiers left on the field of battle. Unable to be rescued by their comrades, the wounded men screamed in agony as the flames engulfed them. Some of the rebel defenders threw down their weapons and ran to the helpless Federals, pulling them out of the deadly fire. Like many good deeds in times of war, the selfless, humanitarian efforts of the rebels did not go unpunished. Yankee sharpshooters, looking for easy targets, drove the would be rescuers back into their rifle pits, leaving their wounded comrades to the mercy of the flames. George, Eli and every other soldier, blue or gray, stood and watched a scene unfold that they would never forget.

A burly sergeant with a bushy grey beard thrust a canteen into his face. "You look like you can stand a drink of water. You done good, son. We heard you boys was new recruits for the most part, so we wasn't sure if you'd be much help, but the lot of you done okay. We gave those Billy Yanks a good whuppin' today."

After a long drink, George handed the canteen back to the sergeant. "Much obliged."

The sergeant tipped his hat and moved on to the next soldier.

The rebel garrison at Donelson was well armed and had ample supplies. The fortress itself was a big improvement over the ill-designed and unfinished Fort Henry less than a dozen miles away. Donelson was situated on high ground with a commanding view of the river. When George Spears and the other reinforcements had arrived at the boat dock, he noticed two tiers of well-placed water batteries, mounting about a dozen heavy guns which could menace any river access by the enemy from above and below the fort. Away from the river on the fort's land side, an outer defense perimeter lined the fort with entrenchments that stretched nearly two miles along high ground from Hickman Creek on the right to the town of Dover on the left.

With the arrival his regiment and other troops from Clarksville, and a brigade of Virginians who had arrived several days earlier, the fort's garrison grew to 15,000 men. As far as numbers tell the tale, rebel infantry appeared to closely match U.S. Grant's Northern forces. Confederate artillery batteries were well positioned on the elevated shoreline which offered the fort a commanding view of the waterway. By February 13th, Grant had moved the bulk of his force from a semicircle spanning the hills near the Donelson works down a short distance where he ordered them to spread in a thin line not far from the rebel's rifle pits.

Judging the Confederate defenses too strong for an immediate assault, Grant decided to wait for more reinforcements. He knew he would be receiving additional troops with each passing day, allowing him to extend his right flank closer to Lick Creek. At that rate, the rebel defenders would soon be completely encircled.

Grant's field generals knew that the commanding position of the rebel batteries spelled trouble for the Union gunboat flotilla, which was steaming its way through the Cumberland's cold and fast moving waters toward the rebel fortress. Flag Officer Andrew H. Foote was in charge of the fleet, which numbered four ironclads and two timberclads.

As the Federal gunboats closed in, Grant stood ready with over 27,000 troops positioned within easy striking distance of the fort. The rebel bastion looked intimidating to the Union soldiers, tired and cold from a week's march over muddy, rain-soaked roads. What they saw was an imposing fort surrounded by rifle pits stretching over several miles of hills and hollows. On February 13th, Grant moved his land force from the semicircle spanning the hills near the fort down a short distance and to the land approaches closer to the Confederate rifle pits. Still judging the rebel defenses too strong for an immediate assault, he decided once more to wait while reinforcements bolstered the line.

Four generals peered at a map by lantern light, talking quietly among themselves when the door flew open and a tree trunk of a man walked in.

General Gideon Pillow looked up from the map. "Colonel Forrest, it's about time. What do your scout's say Grant's up to?"

Nathan Bedford Forrest threw his gloves onto a nearby table. "I'll tell you as soon as your adjutant pours me a cup of that hot coffee—or whatever's passing for it."

Sipping the coffee, Lt. Colonel Forrest warmed his hands on the tin cup.

"My boys tell me more Union troops are arriving daily."

General John Floyd lit a cigar. "Gentlemen, I think Grant may be getting ready to lay siege on us."

General Simon Buckner continued to study the map. "That's not Grant's style. I've known him since West Point days. He takes his time, but when he thinks he's ready, he will attack."

Gideon Pillow unscrewed the cap from a silver flask and took a quick sip. "We have about 15,000 troops. If they don't get that many more reinforcements, I think we can throw back anything they come at us with."

Forrest drained the last of his coffee. "You can forget the idea of a siege or us defending Donelson for long. A farmer taking a look off a high bluff spotted some gunboats and troop transports heading this way. One of his boys was intercepted by my scouts with a message for us. The long and short of it is that within 24 hours, those troop transports will tip the balance in Grant's favor. If General Buckner is right, we can expect an attack as soon as day after tomorrow."

General Floyd relit his cigar. "We need to hold this fort. And Gideon, your point is well-taken. Even with Grant's reinforcements, we still control the waterway and the high ground on land." The general blew a plume of smoke into the air. "Still, it is also incumbent that we have an exit strategy should, God forbid, it come to that."

"You've got a point, John. I've got a plan in mind to send those bluecoats scurrying back to the river. If it's one thing I know, it is tactics, but as usual the leaders of this war are often too late with too few reinforcements. If we had more time and more men to implement my plan, we could stop Grant in his tracks."

Nathan Bedford Forrest glanced at Simon Buckner with a knowing look somewhere between disgust and amusement.

"What do you think, Bushrod?" General Floyd queried. "You're the one who had a big hand in designing and building this fort."

Brigadier General Bushrod Johnson paused before answering.

"While of course I would defer to your and General Pillow's strategy. I can vouch for the fort's readiness. It's well constructed and the gun placements and batteries can hold their own against whatever the Yanks throw at us. Our rifle pits are also well positioned on high ground. We're in good shape. The question is how many men can Grant send against us?"

General Pillow looked at the men gathered around the map table. "We'll know soon enough."

George and Eli stared out into the cold, starlit sky. George packed his pipe with some Virginia burley while Eli lit a cigar.

Blowing a thin stream of smoke into the frigid night air, Eli said to himself as much as to George, "There looks to be about as many Yank campfires as there are stars in the sky."

George lit his pipe. "How many Yanks you reckon are down there?"

"It's probably better that we not know," replied Eli with the hint of a smile. "If we knew, it might cause us to lose some sleep."

George nodded. "That it would. Speaking of sleep, I need to get me some. Tomorrow could be a trying day."

Eli ground out the butt of his cigar with the heel of his boot. "Couldn't have said it better myself. Night, George."

"Goodnight, Eli."

At dawn, after a numbingly cold night, the attack against Fort Donelson got underway. It began in the wind-whipped rain and sleet with gunboats launching a fierce bombardment. Grant delayed moving the infantry forward while shelling from the gunboats continued. His strategy was similar to that which he successfully employed a week earlier against Fort Henry. Grant would have Flag Officer Foote first knock out the fort's artillery, then follow with a ground assault. It was a good enough plan, but he had not counted on the effectiveness of the rebel artillery. The strategy failed and by nightfall it was not the Fort's water batteries, but the Union gunboats that had taken a pounding. Since the Ironclads' guns couldn't reach the uppermost batteries, the rebels suffered no serious casualties. Foote's gunboats weren't so lucky with 54 men killed or wounded. Having sustained extensive damage, they were forced to withdraw. By the evening of February 14th, Grant realized that if he were to succeed in taking the fort, it would have to be through a ground assault. And, given the 15,000 rebel defenders positioned inside and around the fortress, that would be no easy task.

George and Eli sat on snow-covered ground with other men from the regiment, eating their supper. Union sharpshooters made even a small campfire a risky proposition. The men wrapped themselves in their thin blankets, trying to keep from freezing.

Private Bohannon sopped up the last of his cornmeal mush with his fingers and licked them clean. "You put a little fat back in some cornmeal and cook it up good and it'll fill you right up. Only thing missing on a cold night like this is a hot cup of real coffee."

"Chicory will have to do," quipped another soldier, shivering as he spoke.

George lit his briar pipe. "Lieutenant, looks like we got those Union gunboats on the run."

Eli Forrest rapped his gloved hands against his thighs in a feeble attempt to warm himself. "It appears so, but today's victory does not necessarily ensure tomorrow's battle. The gunboats are one thing, the Union troops landing daily are another. My guess is like most generals, Grant would prefer to take Donelson like he did Fort Henry—bombard us into submission with minimal casualties on his end. He knows it won't be easy taking the fort with a ground assault."

"How long do you think it'll take Grant before he figures it out?' George asked Eli.

"Sooner rather than later," Eli replied. "Sooner rather than later."

Behind the rebel fortifications, the mood among the Southerners was cautiously optimistic, at least for the time being—at least until tomorrow.

"I've got some bad news gentlemen. General Hardee has pulled his troops out of Bowling Green, leaving the town and its inhabitants to the enemy," General Floyd said, pointing to the map.

"Sounds like Hardee," Gideon Pillow interjected. "Just when we needed him to hold his ground, he up and high-tails it to Nashville."

Simon Buckner looked out into the darkness. "At the rate they're landing reinforcements, it won't be long before Grant has us and the town of Dover completely surrounded."

"I designed the fort to withstand pretty much anything from the river. The rifle pits are on high ground, but without the heavy guns, they're more vulnerable," Bushrod Johnson interjected.

General Pillow cleared his throat. "Our boys are a stout lot. They have plenty of fight in them. We've got a sound strategy. I went over the tactics again earlier this afternoon. General Floyd and I both agree that we have the provisions, ammunition, will and leadership to hold our own."

General Floyd, wiping a small bead of sweat from his forehead, looked at Simon Buckner and Bushrod Johnson, then back at Gideon Pillow. "As commanding officer, I believe General Pillow has a sound plan. Since he has more combat experience, I think we should see where his plan takes us."

"How about straight to hell," an exasperated Simon Buckner responded.

Gideon Pillow turned red-faced. "Remember your position, Sir. You are not in command here."

Buckner regained some measure of composure and continued. "It's clear the weather's turning colder by the hour. The wind is picking up and snow clouds are forming. Most of our men don't have adequate winter clothing. Freezing soldiers think more about getting warm than fighting. We need to find the weakest link in their line and punch an escape route through it before it's too late. Time is running out and if I know Colonel Forrest, he is not about to sacrifice his troops for our folly."

The generals grew silent. The only sound accompanying the howling wind outside was the pop and crackle of the pot-bellied stove.

Finally, Bushrod Johnson spoke. "I agree with General Buckner. Our land defenses aren't strong enough to withstand a sustained attack more than a day or two. And without Forrest's troops, we would have no chance to break through the Union lines."

"Colonel Forrest can't leave without my authorization. He's under my command," exclaimed General Floyd.

"I'll let you tell Forrest he can't leave," Buckner replied with a wry smile.

Gideon Pillow began pacing back and forth. Suddenly, he stopped and turned to the other generals. "I've got it, Gentlemen. We can in a sense, be victorious even in retreat, if we can get the bulk of our forces out and give the Hessians a thrashing for good measure as we leave. If we escape, Grant won't get what he won at Fort Henry—an easy victory. By God, it may not be ideal, but I do believe we can leave with honor if we do it right. Let's look at the scouting report one more time. The key is to find where their encirclement is the weakest. General Johnson, go check on the readiness of our troops to move out. While you're at it, let Colonel Forrest know of our change in plans. Meanwhile, we will decide on the time and place."

At the end of a long night, the three ranking Confederate generals decided a massive attack against the Union position on the Confederate left toward the enemy's southern position was their best chance to break out. If the enemy line could be broken there, one of the generals would be able to lead his division in a surprise escape from the fort and flee to Nashville. The rest of the command would provide cover for the retreat, and then follow with their divisions. The three men drank a toast and retired to their quarters for a few hours rest. Tomorrow would tell the tale.

BREAK-OUT

At 5:00 a.m. on a cold and dark prelude to another day, General Pillow's division moved forward aided by General Buckner's division and Lieutenant Colonel Forrest's 500 mounted troops. Their combined force totaled about 6,000 rebel soldiers hailing from the states of Virginia, Kentucky, Mississippi, Tennessee, Texas and Alabama.

The men in George Spears's Tennessee regiment marched in silence, each man left to his own thoughts. The only sound was the crunching cadence of their march toward battle and the occasional order sounded by officers in urgent whispers.

"You ready, Private Spears?"

George looked to his right and realized Eli Forrest was marching next to him.

"I hope so, Lieutenant. Guess I'm as ready as I'll ever be."

Eli pulled up the collar of his coat and leaned into George. "Just remember what I told you. Stay low when the fighting starts and move with as much cover as you can. Always keep moving and stay focused. Shoot deliberately and aim for the enemy's middle—belly and chest area. It'll give you a larger target."

"I'll do my best," George replied nervously.

"I know you will," Eli said. "You'll do just fine when the shooting starts—your training and instincts will kick in. You already had a taste when we first got here. The first fight gets you ready for the next one."

Eli reached in his coat pocket. "Here, take this." He handed George a chew of tobacco. "It'll calm your nerves." Looking over his shoulder as he moved on up the line of marching men, Eli whispered, "God willing, I'll see you later."

Pillow's and Buckner's divisions welcomed the first streaks of a new day's cold dawn with the roar of rebel yells. They charged head-long into the Union positions. An explosion of musket and rifle fire shattered the early morning calm. Again and again, Confederate soldiers hurled themselves against surprised Illinois infantry regiments. The Yankees held their ground at first, reacting with a desperate defense. The loud crack of continuous gunfire pierced the bitter cold, rising above shouts and curses as the enemy repulsed one attack after another. Smoke clouds drifted above snow-covered trees and the smell of gunpowder permeated the frozen woods.

To George Spears's right, the soldier nearest him screamed and dropped his weapon. The young Alabamian clutched his blood-soaked coat and crumpled to the ground. The entire front line was fully engaged. Tennessee and Alabama sons of the south were fighting shoulder to shoulder against their Illinois adversaries. The momentum of battle carried the giant wave of blue and gray one way and then another as the ebb and flow of battle evolved toward its conclusion.

The initial charge against the Union's right line was repelled. Spears and the others in his company fell back, leaving many of their fallen comrades behind. They quickly regrouped and advanced toward the Yankee position a second time. The second assault proved to be even more costly as Union artillery zeroed in on them. Repeatedly, the rebel forces surged forward, bending the Union defenses, only to be pushed back as reserve troops were rushed in to shore up the Yankee line. At one point, the opposing sides closed to within twenty-five yards of each other, firing at point-blank range.

By mid-morning, the resistance of the Union lines began to waver. With the help of Forrest's hard charging horse soldiers, Union infantry units began to fall back. The fiery Confederate cavalry commander galloped back and forth, exhorting his fellow Tennesseans and the three mounted companies of Kentuckians forward.

As the Yankees began to retreat, the exhausted rebels rushed after them in an adrenalin-charged frenzy. Confederate officers shouted encouragement to their battle weary troops. "Close to the right," "They are moving back," "Keep your eyes on the colors," "Come on boys, forward!" The butternut clad foot soldiers seemed to get their second wind. George heard a primordial sound coming from deep within him. It was something he had never experienced before, born of a strange mix of fear, desperation, rebellion and jubilation. Out of his gut, for the first time, George gave voice to a blood-curdling rebel yell. Some of the Yankee units tried to make an orderly retreat to more defensible position, but while running might be a natural survival instinct, it was the worst thing they could do. Forrest's men pursued them with wild abandon as did jubilant rebel infantrymen.

When George and his compatriots reached the road, their pursuit was halted. The rebel soldiers reveled for a time over their hard-earned victory. Some knelt in prayer and gave thanks to the Almighty for being spared in battle. The laughter and shouts of celebration gave way to remembering their fallen comrades who had not made it to the road. The pounding roar of rebel and Union artillery in the distance reminded them that the battle for Fort Donelson was not over.

George and Eli rested on an overturned Union ammunition cart and marveled at how they had come through the fighting in relatively good order. George's cap and coat hadn't fared so well. A minie ball had torn through his coat on the left side above his waist, leaving a blackened hole where it had passed through. His and Eli's caps were black from the smoke of gunfire. The smell of sulfur hung heavy in the air.

"Is my face as black as yours and the others?"

Eli looked at George with a weary grin. "Blacker."

The two friends drank from their canteens and ate some cold cornbread as they observed the remnants of the battle. Yankee and Confederate dead lay everywhere, their blood reddening the snow. Some looked like they were resting in a peaceful sleep while the bodies of others were contorted in unnatural shapes. A shattered arm rested atop a dead horse while a shoeless foot seemed to be standing at attention next to a disabled canon. George and Eli finished their cornbread in silence. George looked at his friend, gesturing at the carnage before them.

"Eli, you reckon this is what hell looks like?"

"I expect so, George, I expect so."

A panting young Confederate officer, his face covered with grime and a blood-stained bandage wrapped around his forehead saluted. "Lieutenant Colonel Thomas Gordon reporting, Sir."

General Buckner continued peering through his field glasses on the rise of a hill near the fighting. "Major, give the colonel a drink of water."

After Gordon had taken a long drink from the canteen offered to him, Buckner, continued. "What's the situation on your front, Colonel?"

"The Yanks put up a hell of a fight, General, but we broke their line about an hour ago. We got the Third, Eighteenth and Thirty-second Tennessee regiments across an open field to the right of Wynn's Ferry Road."

Buckner lowered his field glasses and looked at Gordon. "Sounds like the enemy had some artillery firing on your flank."

"That they did, General. It was positioned on the road—but it didn't stop our boys. We kept the heat up and the Yanks finally took off and left us the battery."

Simon Buckner smiled for the first time that morning. "Well done, Colonel. Well done, indeed."

Nathan Bedford Forrest slapped his gloves against the side of his trousers. "We have done a good morning's work. Four Yankee brigades are on the run and my scouts estimate they've left about 800 dead and wounded in the field. We now own Wynn's Ferry Road and have our escape route secured. We can start evacuating Donelson. Gentlemen, it's time we light out for Nashville and live to fight another day."

"I don't guess you have heard the news, Nathan. General Pillow has ordered Brown's men to fall back to the rifle pits," a crest-fallen Bushrod Johnson replied.

"Return to the trenches?" Forrest exploded. "Has he lost his mind along with his manhood?"

Eli, George and the other men of the decimated regiment sat exhausted in their rifle pits and ate rations of cold beans and cornbread.

Sergeant Gene Hill bellowed his disgust through a mouthful of beans. "Who the hell is in charge of this blasted army? We have the bastards on the run and what do we do—we retreat. I tell you, it's more than a man can take."

Eli Forrest knew the men were both confused and exhausted, not the best combination for motivating them to fight on.

"Sergeant, if nothing else, we fight for each other. None of us planned on returning here. But whether we're here or there, we won the morning. Now, let's try to get some rest before the next round...."

Eli never finished his sentence. Three soldiers from the rebel picket line jumped into the trench. "There looks to be a whole damned Yank division coming through those woods about five minutes behind us."

The Union troops from C.F. Smith's Second Division quickly over-ran the outer rifle pits as all hell broke loose. Eli, George and the other soldiers in their regiment were fighting for their lives. Survival-fueled adrenalin surged through their bodies as they attempted to fight off the Union offensive.

Major Adkins grabbed Eli Forrest by his jacket collar and shouted, "Lieutenant, get some of your boys down to the right of our line. It's about to collapse. If it falls, our river batteries are exposed. And you..." At that exact moment, a minie ball shattered Adkins' skull before he could finish his sentence, spraying blood and brain matter on Eli.

Eli grabbed George and two dozen men from his regiment and rushed toward the end point of their right flank. In the fierce fighting they encountered there, it was unclear who controlled the line. Blue and Gray intermingled in a bloody dance of death. Close range musket fire and hand to hand combat took its toll on friend and foe.

George felt like a cornered, wild animal as he tried to hold his position. Running out of cartridges, he broke the barrel of his musket on the head of a huge Union soldier charging at him with a bayonet. Dazed only momentarily, the Yankee shook his head to clear the cobwebs while George looked frantically for a weapon. With the Yankee still clinging to his musket and leveling it to fire, George threw his empty canteen at the man's head. George felt the errant shot whiz by his face as the Yankee charged, thrusting his bayonet forward. Time slowed down as George's feet seemed stuck where he stood, the point of his enemy's bayonet bearing down on him. In times of war, luck as much as anything else decides the outcome of a man's survival. The charging Union infantryman tripped over the body of a dead rebel soldier and, losing his weapon, fell to the ground. Snapping out of what seemed like a trance, George picked up the Yankee's rifle and raised it above his head. As he prepared to plunge the bayonet into his enemy, the terrified soldier raised his arm as if to stop the game of violence that he was about to lose. Blinded by fear and a primal survival instinct, George didn't hesitate. Using both hands, he stabbed the bayonet into the soldier's chest, not once but three times before he collapsed in an exhausted heap.

"George!" George looked toward the sound of his name and saw Eli helping a wounded soldier. "Come on, George," Eli shouted. "We've got to get out of here. The Yanks are everywhere. The whole damn line's collapsing."

By the end of the day when the fighting had finally subsided, the temperature was well below freezing. With more than 2,500 Union troops and more than 1,400 Confederate soldiers killed, wounded or missing, a bloody day turned into a frozen night.

The pot-bellied stove popped and crackled once more at Confederate headquarters. General Floyd paced nervously back and forth across the room while General Pillow stiffened his resolve with an occasional drink from his flask. Simon Buckner and Bushrod Johnson stared at the map on the table as if it might offer some magical new escape route. Nathan Bedford Forrest stood near the stove, his back to the other officers.

Floyd stopped pacing and looked at Gideon Pillow. "Why in God's name, did you give the order to relinquish Wynne's Ferry Road after we had fought so hard to secure it? We lost eleven percent of our forces today—more than a thousand men—and McClernand's division, with help from Lew Wallace's Third Brigade, retook the ground we won this morning. To make matters worse, they have extended their line around our left flank. If you had held your ground instead of pulling your men from their positions, we might have had a chance."

Taking another drink of whiskey, Pillow offered the flask to Floyd, who refused. "I thought it best. It was a temporary, tactical withdrawal in order to resupply. I'll tell you one thing. Our boys fought valiantly. Our tactics were sound. We just didn't have enough fire power. Besides, if General Buckner had come up in time, I am confident we would have routed the Yankees."

Simon Buckner turned red-faced. "You gave the order, General Pillow, not I. Even after I questioned the wisdom of it, you still gave the order."

A seething Forrest turned from the stove and faced the other officers. "You—especially you, General Pillow—are a disgrace to the uniform! We had the escape route secured. You diddled and dawdled your way into the sorry mess we're in now."

"I remind you once more, Colonel Forrest, you are not in charge here. General Floyd…"

Forrest interrupted the sputtering Pillow. "Neither you nor General Floyd could command your way out of a privy."

General Floyd cringed as Gideon Pillow bellowed, "How dare you....."

Simon Buckner raised his hands for quiet. "Gentlemen, compose yourselves. Time is short. The men are freezing and we have to bring this matter to a conclusion. It has been a long day, starting with promise, but ending in futility. It is clear that we can no longer hold out against Grant's forces. We must surrender."

John Floyd was clearly agitated. "As a former Secretary of War for President Buchanan, I most certainly will be tried for treason if I surrender to Grant."

"And Grant would like nothing better than to get his hands on me. Besides, I'll be needed to help develop a defensive strategy for Nashville," added Gideon Pillow. "I'd like to stay with the men. I continue to believe we could cut our way out, but it won't do our cause any good for propaganda purposes if I surrender. Gentlemen, surrender is not an option for me. I will escape with General Floyd and live to fight another day.."

Floyd and Pillow turned to Simon Buckner. Buckner offered Forrest a knowing glance before he replied to the generals. "I'll do it."

After Floyd and Pillow left the room, Buckner turned to Forrest. "What are you going to do?"

Forrest looked at Buckner and spoke matter-of-factly. "You know what I'm going to do. I'm going to gather my men and anyone else who wants to escape this hell-hole and leave. I'm in the business of killing Yankees, not surrendering to them."

Forrest picked up his hat. "What kind of terms do you reckon Grant will demand?"

"Not sure," Simon replied. "I knew him at West Point and helped him out once with a loan. I'll see what kind of terms I can get."

Late that night, Gideon Pillow escaped in a small boat across the Cumberland River. John Floyd took two of his Virginia regiments and escaped on a commandeered steamboat.

Snow was beginning to fall again as George and Eli along with two other soldiers attempted to warm themselves next to a small cook-fire in the rifle pit where they stood.

"Word around the regiment is that we're getting ready to surrender the fort," George said.

Eli took off his gloves and rubbed his hands together over the fire. "I'd say it's just a matter of time."

A horse suddenly pulled up next to George and Eli, snorting a frosty vapor from its nostrils. The rider leaned forward in his saddle. "Lieutenant Forrest, may I have a word with you?"

The mounted officer talked in hushed tones with Eli for a short period of time. After shaking hands with Eli, the rider galloped off.

When Eli returned to the fire, George looked at him. "Wasn't that Colonel Forrest?"

Eli stared at the fire and nodded his head.

"How do you know Colonel Forrest?.....wait a minute....your last name's Forrest."

"I know Colonel Forrest as Uncle Nathan," Eli replied, continuing to stare into the fire. "General Buckner will be surrendering to Grant tomorrow so Uncle Nathan and his men along with some other stout hearts will be leaving after midnight."

"You going with him?" George asked his friend.

"Don't know. Thinking about it. What about you, George. You want to come along?"

"Where's the colonel heading?" George queried.

"Nashville. He says that's where the next big fight will be."

George threw another piece of kindling onto the fire. "Don't reckon I'll be heading to Nashville."

"Why not?" Eli replied. "Uncle Nathan will get us out of this place. Wouldn't you agree that at the moment, Nashville sounds a lot better than freezing to death in Fort Donelson or on some Yankee prisoner of war transport?"

George smiled at Eli. "I sure can't disagree with you on that point." A more somber expression clouded his face. "Trouble is, I got two brothers, A.F. and Will, who are in a regiment down New Madrid way. I think they might be part of the garrison on Island No. 10."

George's hands began to shake as he warmed them over the fire. "After witnessing and participating in all this killing, I need to get down there and make sure they're alright….You know, Eli, I ain't never killed a man face to face until yesterday and it's weighing heavy on me."

"I know," Eli responded as he pulled a bottle from his coat pocket. "Here, take a sip or two of this. It'll calm your nerves. A little corn whiskey will take the edge off things."

George sipped the whiskey while Eli continued. "I don't have any brothers. Just my crippled father down in Memphis. If I were in your shoes, I'd want to check on them, too."

George handed the bottle to Eli who turned it up and took a long pull. "We're an odd pair to be friends—me a private and you, an officer. But I want you to know, Eli, you're as good a friend as a man could ask for and I hate to part company with you. That said, I need to see to my brothers and you need to go with your uncle."

Eli handed the bottle back to George. "Finish it off, friend. I wish you would come with us, but I understand. We may be parting ways, but by the grace of God, I do hope we meet again, in this life or the next."

On Sunday, February 16th, Grant's forces—27,000 strong—continued to shell and take sniper-shots at what remained of the encamped rebel force. A lone messenger on horseback emerged from Fort Donelson under a white flag of truce. He carried a note to Simon Buckner's former West Point classmate and friend requesting "terms." Grant's written reply became a watchword throughout the remainder of the war: It stated: "No terms will be accepted other than unconditional and immediate surrender. I propose to move immediately upon your works." When General Buckner read Grant's message, he considered Grant's response unscrupulous, but he had no choice if he wanted to avoid further bloodshed. He accepted Grant's terms.

As Federal regiments prepared to advance on the fort's breastworks, a lone Confederate bugle sounded as a white flag was raised. Before noon on that day, 12,000 rebels, their fort, field guns, artillery and considerable stores of ammunition were in Union hands.

It had been three days since the surrender of Fort Donelson. U.S. Grant poured a glass of whiskey for his former West Point classmate and filled his glass again as well.

"Simon, I know you hoped for something better than an unconditional surrender, but I also have to consider political issues. Some of the scoundrels I have to deal with want to treat captured rebel soldiers as criminals and not prisoners of war so I'm restrained when it comes to situations like the surrender of Fort Donelson."

Simon Buckner raised his glass to Grant before he emptied it. "I was disappointed, but as you know, we have our share of political scoundrels in the South as well."

Simon placed his empty glass on the table next to him. "Speaking of scoundrels, you might find General Pillow's reasons for needing to escape, amusing."

Grant took a sip of whiskey. "I can only imagine."

"General Pillow was convinced that his capture would hurt the Confederate cause—that you wanted him more than any other Confederate general."

Grant laughed. "Poor Gideon. If I had captured him, I would have immediately released him. He's much more valuable to the Union commanding rebel soldiers than sitting in a prisoner of war camp."

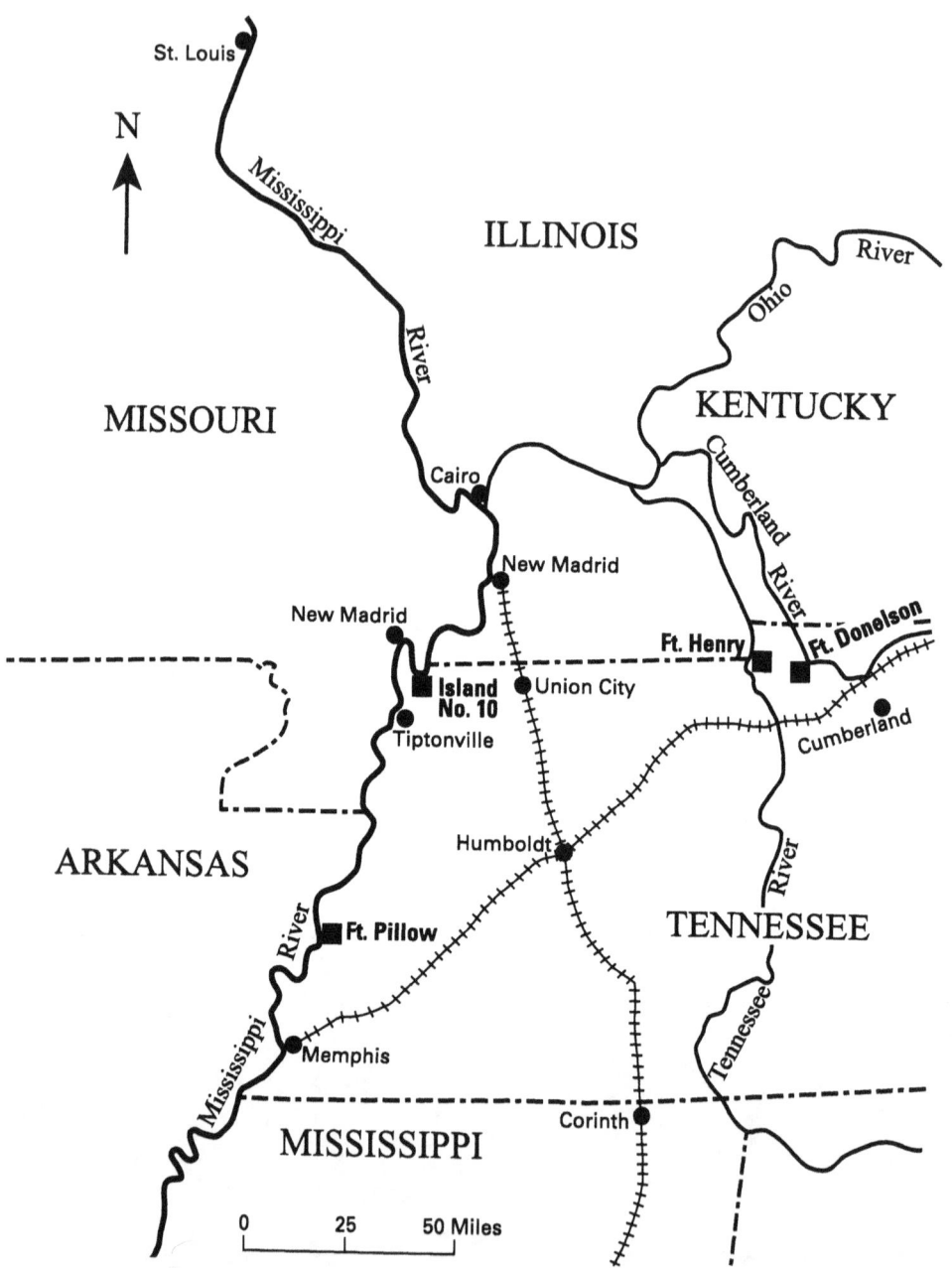

MAP 2. TRANSIT—DONELSON TO ISLAND NO. 10

ELUDING CAPTURE

In the confusion surrounding thousands of Confederate soldiers being taken prisoner, some of the fort's defenders managed to simply slip away in the predawn darkness. Like ghosts, they disappeared into the snowy mist. Among them was a twenty-three-year-old Alabama private named George Spears. George Washington Spears had fought at the fort under the division command of General Simon Buckner, now a prisoner of the Union army. In civilian life, Spears helped run a large plantation in Choctaw County, Alabama. He was the first of four brothers to serve in the Army of the Confederacy. He had left with the blessing of his father, who owned a small farm not far from the vast Cullen Roberts estate where George was employed. A brother with whom he had a special bond, Alexander Franklin (A.F.) Spears, was generally considered "slow." He had a sweet spirit about him and a quick smile for friend and stranger alike. A.F. was handsome enough. Over six feet tall, his head seemed too small for his well-proportioned physique.

Although A.F. moved with a slow, deliberate pace, he was strong as an ox. He could barely read, but could scratch out his name. The last letter George received from his mother indicated that A.F. and Will, his middle brother, had ended up as infantry soldiers, among sixty-seven enlisted men and boys in a company known as the Griffin Rifle Company. Their regiment had apparently been sent to New Madrid and Island No. 10, a place where Tennessee, Kentucky and Missouri were separated by the Mississippi River.

When George Spears walked away from his comrades in the bitter cold of the Sunday morning after the surrender, he knew that although the battle for the fort had been lost, his ordeal was not over. His mood and that of other rebel soldiers was as cold as the frozen ground he walked on. With

Eli gone, a dark cloud of loneliness swept over George. He was tired of war. He wanted to go home—back to West Alabama. He could almost smell the smoke rising from the home-place chimney and his mother frying potatoes. He would have liked nothing better than to hide in the woods along the river until it was safe enough to start the long and arduous journey toward Choctaw County. Instead, he was headed in a different direction, westward toward New Madrid, Missouri, and God only knows what else.

George picked up the pace in the predawn darkness, hoping to put as much distance between himself and Union patrols as he could. He thought about the turn of events that had led him to the time and place he found himself in. He had his fill of the war. He had seen too many good men die or become horribly maimed. Doubts about whether it was all worth it began to worm their way into his thoughts. George had never really been quite sold on the idea of going to war. Unlike many families who cultivated tracts of land and made a living in the South from cash crops, the Spears family had no slaves, even though his employer owned almost a hundred. Yet, like many Southerners, he deeply resented the Federal government's attempt to deprive Alabama citizens the right to do as they pleased—even if it included owning another human being. He also believed Jefferson Davis who pointed out that the politicians in Washington, D.C. had no constitutional right to force the new Confederacy to disband.

Although there was growing talk of war when Alabama had seceded in January of 1861, George was not one of those stricken by the first wave of war fever that overran his native state. In the midst of flag waving, drum rolls, and marching bands, many young men had heeded the call. With knapsacks and duffel bags in hand and shouts of hurrah, they had gathered at county courthouses across the state, ready to pursue high adventure and glory. Once they were mustered into the army, these sons of the south were organized into companies of the First Alabama. In the midst of more parades, swooning young women and long-winded speeches from proud politicians, they were marched off to a training camp in Pensacola, Florida. Some carried their own muskets, but many went off with no weapon other than their hunting knives.

When Union troops were poised to march from the north into neighboring Tennessee, it became apparent that the war would not end quickly. That was the time George Spears decided to do his duty. He said goodbye to his family and traveled by road and river to Mobile where he joined a company that would become part of the Twenty-seventh Alabama Infantry. After a brief stint at a training camp, his regiment was mustered into the Confederate Army and attached to General Albert Sidney Johnston's Western Military Department. George and the other regimental members were sent to Tennessee in late January of 1862, less than two weeks before they lost their innocence and many, their lives. There were no parades for the dead.

When Eli had confirmed that they were to lay down their arms and be taken prisoner by the Yankees, George knew he couldn't afford to wait any longer. After Eli left, he gathered his bedroll, put some rations in his haversack and filled his dented canteen with water. After saying a quick good-bye to his brothers-in-arms, he grabbed his musket and cartridge box and began to make his way up and around the earth works.

The rebel earthworks where his company was positioned were a short distance from the enemy's position. George moved slowly and deliberately until he was able to hear Union soldiers talking. He slipped quietly through their lines in the freezing pre-dawn mist. Avoiding the main road, George was careful as he quietly made his way over the snow-covered ground. Twice he was nearly detected by outlying enemy pickets.

George emerged from a thicket on the edge of the main road in order to get his bearings. The first hint of the new day's light changed the dark of night into the gray that comes before the sun rises, making visibility a little better. Fishing a piece of dried beef out of his haversack, George chewed on the tough meat as he looked up and down the muddy, snow-covered road. With no sign of any Union cavalry and poor visibility still providing some degree of cover, George figured he could make better time walking the road for a while. Rounding a curve in the road, he stumbled into another soldier. The collision sent both men sprawling to the ground. George jumped to his feet before the other man could collect himself and instinctively swung his musket against the head of the potential assailant. His blow sent the poor fellow backwards into the snow and the mud. George pulled his hunting knife from his belt when the man raised his arms in protest.

"Hold on there! I'm Confederacy."

George looked more closely at the young man holding his bloody head with one hand and pleading his case with the other.

"Where you headed?"

"To Command Headquarters in Dover with a message for General Buckner from General Johnston. I took a wrong turn so I lost a day, but I I'm headed in the right direction now."

George pulled the soldier to his feet. "You're too late. Buckner's already surrendered."

The young courier reached out his hand. "Names Otis Stevens—Private Otis Stevens from Kentucky."

George shook his out-stretched hand. "George Spears…from Alabama."

Stevens looked inquisitively at George.

"I know what you're thinking, Stevens, but I ain't deserting, just heading to New Madrid, Missouri to join my brothers' regiment."

Stevens shook his head in acknowledgement. "I don't reckon there's no point in me going any further. My horse pulled up lame two days ago and I been walking ever since."

George picked up his haversack, canteen and musket. "Just stay off the main road as much as possible. There's plenty of Union patrols out and about."

"No doubt," Stevens replied, "but it's mighty slow going through the woods. I can make better time staying on the road and keeping a sharp eye for Yankees."

George looked at Stevens and shook his head. "Suit yourself."

He pulled a twist of tobacco from his pocket and cut a chew, handing it to Stevens. "Here, this might help with the headache I just gave you."

Private Stevens popped the chew in his mouth. "Much obliged."

George tipped his hat. "God-speed, Stevens."

"You, too," Stevens responded as George disappeared back into the thicket.

Hunched over and creeping at a slow pace, he made his way through the woods. The morning began to give way to afternoon and Spears could see no traces of the enemy, only trees and thickets. The snow had stopped and the clouds began to break. From time to time, George would check the road for signs of enemy activity. Around mid-afternoon he decided to rest on a rock out-cropping that was relatively dry. He lay back on the large, flat rock and chewed the last of his dried beef, letting his mind wander back to West Alabama. His reverie was abruptly interrupted by the sound of gunfire. Reaching for his musket, George turned toward the sound of the gunshots. He estimated the shooting to be about five hundred yards east of where he was—back near the main road. Picking up his musket and staying low to the ground, he worked his way through the brush to a stand of trees near the road. George waited patiently for a sign of enemy activity. Finally, when he felt it was safe, he looked up and down the road. No sign of Yankees. Several hundred yards to his left something in a shallow ravine caught his attention. Making his way through the woods, George could feel the bile rising in his throat. There, laying face down was Private Otis Stevens, shot in the back. George rolled him over and found a letter from someone who sounded like a girlfriend. Maybe he could write her a note when he got to New Madrid. No time for a grave he thought, as he covered him with the dead soldier's blanket.

"God-speed, Stevens, God-speed."

As George re-entered the woods, he thought to himself, "It don't matter how quickly you travel, if you never arrive."

As the afternoon wore on toward evening, the ground began to look swampy. George figured he was nearing the backwater of the Cumberland River. Now he had to move even more carefully, guessing which part of the icy slough was frozen enough to support his weight. He was also keenly aware that he was more exposed as the trees and brush became more sparse. Finally, in late afternoon, he reached the channel's edge, which he followed inland until it was narrow enough for him to cross.

The temperature was beginning to drop again as he crossed flat rocks protruding from the frozen stream. He continued to follow the backwater channel until it reached the Cumberland River. From there, he followed the river's edge on a narrow path as he traveled in the opposite direction of the current. George was determined, for the time being, to avoid a chance encounter with any human, be they civilian or military. As to the latter, he feared being shot or captured by the Yankees. But he also feared being taken by the Confederate army which might not believe he was headed to join his brothers' regiment on the Mississippi. He could easily be mistaken for a deserter.

Late in the afternoon he turned away from the river path, and walked several miles through dense woods until he came upon a narrow road. He followed the road until he came to an old grist mill, fast going to ruin. At first, he saw no signs of life about the place, but then he spied an elderly Negro male straddling a sorrel mule near a shed that looked ready to collapse with the next strong gust of winter wind.

THE ROAD TO HUMBOLDT

The old Negro sat on his mule, cautiously observing the approaching Confederate soldier. He explained that he lived at the mill, which had been shut down for some time. He also indicated that several hours earlier, two Yankee scouts on horses had come through. The man told Spears he had never seen a Yankee before, and was uncertain what they would do to him.

"I sho' didn't know what was what. Massuh Evans told us field hands more'un once that dem Yankees was da devil's spawn. Said they'd kill us and eat our young. 'Course the Massuh stayed purty likkered up so I'se can't vouch for his good judgment."

The old man went on to tell George the two riders looked around and asked about the condition of the road and if he had seen any Confederate soldiers in the vicinity.

Making a point to check his musket, George looked at the elderly black man.

"What name you go by?"

The old man looked nervously at the rebel soldier in front of him tinkering with his gun.

"I'se belong to Massuh Evans and goes by 'L'il Tom.'"

George slung his musket over his shoulder. "Well, 'L'il Tom,' what do you think I'm gonna do with this here musket if I find out you reported me or any other Confederate soldier's whereabouts to the Yankees."

Little Tom's eyes grew wide. "I spect you might shoot me."

George looked at the old man with all the seriousness he could muster. "That's exactly what I will do. If you say a word to anybody about seeing me, I will find you and I will kill you."

Little Tom beseeched George to spare him. "No need to shoot ol' Tom,

Massuh. L'il Tom don't say nuthin' to no one. L'il Tom hates dem Yankees. Massuh Evan's been good to L'il Tom. L'il Tom's…."

George interrupted the old man. "Words won't help you if you don't keep quiet. Just remember, if you mention to anyone you saw me, you'll be a dead man."

George watched the old slave mount his mule and scurry around the bend of the road before resuming his journey. He wanted to believe his threat had worked, but he wasn't sure. Slaves knew what to say and how to act around their masters and white folks in general. The old man's response to George's threat was convincing, but was it real? The slight twinkle in Little Tom's eyes as he proclaimed his hatred for Yankees hadn't gone unnoticed by George. Besides, what was he doing on the road, riding a mule? George quickened his pace as he passed one deserted cabin after another. The occupants more than likely fled when Union cannon-fire began to bombard Fort Donelson. In their haste to depart, many had apparently left their livestock to fend for themselves. As the sky began to turn dark, he came to a large log house with a handsome forefront. Unusual for this region, it had a fine little grove of cottonwood hung thickly with mistletoe in front, and an extensive plot of land that showed signs of having been cultivated in warmer months. It stretched behind the house all the way to the edge of a line of thick timber. Two Negro males, one whose close-cut hair was white as snow and the other not yet twenty, stood on the front porch of the house, staring at the solitary Confederate soldier walking up the pathway. A mule was hitched to the gatepost and two sleepy looking hounds rested on the porch of the house, lying motionless in front of a wooden bench. The two individuals eyed Spears with obvious suspicion as he stopped at the foot of the stone steps.

George addressed the older man. "Where's the owner of this here house?"

The old Negro leaned on a walking stick. "Mastuh MacDonald's taken his wife and chillun' and headed to Clarksville to stay with family. Took my Missus with him to see after the young'uns. Left me and my boy, Jeremiah, to look after the place."

"And you would be?" George replied.

"Folks 'round here call me 'Preacher'."

"Preacher?"

"Tha's right. Ever since Mastuh MacDonald taught me to read the 'Good Book,' I've done the marrying and burying and some preachin' to Mastuh's slaves."

George rubbed the stubble on his chin. "He taught you to read?"

"Shur' enough. Mastuh MacDonald different from the other Mastuhs round here. They don't much like him, 'specially with him teachin' me to read a little. But I learnt so many verses 'cause of my deep yearnin', he 'cided to teach me to read the rest."

George took a drink from his canteen.

"Seen any Yankees or Confederates around here of late?"

"Ain't seen no Johnny Rebs, but two Yankee scouts showed yesterday and helped theyself to some cured hams and Mastuh MacDonald's sourmash whiskey. Nosiree, Mastuh MacDonald won't take kindly to them stealing his whiskey."

George slowly screwed the cap back on his canteen. "Met a slave on the road back a ways. Goes by the name, 'Little Tom'. You know him?"

Jeremiah's face screwed up in disgust. "He no good. That go double for his Mastuh. Little Tom's a low down sneak. Could be watchin' us from the woods rite now."

Preacher cast a stern look toward his son. "You best keep quiet, boy, if you know what good for you."

"I ain't aiming to cause you trouble. Just tell me the truth about Little Tom," George interjected.

Preacher looked at the solemn soldier standing before him and sighed. "Little Tom got no qual'ty. He steal if he get a chance…stole a mule from Mastuh's barn jus' two days past. My boy saw him ridin' off. Ain't seen him since. Best keep yo distance from his kind."

George looked up at the coming night sky.

"I'll need a place to stay the night….and some food."

Preacher pointed to the house. "We got's cold biscuits. Rabbit stew warmin' on the cookstove. No coffee left. Plenty sweet spring water. Room to sleep next to the fireplace where it warm. How that sound?"

George looked at the old black man and his son. "Sounds better than sleeping in the woods."

Reaching in his knapsack, George handed Preacher a small parcel. "Here's a little chicory coffee to boil up for after we eat."

George sopped up the last of his stew with a piece of cold biscuit as Jeremiah handed him a cup of steaming coffee. After supper the three men sat around a crackling fire and talked. At first the conversation was guarded and uneasy, given that Preacher and Jeremiah were slaves and George Spears was a rebel soldier and before that a plantation overseer used to giving slaves orders, not having after-supper conversations with them. George thought about the upside-down circumstances of war as he listened to Preacher's commentary on the Good Book. Two slaves offering shelter and food and him sharing his coffee with them.

Preacher told him about a neighboring tenant farmer and his son who had lived in one of the deserted cabins Spears had passed. When his seventeen year-old son was pressed into the service of the rebel army, the old man was told he would see the boy home in three months. Four months later, the boy returned home. He wanted to leave the army, but was told he would not be allowed a discharge until he had completed one year of service. When the first opportunity presented itself, the young private had run away and returned home anyway.

Mounted militiamen came after him and caught him hiding in the woods behind his father's cabin.

Preacher shook his head. "They whipped that po' boy half to death in front of his daddy and neighbors. Took all his daddy's livestock and valubles."

"Laughed while they was doin' it," Jeremiah added. "We seen 'em from the woods."

Preacher took a sip of coffee and continued. "They put the boy…don't know if he was dead or alive… on a horse and rode off. His po daddy…an' some of the neighbors too, cried 'til they eyes run dry. They cussed Abe Lincoln, Jeff Davis and Gov'ner Isham Harris…the whole lot of them. I looked in on him from the wood to see how he was a few days later."

Preacher paused and stared at the fire in silence.

"How was he doing?" George asked.

Preacher sighed. "He gone. Ever'thing taken from him. No hope. Time to leave. Nothin' good come from fightin' and killin.' Lawd have mercy."

There was nothing else to say. That night George Spears slept next to a warm fire on a pile of homemade quilts, his rifle within arm's reach and his sheathed knife next to him under his blanket.

Early the next morning, he rose, put on his worn shoes, washed his face in a basin of cold water, filled his canteen and quickly ate several biscuits. He wrapped three more in a piece of cheese cloth and placed them in his haversack. Standing on the front porch, George thanked Preacher and Jeremiah for their hospitality.

He pulled two greenbacks from his coat pocket. "Here, take this Preacher. It ain't much, but it might come in handy to you."

"Thank you kindly, Mistah Spears, but you best keep yo' money. You a travelin' man with miles to go. We stay put. We be alright."

George tipped his hat to the two men. With his haversack slung over his left shoulder and his musket in his right hand, he stepped outside into a cold, clear Tennessee morning. Before he made it to the road, two Yankees on horseback riding at a full gallop came into view. They were coming for him. George dropped his haversack and rifle and ran toward the cover of the woods. As he ran for all he was worth, he calculated that his best chance lay 150 yards away. Sweat was pouring down his face as he ran. One hundred yards. Fifty.

The flat side of the Yankee's saber caught George squarely on the back of his head, sending him sprawling and unconscious less than twenty yards from the woods. His next sensation was being doused with a bucket of cold water. When he came to and regained his vision, standing over him with an empty bucket was Little Tom.

The two Yankees on horseback were laughing. The one who had run him down pointed his saber at George. "Johnny Reb, you're one lucky rebel. I had half a mind to run you through."

The other Yankee spit a stream of tobacco juice at George. "Sarge, he ain't gonna do nothing but slow us down."

"Settle down, Hawkins. We got time to decide what to do with our prisoner after we eat and rest a spell."

The Yankee in charge threw a burlap bag to Little Tom. "Hey Blackie, while Private Hawkins here secures our prisoner, you go in and cook us some breakfast. And I damn sure better not find any of that ham missing."

"Yassuh, Massuh Sarge. I'se cook you and Massuh Hawkins up a fine mess o' breakfast."

George Spears's head hurt and the rope around his wrists was cutting off circulation. He saw no sign of Preacher and Jeremiah. They had the good sense to disappear when the Yankees arrived.

After they finished eating, the Yankee sergeant belched loudly. "Blackie, throw another log on that fire. I think me and Hawkins might need a little nap before deciding what to do with our prisoner. If he makes a move, you wake us up. You guard him good and I'll slice you off a nice piece of that ham."

"I watch him good, Massuh Sarge, I watch him real good."

With his hands and feet bound, a splitting headache and Little Tom keeping a close eye on him, George knew any attempt to escape would be futile.

Several hours later, the two Yankees awoke.

Hawkins stretched. "I feel a whole lot better, Sarge. A full belly and a good sleep makes a man feel ready to deal with Johnny Rebs."

"True enough," Sarge replied. "Blackie, go fix us another pot of coffee before we go."

Hawkins looked at George. "What we gonna do with him, Sarge. Like I said, he's just gonna slow us down. We could let him make a run for it, like we did that other rebel."

Sarge crossed his arms and winked at Hawkins before turning to Spears. "What do you think about us giving you a sportin' chance to get away....only if, of course, you promise to go home and not fight anymore. I 'spect you'd rather be farming than fighting anyway."

George had no illusion about them letting him get away. He would have the same chance poor Stevens had.... a bullet in the back.

"Blackie, is that coffee ready?" bellowed the Yankee sergeant.

As Little Tom poured the sergeant and Private Hawkins fresh cups of hot coffee, a voice from the door way calmly said, "While you're at it, Little Tom, why don't you pour me and Private Spears a cup as well."

The two startled Yankees rose from the table and reached for their weapons.

"I wouldn't do that, gentlemen. That is, unless you would like an extra helping of double-barreled buckshot to go with that coffee."

George Spears couldn't believe his eyes. In the doorway stood Eli Forrest, grinning and pointing a cocked, double-barreled shotgun at the two Yankees.

George rubbed his wrists as he looked out from the cabin's front porch. The two Yankees were tied to the hitching post.

Little Tom dropped to his knees and clasped his hands together. "Please, Massuh, Don't shoot L'il Tom. Dem Yankees made me do they biddin'. I was scared they'd kill me. Please, Massuh, have mercy on old Tom."

Eli looked at George. "Well, Private Spears, we gonna shoot him or not?"

Little Tom began to wail louder, pleading for mercy.

"He deserves to be shot," George replied, "but he aint worth the cartridge it would take to kill him. What do you think we should do with him and the two Yankees?"

Rubbing his beard, Eli looked at the two sullen Yankees and Little Tom.

"Since these men are Union soldiers, I think we should limit their dress to their union suits. It will be a little chilly, but if they walk fast, they should be able to retain a good bit of their body heat. And Little Tom could keep them company in the lead."

"I'se don't want to go with those bluebellies," Little Tom pleaded.

George's eyes narrowed. "Would you rather be dead?"

Little Tom dropped his head. "No suh."

"Best I can figure, these 'bluebellies' are about a six to eight hour quick march back to their base camp. I skirted it earlier," Eli continued. "We'll string them together with Little Tom in the lead on the main road. He can carry a canteen in case they get thirsty. We'll take their horses and the mule with us and dispose of their uniforms."

George tamped some tobacco in his pipe he had found in the Yankee sergeant's saddle bags. "Their saddle bags are full of valuables they've stolen from civilians."

Eli nodded his head. "Yeah, I noticed. Not much we can do about that."

"That mule belongs to an old Negro slave by the name of Preacher," George replied, lighting his pipe. "We could leave the mule tied to the hitching post with the saddle bags. My guess is that he will know who the valuables belong to and will return them to their rightful owners."

"Sounds like a plan, Private, with one exception."

"What's that?"

Eli smiled at George. "I think those two bottles of Tennessee sour mash and the rest of that cured ham should go with us as a reward for our good deed."

George exhaled a plume of smoke. "Sounds reasonable to me."

From the woods, Preacher and his son, Jeremiah watched the procession move toward the main road—Eli in the lead, riding a grey roan, followed by two Yankees in their underwear with Little Tom in the lead. George brought up the rear, riding one of the Yankee mounts with the other horse following behind. The two slaves looked at each other and began to laugh.

"Lawd have mercy. Have you ever seen such a sight. If'n that aint some parade goin' down the road. Little Tom done got his due. He shor 'nough got his due." Preacher looked at his son. "Let's go get our mule."

THE WIDOW'S KISS

George and Eli maneuvered the winding, muddy road they hoped would lead to Humboldt as quickly as they could. While uncertain regarding their precise location, both men felt they were at least headed in the right general direction. Eli took the lead and George followed, riding one of the Yankee scout's horses. The other union horse, tethered to George's saddle, served as a packhorse and brought up the rear. The two rebels enjoyed the warmth of the sun which had cracked the frigid, gray skies of February. From time to time, Eli would raise his hand, signaling George that it was time to stop and listen for the sounds of approaching horsemen. Although some might question Eli's extra measure of caution, he had learned while riding with "Jeb" Stuart's cavalry regiment that stopping to listen and paying attention to one's surroundings in time of war was always a good idea. On more than one occasion, startled Union detachments had paid the price when Stuart's troopers had arrived unexpectedly.

Chewing on some Union hardtack, Eli pointed to a spring located on the edge of a poplar grove.

"Looks like a good spot to water the horses and stretch our legs a spell."

George nodded in agreement as he turned his horse and the packhorse toward the watering hole.

George tamped some tobacco into his pipe and lit it.

"You can't beat the smell of a pipe," Eli said, smiling at George, "Unless it's the smell of a fine cigar," as he fished a stogie out of his coat pocket.

George exhaled a plume of smoke. "I think I'll stick with my pipe. Come to think of it, how is that Yankee cigar?"

Eli grinned. "I wiped the Yankee off it before I put it in my mouth."

The cock of a shotgun interrupted George and Eli's banter. Standing less than twenty feet from them stood a middle-aged man who looked to be a farmer. His greasy hair hung long and black, highlighted by a scraggly, gray beard. Next to the man, stood a young boy not more than twelve years of age, pointing a musket in their direction.

The man spoke. "Why don't you fellers raise your hands above yer head while Sonny here relieves you of your guns lest I blow the both of you straight to hell."

After the boy had taken their weapons, he tied their hands behind their back with a piece of rope.

"Now that things are a might more secure, why don't you two tell me what you're up to."

George and Eli guessed the intent of the question. After all, they were two soldiers traveling alone. Everyone in the area must have been going downriver and they knew they looked to be deserters.

"We're no deserters if that's what you think," Eli replied. "We escaped from Fort Donelson when the Yankees took the fort, along with Fort Henry ten days earlier."

The farmer walked closer, but still kept a steady bead on the two men.

"What unit you with?"

"Forty-second Tennessee, Colonel Quarles, Eli replied."

"You say the Yankees took the fort? How long ago?"

"Three days."

"What about the men in the garrison?"

"Taken prisoner. Some got out. General Floyd took his Virginians, about 3,000, out on the steamboats. Colonel Forrest led a thousand horsemen—me included—across the icy slough—George here lit out on his own.

"That so?" the farmer replied, looking at George with suspicion.

"Yes Sir," George continued, "I managed to slip away unnoticed. It wasn't easy. There were Yankee patrols all up and down these roads and gunboats on the river. Fact is, I got captured by Yankee scouts. If Eli hadn't come looking for me, I wouldn't be standing before you. More than likely, I'd a been shot in the back."

The man looked visibly upset. He seemed to be thinking about what Eli and George had told him and was pondering what to do next. After a time, the farmer looked at the two men standing before him and said, "As best I can figure, you two fellers have no reason to lie. I mean you no harm."

Having said that he lowered his shotgun, released the hammer, and motioned for his boy to untie George and Eli.

"You two hungry? I have some vittles if you are."

"We'd be obliged," George replied, rubbing his wrists.

They walked ahead a short distance through the woods until they came to a natural clearing where a haunch of venison was roasting on a spit over a bed of hot coals. The three men ate and talked while the boy stood watch.

The farmer was from near Palmyra, about ten miles southwest of Clarksville. He had two sons in the Confederate army. His name was Absalom Jenkin and he and his youngest son had been hunting for fresh meat before he left for Dover and Fort Donelson to gain some word about one of his sons, who was with the Thirtieth Tennessee, serving under Major James Turner. Eli told him how the Thirtieth had held off the enemy's counter offensive aimed at retaking the portion of the Yankee line that he and George had helped to break earlier in the day. Absalom Jenkin took in each and every word Eli spoke, as he described how there had been stubborn fighting lasting an hour and a half.

"It was the extreme right of our troops fixed there," Eli explained as he described how their position was actually in back of the rebel batteries placed on the river shore and behind a considerable amount of rebel field artillery.

"The Thirtieth came in support of the Second Kentucky, as did other regiments."

The farmer pressed Eli and George for more details of the fight and the two men accommodated him with everything they could recollect.

George took a sip of chicory coffee. "Your son's regiment fought bravely. The Yankees made repeated attempts to storm our right line, but artillery bursts and heavy musket fire from our infantry pushed back their charges and forced them to take cover."

Absalom listened even more intently as George explained how the sheer numbers of the enemy eventually forced the defenders to retreat after they were overrun.

"If it makes any difference, there were Yankee bodies from one end of the place to the other, dead or dying."

The man looked sadly to the ground, deep in thought.

"What of our losses?"

"Although we lost more than half of our gunners due to their exposed position, the casualty toll on the infantry was said to be light," Eli replied.

"Do you know if my son—his name is William Jenkin—Private William Jenkin—was killed or wounded?"

"I'm sorry, Sir, I do not, Eli replied softly."

Absalom began to rub his hands together as his boy moved close to him. "If he is alive and held captive, do you know where that might be?"

Eli looked at the cook-fire. "I have no way of knowing. I wish we could tell you more. We have friends who are no doubt prisoners along with your boy. George and I will try to find out where you boy is and get a message back to you. You have our word on that."

"I thank you. I would be most grateful for any news about my son's whereabouts."

Since George and Eli had little idea of where the road they had been traveling led, they were glad to have the farmer's advice and counsel. Jenkin told them they had a day and half a night's travel left before they would reach Humboldt. They learned they had made the right decision in not following the river's edge, since much of that way was marshland and impassable on foot. Asked if the railway was still open, the farmer replied that he last heard that it was, but that was nearly a week ago. Jenkin gave the two rebels the name of a storekeeper in Cumberland Crossing who would help them if they mentioned the farmer's name.

Jenkin was determined to continue his journey to Dover, despite Eli and George's warning that it would be under Federal occupation. If his son lie wounded in a field hospital in Dover, he wanted to be with him. If he were dead, he wished to bring him home.

The three men shook hands and parted.

Eli and George mounted their horses and followed the road until they came to a fork. They had been told by Jenkin to keep left and follow the road back to the river until they arrived at the spot where it branched off in two directions. There they would need to follow the road along the wider water's edge. According to Jenkin, they would eventually come to a small inn in a place called Cumberland. The innkeeper was Silas Etheridge and would not question them or cause them any trouble if they told him that Absalom Jenkin had sent them.

George and Eli made good time from the turnoff in the road as they made their way toward the river. They felt fortunate to not have encountered any Yankee patrols. On two occasions they saw smoke coming from the chimneys of log cabins they passed. From one of the dwellings, a young girl wearing a tattered dress emerged, followed by a growling dog. George was prepared to greet the approaching canine with the butt of his musket, but that proved unnecessary when the girl shouted for the charging animal to return to her.

When she came closer, she asked George and Eli if they were soldiers. George smiled at the small child and said that he was. The little girl waved goodbye. Suddenly George turned his horse back toward the little girl who was still waving. He took something out of his saddlebag and handed it to her. When the two men resumed their journey, George looked straight ahead.

"I gave her the venison and Johnny cake, the farmer wrapped up for us. Looked like she hadn't eaten in a while. I expect that also goes for whoever else is in that cabin."

Eli replied by spurring his horse. "We need to get as far as we can before dark."

Late afternoon, the road drew near the river and became partially submerged in spots. Avoiding the deep puddles and muddy parts required considerable effort. Toward evening the road improved. Eli and George rode at a steady pace until they noticed the outline of a barely visible small cabin notched in the woods and set back several hundred yards from the road. The two men left the wagon path and cautiously advanced toward the cabin. There was no light coming from its two visible windows and smoke could not be seen rising from its chimney. Eli sat on his horse with his shotgun cradled in his arms while George cautiously opened the front door and stepped inside.

It was apparent that the place had recently been abandoned. Aside from an old pot, brown table, chair and some items of clothing scattered on the floor, the small cabin was empty. There were no signs that animals from the nearby woods had found their way inside and the good condition of the roof and windows suggested that the occupants had probably left the cabin not long before he and Eli had arrived.

While Eli got the horses watered and settled in a ramshackle shed adjoining the cabin, George used some dry kindling wood to get a small fire going in the fireplace and boil some water for coffee. After pouring the coffee, he began to warm up some beans in a small iron skillet that he had cooked the day before.

Sopping up the last of the beans with a piece of hardtack, Eli smacked his lips. "We should've thanked those Yankee scouts for the provisions they donated for the Southern cause."

"And their blankets," George added. "Yep, those blankets will come in handy once we put the fire out and the night's cold starts to set in. It would be nice to keep the fire going since there's plenty of split hickory in the shed, but no sense in taking a chance on any unwanted surprises from uninvited company."

George wrapped himself in two blankets and leaned against his haversack in the corner facing the door, his musket and hunting knife within easy reach. He yawned and said as much to himself as to Eli, "After those Yankee scouts got hold of me and that farmer nearly shot us, I've had enough surprises to last me awhile."

The first hint of daylight found Eli and George back on the road. A light rain started to fall and the wind began to pick up as they rode at a deliberate pace. The two men noticed more evidence of the river and its late wintertime overflow as well as more cultivated farmland. They also began to see more people—a man holding an axe gave them a quick look as he worked to fell a large oak on the edge of the woods and a woman carrying a basket on the road smiled when Eli tipped his cap and offered a polite "morning, Ma'am."

The road began to slope downward toward a large expanse of river. There were a dozen or so wooden buildings near where the road stopped and a wooden bridge stood. Tied by two thick ropes to large stakes driven deep into the river's edge were several barges loaded with iron ore and a steam-driven vessel that was used to tow the barges. Its single level deck was ringed with a short rail. A cramped pilothouse was situated above the boat's engine section and wheelhouse.

George and Eli pulled their horses to a stop on the outskirts of the tiny settlement and carefully surveyed the setting. They slowly proceeded to a two-story building near the bridge. They observed a single person near the building who was tending to horses in a nearby corral located next to a barn. George guessed that some of the animals were used for a coach and others, a wagon, both of which were parked near the buildings. Just then a figure emerged from the building, a large, clean-shaven man clothed in a mid-coat, which revealed an apron protruding from the coat's bottom. The man was bareheaded and almost completely bald, but carried a round flat cap and wore laced calf boots. He headed toward the corral, paying Eli and George no heed. Eli dismounted and walked to where the man was inspecting the coach.

"Pardon me for troubling you, but would you happen to be a Mr. Silas Etheridge?"

The man turned and faced Eli with a scowl. "What if I was?"

Eli looked at George then back at the unhappy proprietor. "A Mr. Absalom Jenkin recommended you to us. Said you might be of some help as we journey to relocate our regiment."

The man's face softened. "How is Jenkin?"

"He's trying to find his son, William, but I don't think his odds are going to be too good on that count. More likely all he'll find is a road full of Yankees," Eli replied.

"This here war's hard on all of us. Call me Silas," Etheridge said, extending his hand to Eli. "Why don't you two boys come in inside and get yourselves something to eat."

George and Eli followed Silas Etheridge into his Inn. They couldn't believe their eyes.

There were polished chairs and tables and a long mahogany bar, behind which were shelves stocked with liquor bottles of every shape and size. It was early and no one else was in the place except a woman who appeared to be Etheridge's wife. The woman directed the two men to sit down. She brought them two glasses and a large pitcher of fresh buttermilk. Then came the food—boiled beef, country ham, cabbage, and a skillet of cornbread. Eli and George sat quietly and ate while Etheridge and the woman watched them. When they finished their meal, the woman cleared the table and brought them two steaming mugs of real coffee. While they sipped their coffee, Silas Etheridge pulled up a chair. "How you boys fixed for provisions?"

George wiped his mouth with the back of his sleeve. "We have a little money..."

Etheridge leaned back in his chair. "What about your horses?"

"Our horses?", Eli replied.

Silas Etheridge rubbed the stubble on his chin. "Two of your horses are U.S. branded. If you two happened to get caught by Union cavalry riding those Federal owned mounts, it likely won't go well with you. I do a little trading here and there and could dispose of them for you."

"That's fine," Eli said, giving George a quick glance, "but we would still need two mounts."

Silas looked at Eli, then at George. "A good mule, a horse and some dried beans, corn meal and bacon for the two horses seems about right."

George nodded imperceptibly to Eli.

"Throw in two bottles of that Kentucky bourbon and you've got yourself a deal," Eli countered with a grin.

Silas Etheridge rose from his chair and stuck his hand out to Eli. "Fair enough."

Rising from the table, George and Eli began to pull money from their coat pockets. Etheridge waved them off. "Keep your money. Absalom Jenkin sending you here is money enough for me. Humboldt is a full day's ride. Be sure to take a right at the crossroads down aways. There's a giant red oak and a burned-out barn compliments of a Yankee raiding party. You can't miss it."

With fresh provisions and full bellies, George and Eli climbed on their mounts. They heard the woman call out after them, "God Speed", as they rode away.

They rode all night. It was mid-afternoon with the temperature dropping when the two men pulled into Humboldt, a good-sized town with several blocks of storefront and wood-plank sidewalks. They rode up to the railway depot to check on the schedule. The next northbound train had been delayed due to marauding Federal cavalry units.

George and Eli left their horses and the mule tied to the hitching post in front of the depot and made their way along the wooden sidewalk. In a matter of minutes, they found themselves standing outside of a general store on Main Street. Entering the store, they nearly bumped into a young woman holding a basket half-filled with vegetables. She smiled politely when George stepped aside to let her pass. The two men turned to find a gray-haired man with a pullover grocer's apron staring at them over small round spectacles.

"From the looks of it, Laddies, you two might be needing some assistance," the grocer said with a thick Irish accent and a warm smile.

Eli explained to the grocer that they had a little money and some provisions, but needed a place to stay for the night. A hot bath would also be desirable and perhaps, some supper. He told him about the disruption in the train schedule.

"Name's McCurdy—Amos McCurdy and the Yankees aren't the only thing disrupting your and other folks' plans around here. In case you haven't looked up at the sky lately, we got a storm coming in from the west. Almanac say snow and rain. Probably last several days, so you'll be needing a place to stay until it's over and the train returns. You laddies have any prospects?"

George and Eli looked at each other and then back at the grocer and shook their heads.

"We're running a little low on money. We've got some provisions and we'd be willing to work for a few days board until the train comes," George replied. "Even a livery stable with some fresh hay to sleep on would do."

"I may just have an answer to your predicament," Amos McCurdy replied with a twinkle in his eye. "There is a certain widow lass who lives on the edge of town. Her husband was a fine young man. Killed at the Battle of Manassas. She's turned her home into a small rooming house, but alas, with the war and all, she currently has no tenants. She might just be willing to take the two of you in for a few days in exchange for your labor."

Ann Pritchard opened the door on Amos McCurdy's second knock. Barely five feet tall, she stood proud and erect, her brown hair tied in a neat bun. In greeting her guests, Ann Pritchard's blue eyes sparkled somewhere between caution and anticipation.

Eli noticed something else right away. His reserved matter-of-fact friend's face was flushed with surprise at the first sight of the young, prim and proper widow standing before them. As a connoisseur of women, Eli knew what that meant. Whether he knew it or not, George had caught a malady he wasn't familiar with.

In short order, Ann Pritchard agreed to give George and Eli room and board until the train returned in exchange for them making a variety of needed repairs.

That particular day turned out to be a respite in the midst of dark and troubled times—a day to savor and draw strength from in dealing with the hard times to come. That afternoon each man enjoyed a hot, soaking bath, their first in weeks. They put on fresh woolen underwear they had purchased from McCurdy's store and clean clothes that had belonged to her late husband. The widowed proprietress of the rooming house promised to wash and mend what passed for their uniforms. After shaving themselves, Ann Pritchard's practiced hand cut George and Eli's hair.

When evening came, between the provisions they had garnered through their recent trade and the food Ann Pritchard had on hand, a fine meal was prepared. They were joined by Amos McCurdy for supper which consisted of fried eggs, biscuits, beans and onions seasoned with thick slices of bacon. At the end of the meal, they were served hot bread pudding.

Eli leaned back in his chair and placed both of his hands on his stomach. "Mrs. Pritchard, I do believe that is the finest supper I have ever eaten."

"It...it...was fine," George stammered.

Amos laughed. "Indeed, Mr. Spears, indeed."

"Why, thank you gentlemen. I am glad you enjoyed it," Ann Pritchard replied with a demure smile. "Tomorrow, the two of you will certainly earn it."

When she rose to clear the table, she was no less surprised than Eli and Amos to find George volunteering to help her.

The following morning after a breakfast of hoop cheese and biscuits, Ann Pritchard proved to be a woman of her word. Although the temperature continued to drop under an overcast sky, George and Eli had no problem breaking a sweat as they undertook their chores.

Eli wiped the sweat from his brow. "Mrs. Ann Pritchard meant what she said last night. The list she gave us this morning would require four able-bodied men to complete all the tasks by day's end."

George looked at Eli with something between a smile and a grimace as he continued hammering a board onto the chicken coop. "Hard work won't hurt us. Beats killing and being killed."

Eli stopped what he was doing. "You have a point, my friend. Still, building a new fence section, replacing roofing shingles, constructing a new outhouse and rebuilding this here chicken coop seems a mite ambitious to me."

George laughed. "Just keep hammering and thinking about that fine supper we will partake of when our work's done."

And a fine supper among a week of fine meals it was. If she excelled at anything besides assigning tasks, Ann Pritchard proved to be a cook without equal.

Eli stood on the front porch of the rooming house, a cup of fine Kentucky bourbon in one hand and cigar in the other, looking at the bright stars glittering against a cold, cloudless night. He could see George and Ann Pritchard sitting in front of the fireplace. He took a swallow of whiskey and chuckled to himself. Over the course of the week, he had watched their chairs move closer together each night. Now, on the night before he and George were to leave, there they sat—side by side, talking and gesturing about who knows what. Eli relit his cigar and exhaled smoke rings toward the stars. Then it happened—the magic moment. As if on cue, he watched the two talking heads turn to face each other, suddenly coming together in a long, lingering kiss. Eli swallowed the last of his whiskey and sensed theirs was a different kind of kiss than the kind he was accustomed to—the kind that was driven by a desire to take the next step, to see how far he could go. The kiss Ann Pritchard offered George was one of restrained innocence, a kiss born of respect and affection—the kind of kiss that could last a life time. In that fleeting moment of observation and self-reflection, Eli envied his friend.

TRAIN TO COLUMBUS

George and Eli boarded the train after waiting at the tiny depot for its late arrival. When the conductor leaned out the open passenger coach door and signaled for the Humboldt bound passengers to board the third of the three cars in use, George and Eli were surprised to find nearly every space occupied. The conductor looked at the two soldiers as they stepped aboard and mumbled something about needing to see their furlough papers. George nodded approvingly, knowing that he and Eli had no such documents. In an effort to change the subject, Eli quickly asked about the fare. The harried conductor said there was no charge for Confederate soldiers. Eli uttered a polite thank you and the two men walked down the aisle until they found a space at the opposite end of the car. It was on the floor away from the stove. They could pretend to sleep, thereby avoiding any fellow riders who might want to converse about the war. They made themselves as comfortable and invisible as possible in the corner of the crowded coach as the locomotive began to pull away from the depot.

George looked at Eli out of the corner of his eye. "That conductor ain't gonna be none too happy when he finds out we don't have any furlough papers."

Eli yawned and closed his eyes. "Take a look around. What do you see?"

"What do you mean?" George replied as he surveyed their surroundings.

"What you see," Eli continued, "are frightened people—people trying to flee the Yankees with little more than the clothes on their backs. When they look around and see us and the rest of our rebel brethren, they can't help but notice what a ragged, weary looking lot we are no matter how determined we might be to stop the blue flood that is surely coming. That, of course, makes them even more desperate to find a safe refuge should such a place exist. And then there's the conductor, the one who is supposed to manage this mix of civilian desperation and soldierly chaos. Notice how disheveled he is—his bloodshot eyes. My guess is he'd rather flee with the civilians than bother with us. We play our cards right, our lack of furlough papers won't be a problem."

The train soon picked up speed and gradually settled into a steady gait, punctuated with the bouncing rhythm of the rails and every so often, a teeth-rattling jolt. George shut his eyes and listened to the conversation of two men seated nearby on a bolted down bench.

He learned that most of the passengers were indeed fleeing from Nashville. They had boarded steamers to Clarksville and caught the train. Nashville was in something of a panic, set off by the news of Fort Donelson's surrender. Residents jammed roads and rail lines, especially those heading south toward Chattanooga or the Alabama towns of Bridgeport or Decatur. The two men were bound for Memphis, which was to be the new state capital. One of them was apparently a state legislator and he was convinced that Memphis would be safe as long as Beauregard's troops held the Mississippi River below Columbus, Kentucky. In Memphis there would be none of the mob rioting and looting that was taking place in Nashville.

The train continued to rattle along in a southwest direction. The conductor came through and collected tickets from the riders who had boarded at Humboldt. He paid no heed to the two sleeping soldiers, but opened the end door to a loud clattering and a chilled draft of winter air. He quickly stepped through and slammed the door behind him.

Before long, the train slowed down and George could hear one of the nearby passengers comment that they must be crossing the railroad bridge over the river. He, along with Eli, continued to feign sleep. Visions of Ann Pritchard occupied his thoughts as he touched the breast pocket of his coat where he had carefully tucked the photograph Ann had given him when they boarded the train. The train slowed once more, this time for the Obien River, and then picked up speed for about half an hour. The conductor before long announced that Union City was coming up and it would be at least an hour stop to take on water and fuel. Passengers could leave the train and that there was a separate backhouse for the convenience of the ladies.

George and Eli remained in the passenger coach until it was nearly empty before they eased outside.

Eli filled their canteens from a nearby well while George opened the small basket of food Ann had prepared for their journey. They sat in silence and ate the country ham biscuits Ann had packed for them. When they had finished, George lit his pipe.

"That Mrs. Pritchard is one fine cook and a handsome woman as well," Eli casually remarked.

"She's a good and honorable woman," George stammered, his face turning slightly red.

"I meant no disrespect," Eli replied. "She is indeed a good and honorable woman. Surely you can agree that a good woman can also be a good-looking woman."

Puffing on his pipe, George said nothing.

"I noticed you looking at a photograph on the train," Eli continued.

"She gave it to me at the train station."

George took his pipe out of his mouth and looked directly at Eli. "Ann Pritchard is a good woman in every sense of the word and she is the most handsome woman I have ever seen. You might as well know that when all this is over, I aim to return for her and take her back to Alabama as my wife. That, Eli, is all I have to say about the matter."

Eli's face crinkled into a smile as he slapped George on the back. "Well said, my friend. You are one lucky man and from what I know of you, Ann Pritchard is one lucky woman."

George knocked the ashes from his pipe, eager to change the subject. "If we're going to New Madrid, Amos McCurdy said we need to take this line clear through to Columbus, Kentucky. It seems a roundabout way."

Eli nodded in agreement. "Heard a couple officers say the land route from Columbus to New Madrid isn't safe…too many Yankee raiding parties. Best for us to take a river steamer to New Madrid once we get to Columbus."

George looked around and noticed how the landscape appeared flat, not anything like the terrain where he grew up in Alabama. It also differed markedly from the scenic surroundings of Fort Donelson, with its oak, magnolia and holly trees. He had spent January and the better part of February in that region, the Western Highland Rim, located between the Cumberland and the Tennessee Rivers. High ridges, fast running streams, waterfalls, and deep ravines offered a natural beauty now despoiled by war. He was glad to be out of it and into the flatlands of Western Tennessee where he imagined fields of cotton, tobacco, and corn in the summer stretching all the way to the Mississippi River. He even welcomed the sight of cedar bushes that grew along the railway track bed.

George and Eli boarded the coach again and returned to the spot they held since the train had left Humboldt. When the passengers filed back into the car, the two soldiers noticed an unoccupied bench two rows forward. The conductor was nowhere to be seen. Leaving their haversacks, bed-rolls and muskets stacked against the wall, the two men moved to the vacant bench and sat down. The woman sitting across from them was traveling with a young child who kept her too busy to engage in conversation, a circumstance for which they were grateful.

The train whistle sounded and with a pronounced lurch, they began moving forward. After several more stops and a river crossing, the steam-driven locomotive and its retinue of passenger and freight cars crossed into Kentucky as evening approached.

When George and Eli stepped down from the train, which had now pulled to a stop several miles into Kentucky for what turned out to be a very long delay, the night air was cold and damp. Another passenger, a banker from Nashville, stood by the passenger car entrance. He walked over to where George and Eli stood and told them that the train was regularly so delayed. Worst of all, he had heard it on "good authority" that it may no longer be able to run all the way to Columbus because the Confederate garrison there was planning to abandon the fort after hearing the news of the Federal seizure of Forts Henry and Donelson. All hope for keeping the Mississippi River and the rail line open, he said, rested with a successful defense of New Madrid and Island No. 10.

On Saturday, February 22nd, after a cold night aboard the passenger car warmed only by a pot belly stove in the rear of the compartment, the train finally began to move slowly forward. The tired-looking conductor confirmed what George and Eli had heard from the Nashville banker. He announced to the passengers that the Confederate army was indeed planning to evacuate the troops from the garrison of batteries at Columbus, but General Beauregard would be sending some of the units from there to bolster the defense of Island No. 10. Credible reports as well as rumors, he said, had it that the next move of the Yankees would be down the Mississippi and Tennessee Rivers.

George told the conductor that it was urgent that he and his lieutenant get to Island No. 10 as soon as possible. He asked him how close the train would get them to that desired location, assuming that it no longer ran all the way to Columbus. He was pleased to learn that the train would still make it to Columbus. The town apparently was not yet threatened by the Union army—at least not yet. Nor had they hindered rail traffic in that part of Kentucky. Indeed, yesterday the southbound train had been jammed with civilian residents fleeing Columbus in anticipation of its capture by the Yankees.

With transportation to Columbus still an option, the two rebel soldiers would be spared a dangerous two-day overland trek to Island No. 10. Instead, they could proceed as planned, first by train to Columbus, and then by river steamer from Columbus to the island fortress where George's brothers served. If all went as planned, they could arrive at their destination in two or three days.

As the conductor squinted at his pocket timepiece, he assured them that the train engineer would be making good time and they would soon arrive at the Columbus depot. When the train had left Union City hours before, there were far fewer passengers inside the coach in which they rode. The extra space and a well fueled stove made the harder wooden seats more tolerable. Eli sat by a window and watched the countryside slip by as the steam locomotive with its freight and passenger cars in tow puffed northward while George began writing a letter to Ann Pritchard.

It was dark when the train pulled into Columbus. George and Eli left the depot and walked toward the main part of town. There was a large number of Confederate soldiers in the small river town, including some who apparently were on furlough from the nearby army post. More than a few were intoxicated and staggered and stumbled their way along the streets and walkways. Loud talk and curses punctuated the early evening air, followed by occasional fistfights. George and Eli managed to find a room in Columbus' only hotel. That evening they ate what was left of the rations in George's haversack, since they were running low on legal tender. They shared a bottle of cider a kindly woman had given Eli when he helped her and her two young children with their baggage as they departed the train at Union City. Considering their plan to join George's brothers at Island No. 10, both men thought it wise to report early in the morning to the fort's commander lest they be mistaken for deserters or Yankee spies.

The next morning Eli and George left the hotel after a breakfast of grits and black coffee and walked toward the post, passing local townspeople on their way to church. George was impressed with the high bluffs towering above the Kentucky town. Reaching the main gate, he and Eli provided their names and regimental affiliation to the sentry who instructed them to wait. A barrel-chested sergeant appeared shortly and told them to follow him as the three men walked through the parade grounds to the fort's headquarters. There they stacked their weapons and haversacks in the corner of the ante-room and waited with the sergeant who seemed none too pleasant. From the look of his blood-shot eyes and the smell of his breath, Eli guessed his Saturday night wasn't spent in preparation for Sunday services. After a substantial wait, a major appeared and instructed George and Eli to follow him to a back room with a desk. The major seated himself behind the desk and looked at the two travelers standing before him.

In the hour that followed, Eli and George related their experiences of the past week. After they had finished, the major stroked his beard and shook his head in amazement. He wanted to know more about the fighting that had taken place at Fort Donelson. He was impressed that George had managed to escape the fate of most of the other fort's defenders and that Eli had returned to aid his friend. George and Eli learned from the major that 12,000 of their fellow soldiers at Donelson had been taken prisoner and sent by river steamers to Cairo, Illinois. The two men were informed that George's old Alabama regiment, as well as his and Eli's Tennessee unit, were among them.

The major was a Kentuckian in his early forties and the nephew of Kentucky Senator William F. Simms, a staunch supporter of the Southern cause. He made it clear that he admired the two men's courage and determination as well as George's loyalty to his brothers. Moreover, he would do what he could to see to it that George and Eli were able to join the brothers' regiment. Unfortunately, George's information about his brothers' regiment was erroneous. If they were with the First Alabama, Tennessee, Mississippi Regiment, commanded by Colonel Alpheus Baker, they were not at Island No. 10, but were instead at Fort Pillow, a hundred miles or so down the river from that location. Baker's regiment was at Fort Pillow awaiting orders to move upriver as soon as it was properly armed, a problem the major believed would be shortly resolved. The major thought it best that the two men standing before him board the next transport headed downriver to Island No. 10 and wait there. A transport would probably be leaving within several days. In the meantime, the major instructed the sergeant to find quarters for Private Spears and Lieutenant Forrest and to see that they were treated well.

Two days after their arrival in Columbus, George and Eli found themselves down on the shoreline of the Mississippi River at the town's landing. They were waiting for the signal to board a steamboat that would carry them and other reinforcements as well as a shipment of supplies to Island No. 10.

In his haversack, Eli carried a letter from Major General Leonidas Polk, commander of the Confederate garrison at Columbus, to Brigadier General John McCown, newly appointed commander of the defense forces at Island No. 10 and nearby New Madrid, Missouri. The letter introduced Private Spears and Lieutenant Forrest, who were being deployed to the area. It contained a request to McCown that Spears and Forrest be assigned to the unit in which Spears' brothers served. McCown had been detached from Columbus that very day and was actually set to embark for Madrid Bend on the same vessel George and Eli were on.

The commercial steamer was one of two that had been leased by the Confederate government to provide for the needs of the several rebel garrisons positioned along that portion of the great river. As George stood by the railing of the main deck and enjoyed the morning sunshine, a gentle breeze hinted at an early spring. He wondered what destiny lay ahead for him, his brothers and Eli. Would the war ever end? Would he return to the embrace of Ann Pritchard? Looking out over the river, George knew as surely as he breathed, he would find her one way or the other when the war finally ended.

With its boilers pressured up and its engines now at work, the big boat backed slowly from the landing. The huge paddle wheels churned up massive amounts of river water as the craft moved easily with the strong current. Five hours later, the large steamboat, laden with its cargo of Southern men as well as stuffed burlap bags, stacked crates, and large wooden barrels, approached several encampments of Confederate infantry positioned on the eastern shore of the river. Slowly rounding a bend in the river, the steamer came upon a land battery also on the eastern side, which brandished four heavy guns. Within a few minutes, the large boat pulled up in front of the south end of an elongated island in the middle of the river's channel. The pilot was obviously familiar with the location used for a landing, which was not marked, as well as with the current, owing to the expert way in which he navigated the vessel to a mooring area used by the island fortress.

George and Eli waited until the newly assigned general and troop reinforcements disembarked before they departed the steamer. In a conversation with a member of the steamboat crew, they learned that the general would be re-boarding after inspecting the defenses on the island. His command headquarters would be at Fort Thompson, located less than a mile below New Madrid. The troops on the island and nearby shore batteries would be under the direction of Colonel William Travis of the Fifth Tennessee. George and

Eli waited patiently on the island landing and watched the soldiers who were busy unloading the supplies and heeding the orders of the quartermaster in charge.

Finally, after two hours, the task was completed and the commanding general returned, followed by several officers assigned to his staff. Eli thought that it best to present General Polk's letter to McCown after he got settled in at staff headquarters on the island. But when Eli and George discovered that McCown would be at New Madrid, they realized they had lost an opportunity to approach the general on the steamer. As the general approached the waiting vessel, Eli stepped forward and caught the attention of an officer who had apparently heard of their escape from Fort Donelson and the arduous journey they had undertaken to find George's brothers. The officer, Captain Micha Samuels, told Eli and George to stay put while he shared the letter from General Polk with the general. The general had not yet boarded, but was talking to Brigadier General A.P. Stewart and an aide when Captain Samuels approached them. When McCown finally had read the letter, he handed it to Stewart, who also read it and handed it to his aide. Several minutes later, Eli and George stood at attention before the two generals. McCown spoke:

"Lieutenant Forrest and Private Spears, I have but little time. Please be assured that I will do everything within my power to comply with your request. You honor us with your presence, and we are the better for having men with your experience and determination. Major, see to it that these men are placed in the regiment where Private Spears' brothers serve. Then prepare the paperwork necessary to recommend to the colonel of that regiment that the lieutenant's rank be respected and that the private be promoted to the rank of corporal." McCown saluted George and Eli, turned to the boat, and boarded. The steamboat's paddle wheels began to churn and it was again on the river, bound for New Madrid and Fort Thompson.

The journey had been a long one. The two weary travelers would spend that night and the next on the island awaiting the First Alabama, Tennessee, Mississippi Regiment's relocation from Fort Pillow to New Madrid. Meanwhile, George and Eli found a temporary home with a West Tennessee infantry company of the Fifty-fifth Regiment. They were given their own tent to sleep in and would take their meals in camp with their "guest" company. George and Eli found that the men of the Fifty-fifth enjoyed ample provisions and sufficient blankets to keep them warm at night. However, they were poorly armed and some of the men had no reliable weapons despite the efforts of their colonel, Colonel Alexander J. Brown, to procure an adequate supply of muskets.

Having no assigned duties, Eli and George found themselves with more than enough time to explore the island, and no one seemed to care that they did. The day was cloudy, but not particularly cold. They left their muskets in the care of a soldier who lay sick in his tent and who agreed to safeguard them. They stowed their haversacks and bedrolls in their tent. George wore his bowie knife, safely tucked in a leather scabbard and Eli holstered his revolver. Having nothing else to concern themselves with, they left the camp behind them and walked to water's edge, on the island's north shore.

The island itself comprised about 700 acres, most of which was heavily wooded. The head of the island consisted of a square clearing, from which protruded an outstretched bar that was thickly overgrown with shrubs and weeds. Between the bar and the shoreline opposite the island was a wide chute in the deep channel, in which a large side-wheel steamer had been scuttled and partially submerged. A large farm once had stood in the center of the island, before the army had confiscated its crops and livestock. The abandoned buildings remained in fairly good condition. Directly below the farm and on the eastern side of the island, a floating battery with nine large guns was moored along the bank. Below the center of the island there were no batteries, and the land tapered off to the west in a sharp knife-like point. When George and Eli had come full circle and again stood on the north shore, they noticed three transport steamers, each fitted with cannon, several hundred yards from its embankment. George wondered how they had escaped their notice earlier.

Eli had a favorable impression of the prospects for a successful defense of this particular island fortress on the Mississippi.

"Here, take a sip," Eli said thrusting a pint bottle toward George. "It's corn liquor, not bourbon or sourmash, but it'll do in a pinch."

George took a sip more out of politeness than anything else before handing the bottle back to Eli and taking his briar out of his pocket to fill up with the last of his Virginia burley.

Eli took another pull from the bottle. "These man-made fortifications are formidable, both on the island itself and on the opposite shore. The artillery are well-positioned and there is considerable troop strength."

Sweeping his free hand across their view, Eli continued. "There are several advantages provided by the conjoining of land and water. The river and the island together provide natural defenses not found at Fort Donelson, which was located in a place ill-suited for defense. Island No. 10 stands at the bottom of a large double hairpin bend in a section of the river known to be unkind to water traffic. The heavy artillery is well-placed in a position that can effectively prevent Federal gunboats from passing. To make matters worse for the Yanks, the river at this time of year is in flood stage, making a land assault coming from above the island along the eastern bank nearly impossible." George glanced at Eli in amazement, obviously impressed with his friend's military prowess.

Eli took another swig and told George to observe the area between Island No. 10 and the mainland shore. "See those narrow strips of high ground on both sides of the river. They are backed by swampland."

Eli lit a cigar. "One thing's for certain. I'd hate to be a Yankee caught in those swamp bogs under fire from our artillery."

The two men walked back to the camp in time for the midday meal, which they found better than most camp fare. After they ate their fill, George occupied himself by cleaning his musket and finished smoking his pipe. While George cleaned his weapon, Eli read a week old Memphis newspaper and went looking for a card game at the officer's mess. After George washed himself with soap and several camp kettles of heated water, he volunteered to help the cook-of-the day prepare the evening meal. After mess, he finished the letter to Ann Pritchard he had started on the train. George could hear someone playing a banjo as he drifted off to sleep.

The camp environment on Island No. 10 gave little indication that the soldiers were aware of the looming danger that approached from the north. An occasional rumble of cannon from the vicinity of Fort Thompson hinted at trouble on the horizon, but such thoughts were pushed from their collective consciousness. The only exception was the increased attendance at Bartley Sims nightly prayer meetings. Sims was the unofficial chaplain of the camp. His massive forearms suggested his trade might have been that of a blacksmith before he enlisted. His dark piercing eyes were framed by a flowing salt and pepper beard. He could look right through you one minute and roar with laughter the next. His favorite refrain was "the day of judgment will be here before you know it" and from the increased frequency of cannon fire in the distance, more of the men were heeding his warning.

When men were not carrying out sentinel duties, laboring on fortification repairs or attending prayer meetings, they occupied themselves with various leisure-time activities. Reading materials were in short supply and high demand, despite the fact that many men were not inclined to read or were illiterate. Some busied themselves with writing letters to family as a way of alleviating their homesickness. Music was also a pastime activity enjoyed by the enlisted and officers alike. Several soldiers played harmonicas and, in Eli's opinion, a few managed to perform quite well on the banjo. One private from Mississippi was a first-rate fiddle player, which he spoke to by name and cared for as if it were a baby. His best melody was "Home, Sweet Home." After supper, despite the cold and closing darkness, the men stood around the campfires, smoking and talking. Several related stories about home while others listened to music being played, often singing along when a familiar tune was played. No one spoke of the enemy threat to the north. They seemed oblivious to rumors of Federal troops massing several miles from Fort Thompson or of Yankee gunboats steaming down river toward their island fortress.

FAMILY REUNION — THE BATTLE BEGINS

On the same day Private George Spears and Lieutenant Eli Forrest walked into the Confederate army headquarters at Columbus, Kentucky to volunteer for duty at Island No. 10, a thirty-nine-year-old career officer, considered a rising star in the Federal Army, assumed command of the Army of the Mississippi. John Pope was promoted to the rank of Major General and given the objective of shutting down the rebel batteries at Madrid Bend and Island No. 10, which the Northern High Command viewed as a strategic tri-state position that protected the Mississippi River and the Confederate heartland in the west.

In three day's time, from February 28th to March 2nd, Pope moved more than 22,000 Union troops, including artillery and cavalry units closer to New Madrid. Large supplies of arms and ammunition were transported a distance of forty miles, starting from Pope's base at Commerce, Missouri and going to within two and a half miles of the Confederate outpost, which stood downriver a short distance from New Madrid, Missouri.

On March 3, 1862, General Pope and his impressive force began a tenday siege of Fort Thompson and New Madrid. Union artillery unleashed a massive assault on the fort's earthworks as well as on a smaller rebel fort east of the town, where 1,100 rebel infantrymen sought cover. The bombardment culminated on March 13th. Among infantry soldiers who endured the cannonading east of the fort were two Alabama brothers from Choctaw County who, before the Civil War, had never crossed their state's border with Tennessee. After being subjected to the Union bombardment, A.F. and Will Spears wished they hadn't left their home in Alabama and swore never to return to the Volunteer State.

It was the second day of March when George and Eli boarded the wooden gunboat for the ten-mile ride downriver to the mouth of Bayou Saint John where a four regiment garrison of Confederate infantry and a seven gun artillery battery guarded the river approach to New Madrid and Fort Thompson. *The Pontchartrain* was commanded by Captain John W. Dunnington and was one of five Confederate navy gunboats that had been committed to the defense of New Madrid and Island No. 10. Neither George nor Eli found the short trip in the swollen current to their liking, and both were relieved when the boat pulled into land.

The upper fort, positioned on the western side of the mouth of the bayou, was called Fort Bankhead, named after the artillery captain who was in charge of the fort's battery. There were two infantry regiments camped at the fort and two bivouacked in the adjacent town. Construction was still being carried out on the earthworks. It consisted of a sizable parapet ditch, next to a make-shift abatis. The entire battlement made up a straight line, extending from the bayou shore to the bank of the river about 400 yards away. It enclosed in an equal dimensional triangle about eight acres of the town of New Madrid. The portion of the fortress on the river bank was low and muddy.

Captain Dunnington and the two army passengers disembarked and made their way through the camp to the tent of Colonel Alpheus Baker, who commanded the First Alabama, Tennessee and Mississippi Infantry which consolidated four Alabama, two Tennessee and two Mississippi companies into one regiment. The colonel was seated at a small table when his orderly escorted the navy officer into his tent. There was some light-hearted discussion, interspersed with laughter, after which Dunnington left, giving George an encouraging pat on the left shoulder as he walked by. The Colonel's orderly motioned for George and Eli to come forward. They stood before Colonel Baker and saluted.

The colonel, a man in his early thirties, peered through small, rounded glasses at the two men standing before him. A slight man with piercing blue eyes, Colonel Baker gave the appearance not of a regimental commander, but of a lawyer, which in fact, he was in civilian life. He impassively suggested that the two new volunteers set their haversacks, bedrolls and muskets on the ground. Speaking with an accent that George knew to be from southeast Alabama, he asked George and Eli how they came to be assigned to his regiment. Eli explained who he and George were and that they were assigned to the colonel's regiment as a result of General Stewart's orders. Baker had received no word from Stewart or anyone else regarding the two men, so Eli was required to elaborate regarding their circumstances.

Colonel Baker summoned his orderly and directed him to bring the Spears brothers, H. W. Spears and A.F. to his tent. He also told the orderly to inquire if Captain Griffin was available to come as well. In the meantime, Baker briefed Eli and George about the role of the upper garrison at Bayou Saint John. It and Fort Thompson, a mile further downriver, were under the command of Brigadier General Stewart. Stewart had put Colonel Lucius M. Walker in charge of the bayou garrison. Marsh Walker a native of Columbia, Tennessee, was the same age as Baker, but unlike Baker, was West Point trained and had served in the regular army. In addition to Colonel Baker's regiment, Walker's post included his own Fortieth Tennessee Regiment and two others plus a Tennessee artillery battery. The latter consisted of four smooth-bore heavy cannon and an equal number of eight pound field pieces, all of which was under the direction of a young artillery captain also from Memphis by the name of Smith P. Bankhead. The four heavy cannons, 32-pounders, were strategically placed along the earthworks of the fort and the artillery pieces rested on wooden platforms behind the excavated parapet. Fort Thompson was the larger of the two fortresses at New Madrid. It mounted fourteen heavy guns on the earthworks. Colonel Edward W. Gantt, an Arkansas politician turned soldier, ran the operation at Fort Thompson.

A short time later, appearing at the entrance of Colonel Baker's tent was a solitary soldier clad in the butternut-colored shirt and trousers worn by many in the Confederate army of the west. He was a young man of twenty-four, but the smooth skin of his face made him look younger. Blond-haired, light-skinned and beardless, his head and thick neck rested on broad shoulders and an angular body. He was tall in an awkward sort of way. His large hands hung at his side pointing to even larger feet. His rumpled trousers partially covered a pair of badly scuffed, mud-splashed shoes. He had a slouched cap without a cord, which he took off as he entered the tent and now held with both hands in front of him. Looking confused, he scanned the faces of the men in the tent. He smiled broadly as his eyes fixed on George.

Soon after A.F. arrived, a second soldier entered the tent. He was attired in a similar fashion, except for the hat, which was wide-brimmed and tan-colored. At thirty-two years old, H.W. —Will" —Spears was older than his two brothers standing before him. He was shorter and more thick-bodied than the other two, with coal black hair running down to his shoulders and a dense black beard. His eyes were wide-set and dark.

Colonel Baker motioned to Eli to follow him outside the tent in order for the three brothers to have a bit of privacy for their reunion. The colonel wiped his eyeglasses with a tattered handkerchief he pulled from his breast-coat pocket. "So your name's Forrest?"

"Yes Sir."

Repositioning his glasses on the bridge of his nose, he looked directly at Eli. "You wouldn't by chance be related to Bedford Forrest?"

"Yes Sir, he's my uncle," Eli responded.

Extending his hand, Colonel Baker smiled at Eli. "I'm sure we can use another lieutenant, especially if he has an ounce of his uncle's grit. Welcome Lieutenant Forrest."

"Thank you, Sir," Eli replied.

Inside the tent, the two brothers embraced George. Will kept repeating, "How in hell did you get here?" A.F. said nothing, but laughed and grinned.

George pulled back and looked sternly at A.F. Then with both hands he took hold of A.F.'s muscular shoulders and feigned anger.

"I oughta skin you alive for what you've done. Ma must be worried half to death over you running off to join the fighting."

"I know it. It was 'cause I didn't want to miss out, seein' as how you and Will and all the others joined up and got to go," A.F. replied, still grinning from ear to ear.

George shook his head and scowled. "This ain't no child's game. At Fort Donelson, we lost a lot of good men in the fightin'. And the rest of my regiment was captured by the Yanks and taken off to a northern prison."

George looked at his other brother. "Will, you shouldn't have let him follow you."

Just like when they were young boys on the farm, George could never stay angry for long at his brothers, especially his younger brother. Alex, as he was known in the Spears family of seven brothers and two sisters, had the maturity level of a twelve-year old child. Alex decided he preferred to be known as A.F.—said it made him seem more grown-up. He had a kindly disposition and never seemed to entertain a mean or cruel thought. He seemed to view the world in a simple, trusting way that left him vulnerable to those who took advantage of such people. George and Will had always looked out for their younger brother, protecting him from those who would trick or tease him or call him half-witted. George felt a cold chill run up his spine. War was the last place on earth A.F. needed to be

A.F. could barely read and could only write his name and a few simple words. But he loved to hunt and fish and was good at both. He was also a hard worker and seemed to relish those routine, repetitive tasks that many others found boring and required more physical exertion than mental prowess.

Colonel Baker returned and instructed Will to take George and Eli back to the tents and present them to Company B's sergeant, who would get the two new volunteers squared away. George thanked the colonel, who responded with a smile and remarked that he was glad to have one more Spears in the regiment. Baker also said he would inform Captain Griffin of George's addition to his company. Baker then turned to Eli and assured him that an experienced officer such as he would be welcomed by the regiment's officers as well as by the men in the ranks.

After leaving the commanding officer's tent, George motioned for Eli to join him and his two brothers. "A.F. and Will, meet my friend Eli—I mean Lieutenant Eli Forrest."

When Will and A.F. came to attention and saluted, Eli started laughing. He extended his hand to the two brothers. "There's a time to salute and a time to shake hands."

A.F. looked bewildered. "I don't think I'm supposed to shake hands with an officer."

George smiled at his younger brother. "It's okay to shake hands with Eli. He is an officer, but more than that, he's my friend. We've been through a lot together."

Eli and George spent the rest of that Saturday getting acquainted with the other men in their new company, many whom George knew from Choctaw County, where Captain Jonas Griffin had organized the unit. George would share a tent with his brothers and another man, who had been a neighbor of his in Alabama. Eli decided for the time being to throw in with them as well, at least until he could find another junior officer to share a tent with.

The two new members of the regiment discovered that food supplies were plentiful and the quality of the fare was better than he had experienced at Fort Donelson. Blankets were also in ample supply. The only thing lacking was reliable musketry. Over a hundred men in the regiment were unarmed while others were poorly armed with a variety of hunting guns and old flint-locks ill suited for army use. They had been issued 260 new rifles made in a Memphis gun shop, but many of these were defective. Only about half of the regiment had firearms fit for fighting the enemy.

Late that afternoon, Captain Jonas Griffin caught up with Eli and George. Griffin had known the Spears family ever since Archibald Spears, Sr. had moved his brood to Choctaw County. The Griffin plantation was just two land tracts down from the Spears place and both families sent their children to the Male and Female Academy in nearby Desotoville. Jonas was of average height, thin, with red hair, a neatly trimmed beard and deep-set eyes. He was not a man of great wealth or extensive military experience, but still had considerable influence as a fair-minded gentleman planter-turned-officer.

The following day was Sunday. After breakfast, a group of about twenty soldiers gathered near one of the fires for Bible reading prayer. They had not been long into their morning devotion when a burst of musket fire erupted. As the soldiers scrambled for their weapons and ran to formation, another salvo could be heard, followed by the loud percussion of artillery fire. Then, as suddenly as it had started, it stopped and all was quiet. Later, after a rider who had been sent to Fort Thompson returned, the garrison learned that a light skirmish just north of New Madrid had occurred. Pickets from that fort encountered advance units of Pope's cavalry moving southward on the Sikestown road. The mood at the Bayou Saint John fort turned somber. Colonel Walker ordered a heightened alert. The artillerymen took to their stations and awaited orders from Captain Bankhead.

After an hour or two, when it became apparent that the fort would not come under attack, the alert was canceled. Men immediately went to work entrenching. Even though the rain had stopped shortly before breakfast, they struggled with the task, made even more difficult by thick, oozing mud and standing water that comprised the grounds of the poorly placed, low lying fort. They worked until dark, when the bell sounded for the companies to fall in line for their supper.

In the evening, Colonel Baker dispatched Company B to go out on picket duty. George considered it bad luck that he drew picket duty his very first night in New Madrid. For once, he wished he could trade places with Eli who was most likely playing cards in the officer's mess tent. The picket line was set up north of the town where they spent the entire night in the frigid cold. Pickets were scattered several miles alongside a roadside ravine, standing amidst rain-soaked knot weeds, decaying leaves and twigs. It was the most miserable night George had spent in the army, even worse than the night he had slept in the woods while making his escape from Fort Donelson. The wind gusts made the night bitterly cold as they blew in from the river. The young lieutenant in charge rode back to camp at daybreak to report to the company commander that his men were nearly frozen whereupon replacements were sent out and Company B was ordered to return to camp. Shivering and exhausted, the picket patrol headed back to their fort.

On their way back, the weary sentries passed by the flooded streets of New Madrid. They walked in silence, interrupted only by wheezing and coughing. Several of them passed by a shanty where their colonel and Major Couch were staying the night—attended by two slaves. Bleary-eyed and stiff-fingered from clutching his musket all night, George glanced at the chimney atop the small wooden structure. It emitted a steady stream of white smoke that seemed to curl in the crisp morning air, promising warmth inside and a hot breakfast. George and one of his fellow sentries spit in the direction of the cabin as they walked by.

The other infantry companies in Colonel Baker's regiment had spent the night taking turns manning the earthen embattlements in support of the artillery battery. Eli volunteered to relieve one of the duty officers and bring the men hot coffee. Because it had rained heavily the previous morning, most of the approaches were thick mud. The mounds provided little protection against the frigid air that blew in from the river. Even worse, the temperature had dropped steadily throughout the night. The last company on duty remained there, cold and miserable until daybreak at which time they were relieved by men from the Fifth Tennessee, who were now also bivouacked at the Bayou Saint John garrison.

Reports came in from scouts that a Federal division had drawn to within three or four miles of New Madrid. Some skirmishing had taken place between pickets from Colonel Jabez Smith's Eleventh Arkansas, who were positioned north of the town, and advance units of Yankee cavalry. Sporadic musket fire could still be heard coming from that direction by the men on the bayou fort's breastworks. Both the pickets and the mounted bluecoats apparently kept their distance given that the sound of firing remained sporadic.

Toward nightfall an infantry regiment guarding the far west boundary of New Madrid—the Eleventh Arkansas—was ordered to fall back to Fort Thompson. The long anticipated enemy assault had finally begun. As a brigade of Yankee infantrymen moved east across a cornfield toward New Madrid, several Confederate gunboats, which had been steaming in place just south of the town along the flooded shore, opened fire on the advancing enemy. The rebel gunboat barrage continued, joined by cannon fire unleashed by rebel gunners at Fort Thompson. The cannonading continued for three hours, reverberating up and down the river. The Yankees pulled back out of range of the fort's heavy guns, content to set up camp and wait for their own artillery reinforcements.

Meanwhile, at the mouth of the bayou, the men of Company B spent the morning resting from their picket duty ordeal of the previous evening. They ate a cold breakfast of cornmeal mush and tried to get some sleep. George lay in the small white tent and pulled an extra blanket on top of him. His thoughts returned to Fort Donelson, where he had fought several weeks prior. He began to experience the same feeling of impending doom about the South's prospects for Madrid Bend that he felt before the previous battle. As he listened to the loud coughing and labored breathing of sleeping soldiers, he pondered the uncertain fate of his regiment trying to hold New Madrid. The last image that floated through his consciousness as he drifted into sleep was the face of Ann Pritchard.

George was abruptly awakened by the discharge of a rifle and the sound of shouting men running past his tent. He hurriedly exited the tent and asked a somber looking sergeant walking in the other direction about the shot fired. Apparently, a man from Company A had accidentally shot himself with his own weapon which turned out to be from the recently arrived shipment of muskets from Memphis. It was a head shot and he was not expected to live. The sergeant cursed the gun shop workers who made these muskets, many of which turned up with defective springs. He called them Yankee agents who ought to be shot or lynched.

Not long after the men of Company B had finished their mid-day rations, a messenger on horseback road swiftly into camp, dismounted and reported directly to Colonel Walker's headquarters. After conferring with the other senior officers, orders were issued.

The Fortieth Tennessee infantry regiment now under Colonel C.C. Henderson would provide support for the upper fort's fixed artillery on the parapet and in the rifle pits dug in front of the fortress. Eli was placed in charge of the men in these defenses. The fort's artillery captain would take his field guns and accompany Colonel Walker and some of Henderson's men out on the Sikeston Road headed north. For his part, Baker would have his regiment take up a position blocking the road as it entered New Madrid on the northeast side of town. There, he would await orders from Colonel Stewart, who was in command of all troops at both forts in the absence of General McCown. Scouts had reported that Yankee cavalry, estimated at five hundred strong, were heading in the direction of New Madrid. Panicked townspeople, fearful of being caught in the crossfire, were said to be lining up along the river landing, hoping to board a steamer for Memphis. Other residents, however, decided to stay put, hoping for a miracle.

George and his brothers stood toward the middle of the line along the road. They tried to stay warm, but there was no escaping the numbing wind and hard, cold surface of the dirt road on which they stood in silence. It wasn't long before a loud gun blast coming from the river could be heard, followed quickly by another and yet another. Word came down the line that one of the Confederate gunboats had repulsed the Union advance. Colonel Baker ordered a rail fence dismantled and set on fire so that so that the men could warm themselves. Ninety minutes later Colonel Walker and the light artillery returned. It seems that they had encountered a mounted Yankee patrol.

George stood close to the fire and rubbed his hands over the flames as Eli rode up on a borrowed horse. He had been relieved by another officer from his duty in the rifle pits.

"What did you learn, Lieutenant?" several of the soldiers queried Eli.

Eli spat a stream of tobacco juice on the cold, hard ground. "Colonel Baker says that the left wing of Walker's patrol was stationed behind one of the fences of a lane near where the Yankee cavalry was advancing. Our artillery was at the mouth of the lane. Four hundred more yards and the Yanks would have ridden right into Walker's ambush. Unfortunately, the gunners fired too soon—when they were about 1000 yards out. The long and short of it, is that the bluebellies pulled up and hightailed it back in the direction that they came from. Besides, it turns out that they were a reconnaissance patrol, not a full-fledged cavalry unit as Walker believed."

The men of Baker's regiment were ordered to return to the encampment at Fort Bankhead. While heading back to camp, many of the soldiers could not resist the temptation to enter the abandoned houses and shops and help themselves to whatever valuables and mementoes they could carry. George saw one man in his company carrying piles of calico cloth and window curtains in his arms, and artificial flowers sticking out of the band of his cap. George looked at his brothers and shook his head in disgust. No Spears brother would take part in looting another man's home, even though A.F. pleaded with him to join in the treasure hunt. They weren't raised that way.

Company B remained in camp the following day as snow fell most of the morning. The pools made by the previous days' rains had frozen solid. The men took their turn keeping watch at posts along the breastworks while work continued on strengthening the fortification. When they were not standing sentinel or hauling dirt, the men of Company B busied themselves washing clothes, cooking or tending to the general maintenance of the camp.

Around mid-day, the enemy appeared once again in a large cornfield about two and a half miles from the upper fortress. Several Confederate gunboats opened fire on their position. The fierce recoil of the crafts' rifled cannon was heartening to the rebel soldiers listening and waiting at their battle stations. Eli estimated the distance of the enemy to be about two miles from the at-tacking gunboats.

George could imagine the blue line and flags of the Yankee soldiers as the shells fell around them, sending dirt and cornhusks flying in all directions. The firing continued steadily for about two hours, then ceased. As things go, it had been a good day. The enemy had been turned back—at least for the time being. Toward evening, Eli, who had moved to the officers' tents, caught up with George. The two men ate their supper sitting on tree stumps close to a camp fire.

That night, Commodore Hollins, the Confederate commander of the five wooden gunboards, ordered a section of the town at New Madrid leveled. Most of the structures were dismantled for firewood, but a few were burned. What contents of the homes and businesses that had not been removed by their owners and looters, were made off with by the soldiers from the bayou fort. Whatever wasn't plundered was scattered throughout the streets. The excuse for the destruction was that a wide path had to be cleared for the gunboats' line of fire and for Captain Bankhead's heavy artillery when it came time to defend the garrison. In addition, the buildings posed a problem because they would provide cover for the enemy when the imminent attack against the fort began. Gunboat crewmen and several companies from the Fortieth Tennessee carried out the demolition assignment. That evening, a number of Baker's men returned to their tents with armfuls of plunder from the town.

Regarding the looting, Colonel Baker was less than pleased. Great quantities of lard were spread about as well as bacon and, in some places, sugar a half foot deep on building floors. Talking to himself as much as to the officers surrounding him, he looked out upon the scene. "What a waste…costly drugs ruined from a ransacked drug-store and food that could feed our army and hungry civilians," the colonel's voice trailed off.

After the looting and leveling was complete, a strange odor emanated from several of the smoldering structures that had been set ablaze. It drifted into the area of the fort where George stood guard. As he stared into the darkness, he noted the irony of war where the defense of a town such as New Madrid against invaders required its destruction at the hands of the defenders.

"What has become of the world?" he thought to himself. "Has civilized society been reduced to a pack of savages?"

After the evening officers' briefing, Eli stepped out of Colonel Baker's tent and lit the last of his cigars.

"Lieutenant Forrest."

Eli turned to see Colonel Marsh Walker approaching him.

"I understand Bedford Forrest is your uncle."

"Yes Sir."

"At ease, Lieutenant. You may speak freely."

"Yes Sir."

"I knew your uncle and his family in Memphis. You might say we kept different company. Some of my business associates held certain business grievances against your Uncle Bedford and his Uncle Jonathan. They found Jonathan Forrest, in particular, to be unsavory and unreliable. You probably already know this, but Jonathan Bedford perished in an altercation with the Matlock brothers after getting caught cheating or some such behavior."

Colonel Walker cleared his throat and then looked directly at Eli. "I trust you have better breeding than your uncle and his Memphis kin."

Eli felt the blood rush to his face. He was glad it was dark. "He's my uncle, Colonel, and like you, a colonel in the Confederate army with his own command."

"A bought command, Lieutenant—bought by a brawling gambler of ill repute with no professional military pedigree. How about you, Lieutenant? Do you have any professional military training?" Walker replied.

"I attended Virginia Military Institute, but then again, I'm but a shadow of my uncle."

The colonel pursed his lips. "Be thankful for that, Lieutenant. Perhaps there is hope for you yet. Perhaps, with your exposure to VMI and proper supervision, you may yet learn to be an officer and gentleman."

Eli clinched his fists in an effort to maintain his composure. "Perhaps."

Walker smiled at Eli's apparent discomfort. "But that's not likely, is it Lieutenant? If it were, you wouldn't be reassigned here."

Eli remained silent.

"Perhaps, you are more like your uncle than you realize—your uncle who turned tail and abandoned Fort Donelson."

Eli felt a fire growing in his belly. "A lot of folks escaped from Fort Donelson, me included. The first ones who left were two of the commanding officers, one who I believe was professionally trained at West Point like yourself, Colonel."

Marsh Walker's eyes narrowed. "I would be careful if I were you, Lieutenant. Insubordination seems to come as easy to you as it does your uncle."

"Please accept my apologies, Colonel. I thought you instructed me to speak freely."

"So I did," the colonel tersely replied. "It would be good that you remember you are no longer under your uncle's protection. I will do my best to help you remember that fact."

Eli relaxed his fists. "Yes Sir."

"You are dismissed, Lieutenant."

Later that night when the Spears brothers shared a pot of coffee with Eli, he informed them that, during the earlier briefing, he had learned that six or seven thousand enemy soldiers were located in woods northwest of New Madrid and more were on the way. Speculation was that they were waiting for other infantry divisions to arrive, reportedly coming down the Sikestown Road and bringing with them siege guns. Will added that he had overheard the fort's artillery commander say that they might be waiting for their ironclads to come downriver to take on Commodore Hollins' gunboats. George offered that the latter, so far, were doing a good job, together with Fort Thompson's heavy artillery, in keeping the Yankee infantry and light artillery at bay.

A.F. and Will retired to their tent. As George cleaned the coffee pot, Eli finished the last of his coffee and looked at his friend. "Something else happened after the briefing tonight."

George put the coffee pot in his rucksack. "What's that?"

"Colonel Marsh Walker made it clear that he has little use for Uncle Nathan and, by proxy, for me as well."

George wiped his hands on his pants. "You reckon he's got it in for you?"

Eli relit what was left of his cigar. "Could be, my friend. Could be."

The next day, General McCown brought up from Island No. 10 a Tennessee infantry regiment commanded by Colonel Travis. They disembarked shortly before the day's gunboat barrage began. George and Eli knew some of the men from their brief stay at the island fortress. They were part of Colonel Stewart's brigade and their encampment would be on the bayou fort side. Close to midnight, pickets from Fort Thompson skirmished with a Yankee patrol along the Sikestown Road. The rebel gunboats again took aim, this time targeting the position with the help of the flare from the enemy patrol's field guns, which seemed to be randomly firing into the darkness.

When the gunboats fired, the Spears brothers emerged from their tent, carrying their muskets and pulling on their trousers. Every campfire was extinguished as they, along with the other soldiers, took cover. After an hour, the shelling stopped, and they returned to the tents. No casualties were incurred by any of the Confederate units during this late night encounter, but at least one and maybe more of the enemy was reported killed by the gunboat shelling.

A badly wounded Yankee was found lying by a fence just beyond the rebel picket line. He had been shot in the abdomen and after lying all night in the cold mud, was barely alive. Although he was carried back to the fort and tended to by the regimental surgeon, he died soon after.

The ensuing day saw no significant movement from the enemy position that was now encamped only several miles to the northwest. The men of Company B filled their day doing much of what they had done the previous day and the days before that. They worked on the fort's approach trenches which were nearly complete. Their company and the others in Baker's regiment labored on the center portion, while the other two regiments were busy on either side. One of Colonel Baker's captains supervised their efforts. A parapet about ten feet thick with a five foot deep ditch below it was constructed, using mostly corn shucks to keep the boards in place.

Picket skirmishing once more took place between Confederate foot patrols sent from Fort Thompson and their Yankee counterparts venturing down from their encampments. Brief intervals of musket fire could be heard at the bayou fort as the solders there went about their digging and earthmoving in front of the fortress. The work was hard, but the weather at the mouth of Bayou Saint John was better than the previous two days, and the men were grateful for the improvement.

On Thursday, March 6th, beginning at midnight, patrols of about sixty men from each of three Confederate regiments were sent out every twelve hours under the command of lieutenant colonels, majors, and a few of the more experienced captains. George and Will were among the second group of picket guards that left the fort. They crossed town streets and then headed north along the edge of the massive cornfield north of Fort Thompson. It was dangerous duty, made more perilous by the low lying fog that persisted throughout the day. The primary danger was in being flanked and cut off by a much larger enemy force.

The officer in charge of the second picket patrol was Lieutenant Colonel W. T. Avery of Baker's regiment. Avery was mounted on a large bay equipped with an ornate black saddle. The other officers were two captains, one named McLean and the other called Helms, plus a Lieutenant Meads and Eli, all of whom were on horseback. The men on foot fanned out over a wide range of cornfields and wooded terrain. When they had come to within a half mile of enemy lines, they found themselves face-to-face with a band of mounted Yankee scouts who, upon encountering the rebel contingent, turned abruptly and fled. The Confederate officers gave chase, shouting and firing at them as they galloped headlong in hot pursuit. While the rebel horsemen pursued the fleeing Yankee scouts along a wooded lane, McLean caught sight of a much larger party of Yankee cavalry galloping in the opposite direction on the cleared track that ran parallel to the lane where the chase was taking place. He could see further ahead where a cross lane connected the two.

"Hold up," McClean shouted, "that's far enough! Look at that pack of Yankees over there! They mean to cut us off."

The five Confederate officers pulled up and wheeled their steeds around, galloping back toward their picket lines. Finding themselves being overtaken by the enemy in hot pursuit, they halted and drew up their firearms. The Yankee horsemen did likewise. Gunshots were exchanged. Seeing their pursuers come to a stop, Avery, McLean, Helms, Eli and Meads turned their horses and again bolted away. The Yankees continued to fire at them and they could feel bullets whistling around them as they rode toward safety. For a reason known only to him, Captain Helms dismounted and attempted to pull his rifle from its scabbard. In the course of that action, he was hit in the neck. The others, not knowing Helms had stopped, suddenly looked back and saw that he had been wounded. In desperation, Helms grabbed the pommel of the saddle as his horse lurched away. Bleeding profusely, he somehow managed to get back on his mount and save himself.

Helms was spitting blood when he got back to the Confederate picket lines. The first person to reach Helms was Eli, who caught the Captain as he slid semiconscious from his horse. Blood was pulsing from the neck of the badly wounded rebel officer. Captain McClean called for an ambulance wagon while Lieutenant Mead and Eli knelt on either side of Helms.

Eli quickly slipped a knife from his boot and cut a strip from Helms' shirt. Wadding the cloth into a make-shift bandage, he pressed it against the wound in an effort to slow the bleeding. Captain McClean crouched next to Eli. "Lieutenant, I hope you know what you are doing. This man's life is in your hands."

"Captain, I do have some familiarity with such situations," Eli replied as he worked on the wound. "Mead, I would be much obliged if you would maintain light pressure with this bandage while I cut up a fresh one from my shirt. By the time the ambulance wagon arrived, Helms seemed to be breathing easier. Although no one expected him to survive, Captain Helms was taken to Fort Thompson, where he was treated by the chief medical officer and somehow pulled through. That same surgeon credited Lieutenant Forrest's quick action with saving Helms' life.

About 3:00 p.m., several outlying pickets from the regiment spotted their enemy counterparts in a clump of copse wood no more than two hundred yards away. These rebel outliers opened fire and before long, nearly all of the pickets on patrol were firing their weapons in that direction. George saw no sign of Yankees in the thicket, but fired his musket anyway along with the others. The Confederates seemed to fire by companies. He thought the Yankees had quit the field, but they suddenly began to return fire in force and continued to do so for some time. Then suddenly they stopped, and before long, so did the men from the bayou fort.

The picket patrol that George and Eli were a part of maintained their positions in the cornfield and an adjacent patch of woods until dark. There was no further fighting in the area where the skirmishing had occurred, but artillery fire could be heard coming from Fort Thompson as well as from the gunboats positioned close by. When nightfall finally fell, Lieutenant Colonel Avery and the other mounted officers led their tired troops back to Bayou Saint John and their tents.

Eli pulled his mount up next to George as their patrol marched back to camp.

George cast a sideways glance toward Eli. "Heard about you saving Captain Helms' life."

Eli said nothing as George continued. "Lucky for Helms that you were nearby. Word is he doesn't always use good judgment in the heat of the moment."

George looked at Eli, surprised by his reticence. "I reckon Captain McClean was grateful to you for saving one of his own."

"Grateful enough," Eli responded with a smile, pulling a bottle of rye whiskey from his saddle bag.

The main topic of discussion that night came from news that the Yankees had moved what was reported to be an entire brigade from their encampment north of Fort Thompson some fifteen miles southward along a mud-filled Missouri road that ran parallel with the Mississippi River. Their destination was a place called Point Pleasant. There they met no resistance from the handful of Confederates posted in the tiny river town. The Union army occupied what little there was worth occupying, set up a four-gun land battery and made camp a mile away from shore. Their objective was no secret. If their gunners were good enough, they could disrupt the supply transports from Memphis that arrived regularly at the New Madrid river landing. General McCown would be sending several of Hollins' gunboats down river to root them out. But he would have to leave part of the fleet at New Madrid to keep the Federals north of Fort Thompson at bay.

George smoked his pipe while A.F. squatted next to the campfire and poked a stick at the glowing embers. Will had turned in earlier and George had no idea where Eli was.

A.F. lifted the stick from the fire and blew on the charred end until a small flame began to flicker. "George, when do you reckon we can go home?"

George looked at A.F., then into the fire. "I'm not sure little brother. I hope it's sooner rather than later."

A.F. looked at his brother and grinned. "How about sooner?"

"Sounds good to me."

A.F. stood up and threw the stick into the fire. "How about tomorrow? I miss Ma and Pa somethin' terrible."

George placed his hand on his brother's shoulder. "Not tomorrow, A.F., but I'll let you know when that day comes."

A.F.'s eyes grew wide. "Promise?"

"Promise," George replied.

"I'll need to get me some shut-eye," A.F. said, shuffling toward the tent.

He stopped and turned back to George. "I can't wait until that day comes."

George smiled gently at his younger brother. "Me neither."

THE FALL OF NEW MADRID

On Friday, March 7th, the dawn cast a gray light on the marsh fields surrounding the mouth of Bayou Saint John. No bugle had sounded, but the entire garrison—the infantrymen of the Fifth and the Fortieth Tennessee regiments and the regiment in which the Spears brothers and Eli served—was at the ready. The men had been roused from their slumber. They stuffed their shirts into their trousers, threw water onto their faces and ate their army breakfast. Now they stood assembled. A messenger had been sent from Colonel Gantt at Fort Thompson that pickets had returned in the predawn hour with reports that the Federals were massing in great numbers a short distance from the town. They appeared to be moving eastward toward their bayou outpost. The words of Gantt's messenger had quickly spread throughout camp and put a scare that was palpable in the chill morning air.

The Federals had indeed moved troops along the Confederate lines extending from the lower part of the town westward. This maneuver turned out to be a demonstration of force, designed to mask a direct assault from the north against Bayou Saint John. It may also have been calculated to show the defenders there the strength of their enemy and the futility of the rebel position. Aside from its unnerving effect, it fooled no one. Two Confederate artillery batteries firing from Fort Thompson and another firing from the bayou fort hurled shell after shell at the thousands of bluecoats who were now massed in a wooded area a quarter mile north of the upper fort. Union artillery returned fire, but the thunder of the heavy guns from both forts was also a signal for the Confederate gunboats to open fire. They were positioned close off New Madrid's river landing and well within range. The combined firepower of the Confederate gunboats and the land batteries drove back the Federal troops assembled in the town streets and stalled those massed beyond the town in the woods as well. Still, the Union artillery barrage continued from a distance. George and the other infantrymen from Company B stationed at the outpost had not fired a shot the entire morning. Their task was to remain at the works, repel any Yankee ground assault, and protect the land battery. Every Confederate soldier who was not manning the cannon, including those who had been pickets earlier in the day, stood in the fort's narrow trenches or along the river bank, having conceded the town for the moment to the superior numbers of the enemy. By day's end, the enemy had abandoned its positions, which had afforded them little to no protection from the rebel cannons. Once again, New Madrid was saved by the Confederate gunboats from falling into Union hands.

For the next five days, sporadic skirmishing of an inconsequential nature continued between small squads of Federal cavalry and the rebel defenders at New Madrid. The Southerners entrenched behind the earthworks at both outposts were more concerned with the dawn-to-dusk enemy artillery fire that seemed to grow worse by the day. For the moment, the Federals seemed willing to settle for the gradual inroads that they were making rather than risk high casualties in an all out frontal assault against the upper and lower Confederate forts. Each passing day saw mounted Yankee patrols making forays into town and the cornfields to its east, steadily driving back the rebel pickets. The blue-coated cavalrymen were followed by artillerymen who quickly unlimbered their field pieces within range of their targets. From these temporary locations, they sent their explosive missiles in the directions of the two forts. Every so often, an artillery shell would strike one of the two forts' breastworks and bounce to the ground, where it would explode, sending dirt and mud flying in every direction. Miraculously, none of the forts' defenders were killed or seriously injured. The bombardment continued until the return fire of the Confederate gunners drew their location and they were forced to move. Then the ritual repeated itself. Neither army seemed willing or able to deliver a decisive blow. Matters were at a stalemate with both sides having little else to do but watch and wait.

The siege of both forts was only a matter of time. The word around camp was that the Union army would soon have siege guns brought down the Sikestown Road. While Pope's division commanders kept their troops out of range of the rebels' heavy guns, they continued to send out daily patrols to harass the forts' defenders. The patrols consisted of a few squads of cavalrymen who were viewed as more of an annoyance than a threat. Several well placed artillery shells were usually enough to turn them back in short order. As this daily ritual played out, Eli and another lieutenant from Baker's regiment devised a plan to ambush the predictable Yankee horse patrols, but Colonel Walker vetoed the idea as too risky.

The Spears brothers and the others in Company B, including a frustrated Eli, remained on the earthworks for hours at a time each day and watched vigilantly, expecting that every shot fired was a prelude to the inevitable Yankee charge. Yet the real threat did not come from Yankee bullets fired from the rifles of mounted soldiers, but from their unnerving artillery barrage showering the rebel defenders. The thunder of discharging artillery, the shrill cry of the airborne missiles and the thrashing explosions of bursting shells struck terror in their hearts. The air was filled with smoke clouds, making breathing difficult for some of the defenders.

The ground shook and both sides of the earthworks became riddled and punctuated by the jagged fragments of the exploding shells. Men held their hands over their ears to muffle the noise of the explosions and shouted curses at each upheaval of torn earth or distant splash of river water. Near the earthworks where the men of Company B sought cover stood Captain Bankhead's artillery battery returning fire at the enemy. Steadfastly obeying their captain's commands, the artillerymen repeatedly prepared, loaded and then discharged the 32-pounders and eight-pounders at such an amazing pace that it appeared automatic. The artillery exchange continued unabated until nearly dark. With every incoming shell fired at the fort came a shrieking warning, flying over the heads of the men crouching behind the earthworks. Some landed east of the bulwarks and buried themselves in the marsh fields, amid the scrub trees of the bayou. Other missiles were less benign, bursting closer to the fortifications and ricocheting through the earthworks with frightening effect. One exploding shell struck five men, although miraculously none received fatal wounds. Captain William Hallum of the Fifth Tennessee Regiment was hit by sharpshooter fire. The flintlock bullet passed clean through him and word had it that he was still alive but in considerable pain. The captain and the other wounded soldiers were taken to Fort Thompson where they were treated by an army surgeon.

That evening as George sat alone and ate a supper of salt pork and beans, he reflected on the day. He found himself comparing his experience with the artillery bombardment at Fort Donelson to that at his present post. He thought about how each man had hugged his piece of the earthworks while the deadly missiles flew over their heads, not knowing where each would land and whether this one or the next would bring death. He concluded it was worse here because at Fort Donelson his unit was continuously on the move and had no time to think. Here at New Madrid, it was different. He and the others had waited for hours in one place. Furthermore, they endured much more artillery fire due to the greater number of enemy guns.

Physically exhausted and emotionally spent, he retired to the tent he shared with his brothers and another soldier and soon fell into a fitful sleep. George didn't hear the three of them enter the tent shortly thereafter. Even if he had, he was in no mood for conversation. He slept for several hours despite the hacking coughs of two of his tent mates. Sickness from exposure to the cold and dampness at New Madrid was beginning to have a telling effect on the physical health and morale of the men of Company B.

For three days, defenders at the two rebel forts could hear the distant exchange of heavy gun-fire coming from downriver. The prolonged battle at Point Pleasant did not bode well, according to Colonel Baker, who was always straightforward with the men in his regiment. Although the gunboats had failed in dislodging the Yankee artillery battery at Point Pleasant, the navy's mission had not been a total loss. They had provided cover for the supply boats to make it upriver along the Tennessee shore. George later found out that Captain Dunnington's gunboat was there, along with one other. Still, they were thwarted in their attempt to drive back the Yankees. Every time they got within range of the enemy's artillery, they were driven back by small arms fire from their infantry who were dug in along the shore. Dunnington had even incurred some casualties when he ordered his vessel too close to shore.

Believing that the enemy's Point Pleasant battery could not be removed by the gunboats, two 24-pounder siege guns from Fort Thompson were transported downriver and set up opposite the Missouri shore location on the Tennessee side of the river. Separated by a mile and a half of fast moving river water, the more powerful rebel artillery held a slight advantage, but the Yankees were still able to menace river traffic. On Tuesday, March 11th, the Confederate gunboats finally returned to New Madrid to rejoin the others in protecting the town and the two rebel forts.

On Wednesday, Company B was sent out on picket patrol, along with several companies from Walker's regiment. Eli was the officer in charge of the B company pickets. There had been a steady exchange of gunfire most of the afternoon. Captain Laird, who Eli and George had taken a liking to, was making his way on foot to the men of his company who were scattered along the extended picket boundary. Joined by Eli, the two were replenishing each of the outlying pickets' cartridge supply. They had not yet made it to George's location when musket fire rang out near the place where his older brother was positioned. Will had fired at a rider on horseback approaching at breakneck speed. The horseman was struck in the abdomen, but managed to stay atop of the stead. Then he was fired on again by other picket soldiers. He was hit a second time, whereupon he fell to the ground. The rider-less horse continued his gallop headed in the same direction.

When the nearest rebel soldier arrived at where the fallen rider lie, he immediately called out to his comrades. George and Will came running, followed by the captain and Eli. The fallen rider turned out to be a Confederate captain! The mortally wounded man was none other than Captain West, Provost Marshall for the South's forces at New Madrid. Captain Laird assured Will that he was not at fault. Rather, the fault lay with the dying captain because he had previously gone beyond the picket boundary earlier in the afternoon and had returned to report that he had been fired upon by rebel pickets. Laird advised West not to risk doing the same thing again, but West was intoxicated and had ignored the warning. Soon after he had passed through enemy lines and turned to come galloping back to the rebel pickets, he was shot at by his compatriots. Will was still upset, blaming himself for West's death and repeatedly apologizing to anyone who would listen.

The next morning, the enemy opened fire on Fort Thompson with siege guns. During the night, they had planted the heavy weaponry, consisting of several 24-pounders and one 8-inch howitzer, on hastily constructed gun platforms, supported by massive rifle pits on either side. The Federals installed their siege guns and a sizable number of troops no more than 1,000 yards from the lower rebel army post. The upper fort was notified and put on alert.

"Captain Griffin, I'm worried," Baker said when the officer entered his tent. Last night, Colonel Walker asked me to provide him with a reliable man for a risky mission. He needed someone to paddle a canoe down Bayou Saint John with a couple of locals who know the bayou well enough to navigate the shallow waterways. While you were away, I lent him your Corporal Seward. They left at daybreak. It is now nearing sundown and the corporal has not returned. I fear he has been captured or killed by the enemy or has accidentally drown."

Captain Griffin stood in silence as Colonel Baker pored over an area map. Finally, Baker took off his spectacles and rubbed his eyes.

"What do you think about Private Spears taking over for Corporal Seward in his absence?"

The captain took the cup of coffee the colonel offered him. "I'll bring the subject up sometime tomorrow with the men in his company, but I'm confident they will be agreeable. George Spears is well-liked and respected. He carries more than his fair share of the workload in camp."

George was awakened at 1:00 a.m. and together with the others in his company, took up assigned positions within the bayou fort. He and his brothers, along with others from the regiment who were well enough to answer the duty call, were on the west earthworks. Eli nodded to George as he led a detachment of troops toward the north section of the earthworks. Near where Company B was positioned was one of the fort's larger cannons pointed in the direction of the Sikestown Road. Sporadic musket fire could be heard near Fort Thompson, but it was cold and windy and too dark to see much of anything.

At daybreak, it seemed as if all hell erupted at New Madrid when rumbling from the Federals' powerful siege guns shook the entire area. Their first target was the Confederate fleet of gunboats and transports afloat below Fort Thompson.

When the gunboats returned fire, there was a brief pause before the Union artillery began lobbing eight-inch shells at the two forts. The forts' guns reciprocated and the artillery battle was in full. From his position atop the north earthworks, through his spyglass, Eli could see little through the mix of drifting smoke from the bayou fort's heavy guns and the dense fog that hung over the area.

The thunder of the heavy guns and the smashing sound of cannonballs falling dangerously close unnerved the defenders on the bulwarks. Many set their muskets against the ramparts, and cringed as they flung their arms over their heads. The braying shrieks of mortally wounded mules added to the cacophony of terror. Two of the fort's 24-pounders were hit within a half minute of each other, and the screams of wounded artillerymen cast dread in the hearts of the rebel defenders. Lieutenant Forrest's shouts for the men on the north bulwark to stand their positions were largely ignored. Seeing that his urging fell on deaf ears, Eli ran to where the heavy guns were mounted, to assist with the casualties. Four men lie seriously wounded.

At 11:00 a.m., Colonel Baker ordered Company B to regroup along a section of the north wall where a company from Colonel Henderson's regiment was stationed. Enemy movement had been detected nearby in the woods along their position. All of the heavy weaponry that could be moved was hurriedly placed on the north parapet with their muzzles pointed at the woods. Suddenly, an entire division of blue-coated infantrymen charged toward the rebel fort. The fort's artillery peeled off shot after shot in rapid succession while the enemy's field guns responded with little effect. Their siege guns, strangely, remained silent.

Hearing the first exchange, several of the Confederate gunboats steamed upriver to the upper fort and unleashed a fierce barrage upon the attacking Union troops. The shots from the fort and the gunboats proved too much for the bluecoats. They slowed their advance and within twenty minutes, their attack ground to a halt.

The Yankees turned and began to run and stumble back toward the woods. When the men defending the fort realized what was happening, they broke out into a loud cheer. They had held off a formidable enemy assault that morning and sustained only limited casualties from the earlier bombardment.

After the advance against the bayou outpost had been repelled, there was a welcome lull in the action at the fort. The men were allowed extra rations, which were brought forward to their positions. Pork, cornbread, cheese and coffee were eagerly devoured. They had not eaten in over twelve hours. Following their meal, the men rested, smoked and talked about what the Yanks would do next.

Their answer came sooner than they would have liked when the bombardment started up once more. This time, the other fort and the gunboats below it bore the brunt of the enemy's fierce shelling. As with the morning's experience, the gunboats and Fort Thompson's cannon responded in kind. The exchange of fire grew more intense by the hour. Several of the gunboats were hit by Yankee gunners, but none of the fleet's vessels were disabled. The bombardment continued throughout the afternoon into the evening. The bayou fortress was not totally ignored. Occasional shelling was directed its way, followed by long intervals of inactivity. Other than keeping everyone on edge with alerts to report to the parapet, little damage to the batteries occurred and no one in the upper fort was killed or seriously injured.

Toward mid-afternoon, the clouds grew darker and it began to rain. George and the men of Company B were tired and exhausted as they stood at their posts on the bulwark. Between the Yankee artillery shelling and the cold rain, they were physically exhausted and emotionally drained. Hardly a word passed among the men as they stood and looked out over the deserted streets and buildings of what was left of New Madrid.

Shortly after dark, the Bayou Saint John defenders were told that Generals McCown and Stewart and Commodore Hollins were meeting aboard one of the gunboats nearby. Matters seemed to be coming to a head according to the consensus of the rank and file. Would they stay and defend their position or would they leave?

When the meeting aboard the gunboat concluded, Colonel Walker received word to report to General McCown. The time was nearly 8:00 p.m. When Walker came back an hour later, he conferred with Baker, Bankhead and the two Tennessee colonels, Travis and Henderson, to tell them that both forts at New Madrid were to be immediately evacuated. As Colonel Walker hurriedly left the meeting, he caught the gaze of Eli who offered a casual salute, not crisp but professional enough. Walker stopped to confront him, but instead, turned and hurried on his way. Eli's mouth crinkled into the hint of a smile.

The colonel didn't need to respond. His glare had said enough. Maybe, it was in the Forrest nature to rebel against "by-the-book" officers—even if it made them enemies they could ill afford to have.

The plan was to use three transport steamers in the evacuation of the bayou fort, with one of the gunboats providing cover. But the gunboat and only one of the transports, the *DeSoto*, showed up. That meant about 1,900 men, artillery and supplies had to be put on board a single steamer not suited for such a load. The gunboat would also have to be used to transport men.

Nobody voiced any displeasure at the thought of abandoning New Madrid and its two forts to the enemy. Everybody—even the "diehards" as Eli called them—knew that 3,500 rebel soldiers were no match for five times their number of Federal infantry combined with heavy artillery nearly equal to what both forts had at their disposal. With more enemy troops and artillery reported to be on the way, it was clear that the Confederate land batteries and Hollins' gunboats could not defend the area of New Madrid for more than another day or two at most. Besides, the defenders had their fill of being hammered by Pope's siege guns.

It was to be a night time evacuation, with 180 men from Company A of Baker's regiment and another company from Henderson's regiment serving as picket guards positioned beyond the earthworks and in the town. Three infantry companies were placed at the parapet while everybody else was assigned to load the supplies and equipment onto the steamer.

Under cover of night, George and the other enlisted men loaded burlap bags and crates of commissary stores and ammunition onto the boat. The *DeSoto* had put in at the New Madrid landing and a crude plank road had been constructed running from the fort to just west of the mouth of the bayou. The crew aboard the DeSoto assisted the troops in bringing the material aboard. It was hard work under difficult conditions. Many of the weary soldiers grumbled as they labored grudgingly to complete the task at hand.

The wind picked up and the rain, which had been steady all evening, began to come down even harder. It made the loading even more difficult. Two of Bankhead's eight pounders were brought on board, but four 32-pounders had to be spiked and left behind. Some of the shot and ammunition piled on caissons and limbers were shoved into the river along with their two-wheeled transporters.

The captain of the transport complained to Colonel Baker about the excessive amount of human cargo that was to be brought onto the packet. Its waterline was already high from the fort's freight filling its stern, and that was without the weight of the soldiers who lined up, anxious to begin boarding. The *DeSoto's* master wanted a second steamer brought up to take at least half of the men.

Colonel Baker agreed and sent for Walker. Colonel Walker came aboard to inform both men that there would be no other transport. He reminded the boat's captain that the Army of the Confederacy and not the Confederate Navy was in charge of the operation.

A rumor began to spread at the fort and on the picket line that not everyone would be evacuated from New Madrid on the transport—some would be left behind. When all but two hundred of the enlisted men were aboard the boat, some of the soldiers began to panic, shouting that they would not be left to the whims of the Yankees. Despite the efforts of Eli and the other officers to maintain order, the men still waiting on shore rushed en masse toward the vessel, pushing and shoving one another to set foot on the wooden staging. The wooden planks sagged under the weight and gave way with a loud cracking noise. Some men landed in the water where they thrashed about against the current until they were helped ashore. Another staging had to be put into place which took over an hour to prepare.

Weather conditions took a turn for the worse. Fierce winds and a heavy downpour descended on the river, along with the roar of thunder and great flashes of lightning. Defenseless, the rebels dreaded the tempest almost as much as they did an enemy assault. Finally, the platform was in position and the wretched men on shore were allowed to move onto the vessel. George and his brothers were among the last to board the overloaded steamer.

George gave pause as he came aboard, observing the mass of humanity filling the main deck and pouring onto the upper deck. He and his brothers were able to find a few feet on the main deck near the entry. He caught Eli's eye nearby, standing with a group of officers. Surrounded by sullen men in soggy wet coats and dripping caps, George pulled his own coat over his head and cap in an attempt to keep out of the cold, driving rain. Since there was no place to rest their haversacks, bedrolls and muskets, he and the other miserable souls clung to these possessions with both arms, all the while trying to keep their balance. Any lurching of the boat would have a domino effect and they would all be thrown to the deck. Those near the sides might find themselves in the raging water. Luckily, there would be no such mishap, notwithstanding moments of considerable swaying.

At 2:00 a.m., the *DeSoto* backed slowly from the landing at New Madrid. With its paddlewheels stirring up the black inky water and its high stacks emitting clouds of black smoke into the chilled night air, the boat moved ponderously toward the middle of the river channel. The near total darkness was interjected only occasionally by brilliant flashes of lightning that illuminated the entire New Madrid shoreline. It was a beautiful and terrible sight. The thunderbolts also revealed dark storm clouds that hovered above the area. Upon reaching midstream, the vessel forced a wide turn and headed upstream toward Island No. 10. The gunboat, *Pontchartrain*—the one that had carried George and Eli to New Madrid—escorted the slowly moving, overloaded transport. Aboard the transport were Baker and a few of the junior officers from the bayou fort. The gunboat carried Eli and the other officers, the picket guards, and the three infantry companies that had manned the parapet until the transport was finally loaded.

As he stood aboard the steaming gunboat, Eli felt no regrets about leaving New Madrid and returning to the island fortress. After two weeks of being exposed to the cold and wet with little sleep, with long hours of supervising work details and the parapet guards, followed by the nerve-wracking bombardment of the enemy's artillery, he had his fill of New Madrid and Bayou Saint John. He was tired and hungry, but at least had managed to avoid the sicknesses that afflicted many of the men at the fort. George's brother, A.F., had come down with a fever, but was at least strong enough to board the transport with only minor assistance. Many of the men were too sick to stand and had to be carried on.

The *DeSoto* churned slowly upstream as her paddle wheels fought the strong current of the swollen river. The water level of the river was much higher than when Dunnington had taken George and Eli to New Madrid aboard the gunboat *Pontchartrain*. Dunnington had told them that the river contained snags and hidden sandbars and was replete with debris of every kind, all of which challenged even the most skillful navigator. George shuddered involuntarily as he wondered how the pilot manning the wheel would be able to manage the overloaded packet in the darkness of night with the river at flood stage.

Remarkably, several hours later, the transport's pilot carefully maneuvered the large vessel just off shore of Island No. 10, where it proved to be too dangerous for him to try for its narrow boat landing. Instead, the *DeSoto* had orders to land on the first high ground it could find on the mainland shore directly below the island. There was a collective sigh of relief when the steamer pushed slowly to land four miles downriver and came to a stop. The defenders of the upper fort at New Madrid had left the seemingly endless drudgery of digging trenches, repairing earthworks and enduring the infernal bombardment that had been their life at the mouth of the bayou. And they had survived a perilous boat ride on the flooded river. As they waited until daylight and the order to leave the transporter, many could be heard thanking the Almighty for having been delivered from New Madrid. Others cursed the general and whoever else had a hand in sending them to defend that wretched hellhole. Although they were drenched and chilled to the bone, at least they were alive.

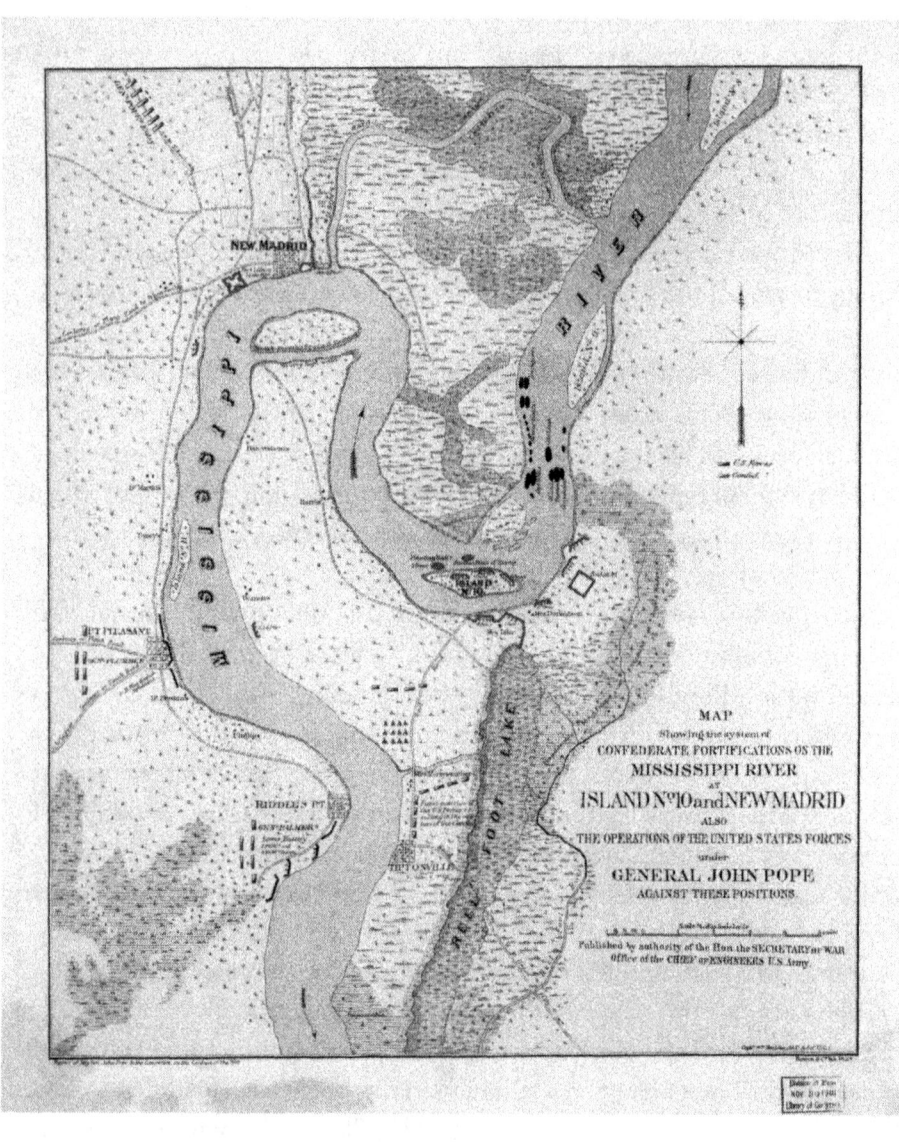

MAP 3. ISLAND NO. 10 & MADRID BEND.

WM. HOELCKE

(Library of Congress)

ISLAND NUMBER TEN

When the survivors from New Madrid stepped on shore, every man among them was drained from the previous two week ordeal. Many were sick and had to be helped off the boat. The Spears brothers and Eli along with several other soldiers found themselves bivouacked in a clover field. The storm of the previous night had thoroughly soaked the ground and a light rain continued to fall. Everything they had carried from the transport was drenched, including a considerable amount of the stores they had aboard. Less than a dozen tents had made the trip from New Madrid and they were quickly set up for the sickest among them.

The evacuees spent the day in the open field, miserable and downcast. The officers among them did their best to encourage them, but it was the plight of the sick that cast a pale over the mud-filled encampment. Many of the sick lay on the wet ground and many others because of exposure to the elements and generally poor conditions were becoming ill. To make matters worse, the river was in flood stage and rising by the hour.

When the rain finally let up, a boat brought a dozen or so Tennessee soldiers over from Island No. 10. George and Eli recognized several from their brief stay on the island. The soldiers brought supplies, mostly food and blankets. The Tennessee volunteers told Eli that they figured matters at the New Madrid forts were not going well when a transport steamer had arrived on the island two days before bearing wagons and teams of horses. While the bayou fort soldiers made hot coffee provided to them by their visitors, they answered questions and chronicled the last days under siege. They also learned from the island soldiers the whereabouts of the regiments who had been stationed at Fort Thompson. Almost all had made good their escape.

Notwithstanding the heavy bombardment and the chaos surrounding their departure, casualties incurred at the lower fort were light. Fort Thompson's surgeon, its provost marshal, a battery officer and eight enlisted men comprised the fort's casualties. At the bayou fort, only Captain Hallum had been wounded, but miraculously no enlisted men were killed by the enemy. One private, a Tennessean from Captain Ragsdale's company, had shot himself to death. Another man from Baker's regiment, Company A, died when his defective weapon misfired. Thirteen other men were reported missing after the evacuation.

By all accounts, the withdrawal from both forts at New Madrid had been a near disaster, owing to the heavy rain, the muddy ground, and the inadequacy of the evacuation plan. The operation proved to be costly in material terms. Twenty-one heavy guns had to be abandoned, fourteen at the lower fort and seven at the bayou fortification. Less than half of the tents were taken aboard the transports. Also, a large quantity of quartermaster and commissary stores had been left behind. No one officer seemed to be in charge at Fort Thompson and the men in the ranks were motivated more by their concern for not being able to board the transports waiting at the lower fort's landing area than by the consequences of refusing an order. Orders were simply ignored. Some of what was abandoned probably could have been saved and McCown was subsequently faulted for that. But he was mostly blamed for not holding onto New Madrid longer. There was still the Confederate fortress at Island No. 10 for the North to contend with, but the plan of tying up thousands of enemy troops in Missouri to keep them from reinforcing the Federal Army of Tennessee at Pittsburg Landing had failed. Someone needed to be held accountable and that someone was General John McCown.

The entire garrison at New Madrid was not sent to Island No. 10. Brigadier General Alexander P. Stewart, second in command at New Madrid, took a brigade of men across the river and south through Tennessee, finally making his way to Corinth, Mississippi. Commander Hollins brought his entire five gunboat flotilla downriver to Tiptonville, with the *Pontchartrain* arriving last. However, several of the transports were subsequently dispatched to the island fortress to be used as needed.

For the few hours that remained before daylight, the tired and wet men who had been at New Madrid slept on their newly provided blankets, crowded around several camp fires. Most of the junior officers slept aboard the transport vessel, which was still tied to stakes driven into the shoreland.

The pre-dawn hours were quiet and untroubled, a welcome contrast to the noise and chaotic surroundings of their previous quarters. George was unable to sleep, so he lay on his blanket watching the fire and listening to the snores and coughs of those around him, waiting for the sun to rise.

"George."

George sat up and found a soaked Eli standing next to him.

"Here," Eli said, thrusting a flask toward him. "Take a drink, you could probably use it."

George took the flask from his friend and turned it up. The whiskey's warmth travelled down his gullet into his belly. Handing the flask back to Eli, he marveled at how his friend—no matter what the circumstances were—always seemed to be able to locate whiskey and tobacco.

Eli took a swallow and squatted down next to George. "Reckon it'll ever stop raining?"

George rubbed his hands together. "At least we're out of New Madrid."

"True enough," Eli replied. "True enough."

The next morning, the senior officers crossed to the other side of the peninsula, headed due north to a riverside plantation known as Watson's Landing, and decided on a location for an encampment a mile back from the river in a large wooded area. From there, they sent for the wet and weary regiments.

The trek across the peninsula was uneventful. The rain had finally stopped and the wind had died down considerably. Major Causler had enlisted the help of area landowners who furnished wagon teams to transport the men who were too sick to walk the five miles to the new camp. The route they followed consisted of a wagon trail replete with water-filled ruts and stretches of barely traversable mud-covered ground. Horses and mules strained to pull the human cargo forward, while the men took turns pushing the wagons from behind. They arrived at the designated encampment around noon. The three regiments occupied a clearing not far from a small schoolhouse. Their closest neighbor was an old woman who lived in a hut several hundred yards from the schoolhouse. Colonel Baker made the woman's acquaintance, while his three servants pitched his tent, tended to his horse, and prepared his and his staff's meal over an open pit fire. Meanwhile, the regiment pitched what tents they had and built fires to warm themselves and cook their rations. While they ate and rested, the thunderous reverberations of mortar shells being fired in the vicinity of the island fortress could be heard rumbling throughout the area. It was not a welcome sound to men who found themselves encamped on a wooded peninsula separated by only a river from an enemy force far superior in number.

The following day saw the overnight occupants of the clearing in the woods busily engaged in establishing their camp. Several cannon positioned along the peninsula's tree-lined Tennessee shore fired toward Yankee positions upriver. Their intent was to warn them that the rebels owned the Tennessee side of the river. In the evening, one of the three regiments—the Fortieth Tennessee, now commanded by Lieutenant Colonel Henderson—was ordered to report to Island No. 10 without delay. They broke camp and moved out that evening, taking the main road that ran down the peninsula. That night, Lieutenant Colonel Minter headed up a sizable picket patrol that deployed along the peninsula's shoreline, following the riverbank for several miles. Their task was to guard against an enemy crossing and, in such event, disrupt them in attempting to gain a foothold on shore from which they could launch an invasion. Everyone knew this was a tall order at best.

On Monday, March 17th, an enormous bombardment was unleashed by Federal gunboats and floating mortars upriver above Island No. 10. The soldiers at the peninsula encampment, including those with George and Will who had just returned from picket duty, listened with apprehension as the ground shook with every blast of the heavy guns and mortars. They and the others waited anxiously for word from the island defenders whether the enemy had launched its anticipated all-out assault on the Confederate fortress and if it had succeeded. In the evening, couriers on horseback road into camp and informed the two regimental commanders—Baker and Travis—that the attack had failed. Even though a redan three quarters of a mile upriver from the island on the east bank of the river had been damaged, the other rebel defenses at or near the island were intact. A cheer went out among the men in camp which more than anything else, signaled a general feeling of relief.

A better understanding of what was expected of the Madrid Bend defenders emerged after the attack upriver that day. Travis' and Baker's assignment, together with a contingent of the Pointe Coupee Artillery under Captain R. A. Stewart, was to guard the river, starting at a point known as Watson's Landing, where two eight-inch siege howitzers and a smoothbore thirty-two pounder stood ready. From Watson's Landing, which lie no more than a half mile from where their camp was located, their orders were to guard a twenty mile area along the river, prevent the enemy from crossing, and stem any attempted amphibious attack. Less than nine hundred infantry and artillery soldiers, with only three pieces of heavy artillery, were tasked with holding off as many as four divisions of the enemy waiting to cross the river and attack the island bastion from its rear. General McCown was betting against long odds.

The chilled, bleak mornings of the first few days spent camped at the upper peninsula gave way to bright sunshine on Monday. By Tuesday, the weather began to turn warmer. The overnight pickets were replaced, and the men in the camp followed what had become routine life at the tented field. Colonel Baker called for an inspection of arms later that day. As the men prepared for review, a courier rode into camp with orders from General McCown commanding Colonel Travis to immediately move his Fifth Tennessee Regiment down the peninsula to Tiptonville. They were gone by nightfall.

The departure of Travis' regiment left the outpost with less than five hundred soldiers, including the artillery crew. Colonel Baker, never one to shrink from the truth, addressed his troops, describing their duty in the defense of Madrid Bend as being "immense and impossible". The enemy was reported to have fortifications at four known places on the Missouri side of the river, stretching from below New Madrid all the way downstream to a point opposite Tiptonville, a total distance of eighteen miles of shore-land. At best, Baker's regiment could post pickets along the river for two miles. The pickets could do little more than fire an alarm should the enemy be spotted crossing the river.

The already somber mood in camp increasingly gave way to despair. Many felt that McCown had decided to sacrifice them to the enemy. Only Lieutenant Colonel Avery refused to be pessimistic. Major Causler and the other senior officers were less upbeat. They knew the rebel position was untenable.

As if to underscore their desperate plight, the hammering of the floating mortars coming from the vicinity of Island No. 10 could be heard throughout the day. They were fired at regular intervals, and from the sound of it, there must have been a half dozen or more of these water-borne implements of devastation. It was said that they could lob shells at rebel positions from a distance of several miles, well out of range of the Confederate batteries on the island or on the opposite shore.

Making matters even worse, one of the enemy batteries planted on the Missouri shore below New Madrid fired a 24 pound shell across the river, hitting the house of Daniel Watson, who had the misfortune of having a Confederate battery located on his property.

On Wednesday, March 19th, the First Alabama, Tennessee, Mississippi Regiment received orders to break camp and relocate to Island No. 10. Much of the evening was spent preparing for the march to the island fortress. At midnight, they finally moved out. For the time being, the artillerymen at the battery and Daniel Watson's people were on their own.

The trek from the abandoned camp to the inland road which ran the length of Madrid Bend's north-south peninsula was difficult and took several hours. Once they arrived at the road, the going became easier. Major Causler was in charge of the troop movement because Colonel Baker decided to remain behind in order to see to the care of Lieutenant Colonel Avery, who had become very sick and was not able to travel. Avery was taken to the cabin of the elderly woman near the schoolhouse and a physician, Dr. Rivers, had been summoned.

On the inland road, Company B brought up the rear of the slow moving procession. There were several wagons loaded with the sick and supplies. Along with the company sergeant, Corporal Spears had responsibility for seeing that the wagons moved along at a reasonable pace.

George took off his field cap and slapped a half asleep young private across the back of the head.

"Bowers, get a move on it. There's too wide a gap between you and the next wagon. We ain't got all day."

"Corporal Spears, I be tired. So tired I near about fell off the wagon two or three times," the bleary-eyed private replied.

"We're all tired, Jesse," George said, putting his cap back on his head. "We'll make camp soon enough. Until then, you got to keep up. Understood?"

The young private popped the reins and hollered at his mules. "Understood, Corporal."

George felt the nose of a horse nudge him in the back. "Watch where you're going, jackass," George shouted as he turned to continue his complaint.

Dismounting from his horse, Eli laughed at his flustered friend and offered him his flask. "Here Corporal, take a tug on this. It will take the edge off what ails you."

"No thanks. I need to keep what few wits I have left to get these wagons to Island No. 10. Who knows how long we'll be there before we're off on another wild goose chase."

Eli took a pull off the flask. "I hear you, Corporal. Our esteemed commanders don't seem to know whether they are coming or going. Of course, they don't want to stand and fight unless they have a chance to win and with the constant increase in Union forces, it's hard to pick a spot for the fight."

The regiment traveled until daybreak and nearing the island, stopped at a meadow owned by a farmer named Harris. Other than a farmhouse, barn and privy, the only other structure at the Harris place was an earthen fortification located at the end of a meadow near the river embankment. A single field piece attended by a corporal and two privates from the Fourth Tennessee Regiment rested at the earthwork. Even though their orders were to proceed directly to the island which was about a mile and a half away, Causler got permission from Colonel Walker to postpone their arrival until his exhausted troops had time to rest. They set up camp in Harris' meadow, where they ate their rations and tried to sleep. Given that they were being serenaded by the intermittent rumble of mortar rounds being fired five miles to the east, sleep proved to be little more than wishful thinking.

Later that evening, George caught up with Eli, who was sitting alone on a felled tree near the field gun, listening to the nearby river. Eli saw George approaching and smiled as the Alabamian sat down next to him.

"Can't sleep either?" George offered. Eli's response wasn't to the question. Instead, he brought up a subject that he had never before discussed with his friend.

"You never have told me, George, what you think of our fine Volunteer State," Eli remarked, with a hint of sarcasm in his voice.

With his characteristic candor, George replied, "No offense, Eli, but I much prefer Alabama to what I have seen of your Tennessee."

"That's because what you have seen of it has been from looking over your shoulder while bein' pursued by the Yankee invaders shooting at you." Eli quipped.

George failed to see the humor in this remark. A minute went by before he spoke again.

"Eli," George asked. "What is old McCown up to? No one voices any confidence in this general. New Madrid could not have been handled any worse than it was and now this mess?"

"George, I don't disagree with you. McCown is not much better as a general than Floyd, Pillow, or the rest of them back at Donelson. Most of your dissatisfied brethren in arms probably joined up with the aim to drive the Northern invaders from our sacred Southern soil, or some such cause. I understand that. I can even respect it. But, for myself, I joined the cavalry service not to defend our liberties, or to save 'hearth and home.' I joined up because I wanted an adventure."

Eli's words seemed not to register with George. He didn't address Eli's point, but remarked, "I am willing to fight in defense of the South. But I prefer to fight under generals who are competent."

Eli decided to leave it at that. He said nothing further and turned toward the sound of the river in front of them. And yet, George thought he saw Eli smile.

At daybreak on Saturday, March 22nd, the entire regiment moved down the road to a landing directly south of Island No. 10. From there, they were transported the short distance to the island. Colonel Baker and Avery, who was still recovering from his illness, arrived two days later.

The First Alabama, Tennessee, Mississippi regiment spent the first days on Island Number 10 setting up camp. Because they had left many of their tents at New Madrid, they were issued tents by the quartermaster of an island regiment and shown where to pitch them. The weather had improved considerably, as had the spirits of the newly arrived Southerners. The availability or shelter from the elements and the island's formidable defenses—both natural and manmade—lifted the men's spirits and gave them a feeling of hope for their prospects, which had been lacking at New Madrid. Even many of the sick seemed to improve.

Although there were several infantry regiments assigned to the island fortress, not all of the men in these units were situated on the island itself. Some were camped on the river's mainland shore above the island. They were there to support the five land batteries. The land batteries' mission was to harass enemy gunboats coming downriver from Cairo, Illinois, and to protect the island bastion from an amphibious assault by Union troops. All of the companies in Baker's regiment, including Company B, were camped on the island. Their job was to provide support to the island batteries and their nineteen mounted guns.

This assignment set well with George and Eli because it afforded greater safety and relief from the high waters challenging the shoreline positions.

They also quickly learned that Island No. 10 rations were preferable to their bayou rations because the island was where the cargo transports from Memphis first unloaded their supplies.

The second day on the island began with an early morning drill for the recent arrivals to make sure that they knew their roles in defending against the imminent Union offensive. There were rumors in camp that General McCown would soon be relieved of his command and that a new commander would be arriving at the end of March.

During a break from drill, some of the soldiers rested while others boiled coffee.

"You been hearing any rumors about McCown being replaced," George said, handing Eli a steaming cup of chicory coffee.

Eli sipped the coffee. "There has been talk around the officers' mess."

George added a little water from his canteen to his cup. "Some folks say it'll be Walker who takes command. He's hot-tempered and he don't have much to do with us in the ranks, but most of the boys say he'd be better than McCown."

Eli continued to sip his coffee.

" 'Course, Walker being in charge could mean more trouble for you," George continued.

"That would be a safe bet to make," Eli replied, throwing what was left of his coffee on the campfire.

McCown was seldom on Island No. 10 and Colonel Walker, who was in line to be promoted to Brigadier General, was already the acting commander of the island.

About mid-morning, the sharp blare of the bugle alerted the island defenders to seize their muskets and take their places at the assigned locations in preparation for an enemy assault. The uppermost mainland battery above the island had sent out an alarm. It had spotted a flotilla of Union gunboats and mortar boats.

An alert at daybreak in the form of a steamer whistle, followed by the firing of alarm guns, had gone out and all of the fortifications down to and including the island fortress scrambled to battle stations. One of the Federal gunboats fired at but missed a Confederate scout steamer. Then in the early morning, the enemy launched a gunboat attack, aiming their blasts at both the battery and the island itself. The Federal gunboats continued firing slowly and methodically throughout the day.

The Confederate artillerymen at the far outpost waited for the Union fleet to pull closer within their range. The enemy fleet, however, seemed content to hold their vessels in the strong current and fire shells from a safer distance.

For twenty-four hours, the Confederate artillery on Island No. 10 held its fire. Company B alternated in shifts with another company in manning the earthworks, retiring to its campsite at midnight. Just before noon on the next day, mortar and cannon fire could be heard coming from a distance up the river.

Soon the bombardment reached the island. The men took cover as best they could, with some of Baker's other units moving to the west where Company B was located. Those on the island's west side were relieved to discover that they were out of range of enemy fire. The shelling continued at thirty-minute intervals all day and into the night. The 128- pounder on the east side of the island returned fire as did the floating battery.

The next day, several Union gunboats, all ironclads, and five mortar boats opened fire against the farthest upper shore mainland battery. They fired one mortar round every minute. The rebel battery being targeted returned fire even though the gunners stood waist deep in the river water. Although there were few Confederate casualties, the intense and prolonged enemy bombardment eventually silenced all but one of its guns. The Confederate artillery struck one of the Union vessels, but did little damage. One of the enemy gunboats sustained casualties when one of its guns exploded.

In spite of their success at reducing the risk posed by the now damaged upper shore battery, the Federal flotilla was not able to penetrate the resistance mounted by the rebel batteries on the mainland shore located near the island fortress. A major obstacle was the river itself. Its strong current posed a danger. If one of their ironclads was hit and became disabled, it would float downstream and be captured. Therefore, the navy commander settled for controlled firing against the shoreline defenses, which he ordered executed from a safe distance.

The following day, the ironclads' guns remained mostly inactive with the exception of the guns on the flagship, known as the *Benton*, which fired an occasional shell into the upper shore battery to prevent the rebels from repairing the damaged breaches caused by the Union bombardment of the previous day. The mortar rafts, however, which had now doubled in number, kept up a continuous if not well directed shelling all day, keeping the rebel defenders on edge.

For the next nine days, the ironclads fired only occasionally and at long range, doing little damage. It was the heavy, thirteen inch floating mortars with greater range that eventually drove the Confederate artillerymen from the upper shore batteries. Their bombardment continued intermittently, forcing many of the defenders to take cover within the caves located along the riverbank bluffs. Gradually, the white tents behind the shoreline fortifications grew fewer in number until they had disappeared entirely. The Confederate encampments were gone, but the main shore artillerymen remained at their posts, firing occasionally at the harassing enemy boats which were just out of their range.

This was not the case, however, with the island batteries. Their bigger guns fired many well-directed shots at the Yankee vessels, even at the longer range. The Belmont heavy rifle in particular was a threat. It even fired over the Yankee mortar boats that hugged the riverbank, all the way out into the middle of the river. On one or two occasions, it barely missed Union transports that were steaming back and forth to supply the mortar boats with ammunition. Its usefulness came to an end one day during the siege when the exchange of fire was especially heated. To the dismay of the island defenders, it blew apart at the third firing. The primary target of the Federal river offensive—the island fortress—was in a state of siege, with the Union army holding the Missouri shore at New Madrid, Point Pleasant and Riddle's Point. The Federal Navy's flotilla of gunboats, mortar boats, and troop transports—the Mississippi River Squadron—was in total command of the upper river. Confederate artillery and the high waters of the Mississippi offered the best hope of keeping the large Union force from taking the island, a hope that was fading fast.

RUNNING THE GAUNTLET

Morale among the five thousand Confederate soldiers camped on Island No. 10 and at the mainland batteries was on the decline. Many of the men were in poor health from exposure to the cold and damp conditions and their nerves were frayed from the continuous bombardment by the enemy. Long hours spent building and maintaining the earthworks had taken a toll. The men were exhausted. It seemed like only a few days had passed since New Madrid had fallen, and now the topic of conversation was how long they could hold out against the superior numbers and gunboats of the Yankees. Rumors were that the enemy had amassed a total of 30,000 troops at New Madrid and were preparing to cross the river.

Once on the other side, they would be able to move by land to a position below the island fortress and launch a ground attack along with a gunboat assault from the river.

The Southerners who camped on the island had been heartened by the warmer weather in late March and the spirited defense of the determined artillerymen of the upper batteries. Disturbing developments in the first few days of April had the opposite effect. On the first day of the new month, as if on cue, an amphibious landing by the enemy finally overran Battery No. 1. The mounted guns of a Union ironclad drove back the small detachment of First Alabama infantrymen who were guarding the redan. They took cover in the nearby caves of the steep cliffs along the river, where they were soon joined by the battery's gun crews. A landing party from the attacking Federal gunboat scrambled up the banks and onto the abandoned, partially submerged parapets. The cheering Yankees planted the Union flag and proceeded to spike the six guns that comprised the battery.

The mainland shore batteries below the one now crippled were not attacked in similar fashion. The gunners there as well as those positioned downriver from New Madrid on the Tennessee shore were still manning their fortifications. Although dispirited by the continuous firing from the enemy's gunboats, the remaining upper batteries were not about to concede their well fortified armed embankments to the enemy. The Confederate gunners had ample food provisions and an abundance of shells as well as infantry support.

A new commander had arrived on the island on March 31st and addressed the men that day, asking them for their support. George and Eli didn't know what to make of him, but figured he had to be better than his predecessor McCown, with whom they had lost confidence during the chaotic evacuation of New Madrid.

During the troop assembly, some of the infantrymen on the island complained that they still had not been given muskets. And several artillerymen reminded the newly arrived general—William Mackall—that one of the island artillery batteries was already submerged and was slowly washing away. To make matters worse, the enemy fired 42-pound rifled cannons, which were more effective than the four smooth bore 32 pounders on the eastern end of the island. General Mackall stated that he was only too aware of these problems and would be conferring with his staff engineer, Captain Shelia, who was assessing the situation.

Men mingled about in small groups smoking and talking about the new general's call for support. The Spear brothers, Eli and several other soldiers stood around a campfire warming themselves.

Will broke off a piece of hardtack and handed it to A.F before turning to his camrades. "What do you fellows think about the general's speech?"

George rubbed his hands together over the fire. "He seemed down-to-earth—straight forward enough, I guess. Don't know what he can do to turn our situation around. What do you think, Eli?"

Eli looked intently at the fire. "Don't really know. General Mackall seems to know the ropes and he knows the deck is stacked against us. Still, I'd say we have a fighting chance with well positioned artillery and decent troop strength. More importantly, Mother Nature is helping out. We have the high ground with swamps behind us and the river in front of us at flood stage. High, fast water makes a Union land attack from the north near impossible. I don't know if Mother Nature will bring us victory, but she should buy us some time."

Grinning from ear to ear, A.F. offered his perspective on the new Commander. "His name sounds kinda peculur', if you ask me. Like one of them jungle birds Aunt Myrtle used to tell us stories about when we was young'uns."

General Mackall would have agreed with Eli's assessment. Peering at the river through a pair of field glasses, he wasn't overly worried about the possibility of attack from the enemy flotilla that commanded the river above the island fortress. He knew that the Federal gunboats would have to fight downstream and given how rapid and massive the river current was at that time, it would be difficult for them to attack.

They could not be anchored in the strong current at a strategic position for effective shelling, but instead would be forced to remain well upstream and fire at long range. If they risked coming too close, one of the ironclad gunboats could be damaged by rebel artillery. If an ironclad lost steam power, it would float downstream and be captured. The prospect of the rebels using a repaired ironclad against Union naval or land forces was a chance the general knew the enemy would not risk.

Mackall was also not terribly concerned about recent information that the Federals were at work cutting a canal across the peninsula opposite Island No. 8, below the mouth of Bayou Saint James. Based upon the opinion of his engineer and others, he believed that they would fail in any such attempt to move their transports below New Madrid. Even if they did succeed, they would need gunboat protection in order to use their transports for crossing the river to the peninsula on the opposite shore. Mackall believed his left flank would prevent a land attack to the rear of the island fortress with the help of the six shore batteries positioned above Tiptonville as well as by the strong current of the mighty Mississippi.

What did worry General Mackall was whether the floating battery and the four batteries on the island plus the four remaining on the main shore above the island could hold out against an extended enemy bombardment. He was also concerned about what would happen if a Federal gunboat slipped past the island. His batteries would be able to prevent this from happening during daylight. But what about a nighttime crossing?

The general handed his field glasses to his adjutant and rubbed his eyes.

"What did John Pope have up his sleeve?" Looking out at the fast moving river, he was certain of one thing—he would find out soon.

General John Pope, the Union Army Commander at New Madrid, stared at the map on the table. The rebel stronghold at Island No. 10 on the Mississippi River was the major obstacle to the North controlling the vast area covered by North America's largest inland waterway. In the early spring of 1862, the removal of that obstacle became of strategic importance. Nearly 23,000 Federal troops were sent to do the job and were encamped primarily on the western shore of the Mississippi from New Madrid to Riddle's Point, Missouri. Since he was the one charged with accomplishing this operation, he had carefully developed a plan. It called for moving his troops across the river to the opposite shore and attacking the fortress from below. With the Confederates' upriver water route effectively cut off by Union gunboats north of the island, and impassable swamps to their east, the rebels would have to move south if they left their fortress.

The only land route open in that direction was an eight or nine mile stretch of road that despite high water was actually in relatively good condition. This road ran inland from the river port of Tiptonville, which was held by the Confederates, to the river shore south of the island. Pope knew that in order to launch his land offensive and at the same time deprive the Confederate island fortress of their supply line and retreat route, his troops would have to cross the river somewhere above Tiptonville. They would first need to find the road, then march south in order to take the town. Pope would also need transports along with one or two ironclads to fend off Confederate gunboat patrols. He knew the Confederates had installed several batteries of heavy artillery along the peninsula shore because rebel gunners periodically fired on the Federal troops encamped on the other side of the river. "No doubt about it," he thought to himself, "our gunboats will be needed to neutralize the threat the rebel batteries pose to a river crossing by our troop transports."

General Pope's planned offensive was also frustrated by the fact that the transports and gunboats he needed were upriver from Island No. 10 and his troops were twenty miles downriver. Any river vessel headed downstream to assist in the crossing would have to get past the island's heavy artillery at a point where the channel swept close to the mainland shore. He made several requests of the navy flag officer in charge of the river fleet to run an ironclad past the island, but the latter refused, preferring not to risk sacrificing one of his boats and the crew aboard.

The Union general had anticipated the problem of getting riverboats past the rebel batteries. Several weeks previously, he asked his command staff to come up with an alternative way of moving the federal troops south of the island. Brigadier General Schuyler Hamilton, along with army engineers, proposed bypassing the fortress by constructing a man-made channel through the peninsula above it. Island No. 10 stood at the bottom of a large hairpin bend in the river. New Madrid, where the bulk of Pope's troops were massed, lay at the top to the west.

The Federal flotilla of gunboats, mortar floats, and transports holding 5,000 infantry controlled the river upstream. By clearing trees in Bayou Saint John on the opposite bend of the river's loop and by navigating the rough, flooded wetlands that discharged downstream near New Madrid, shallow draft transports could circumvent Island No. 10. These steamers could be used to move Union troops across the river. Pope approved the plan and ordered 600 men assigned to the project.

On April 4th, the first transport steamed through the newly constructed channel, making it all the way to dry land on the Missouri side of the river. The satisfaction of having transports available for crossing the river was offset by the reality that there would be no way to protect the transports and the soldiers they carried from rebel shore batteries and gunboats. The river was too wide for the limited range of Federal artillery on the Missouri side to provide effective cover. Without gunboats of their own to soften the enemy batteries and fend off Confederate gunboats, the risk was simply too high. The missing ingredients in the planned invasion were the Union ironclads, which were of no use moored above Island No. 10. The ironclads were simply too heavy to make it through the shallow channel.

John Pope slammed his fist on the map table. His offensive could not move forward. The impasse could only be resolved by running a navy gunboat through the gauntlet of rebel artillery fire at Island No. 10 which seemed to the ranking naval officer positioned with his fleet above the island nothing short of suicidal. Pope continued to pressure him and against his better judgment and the advice of all but one of his gunboat skippers, he finally capitulated. The lone, young naval officer who believed it could be done, volunteered to run his boat past the batteries. His name was Henry Walke. Walke's colleagues in command of the other gunboats thought he had lost his mind. They, like the ranking officer, considered it a suicide mission.

George rested in his tent that evening and thought about Ann Pritchard. There would be no campfire to sit in front of because of the presence of Federal gunboats moored along the river shore less than a mile above the island. The part of the island where his company was posted seemed like one large patch of mud covered with corn husks. In the predawn hours of the previous day, a strong storm and tornado had struck the area, including Island No. 10. One of the regiment's lieutenants and two enlisted men from another regiment had died in the twister. Although the sky was covered by a layer of ominous looking clouds, that night the sky had cleared and stars could be seen. From dawn until dusk, the entire regiment had been on picket duty. George was exhausted. At least the miserable cold and dampness of March had let up a bit, fueling hope among the weary soldiers that milder weather might follow. With the news that Battery No. 1 had been overrun the evening before last, the month of April had started out on a sour note.

Earlier in the day, George had encountered a soldier from Colonel Steadman's First Alabama Regiment who had been on sentry duty at Battery No. 1 when the Yankees drove them back and spiked most of the guns.

The grizzled infantryman popped a plug of chewing tobacco in his mouth. "Tell you one thing, Corporal. As much as I hate to say it, them Yanks caught us by surprise. We was all proud enough to be part of Rucker's Battery even though it wasn't easy duty. On nights when things got quiet, the Yanks in the gunboats liked to give us a hard time—but we gave as good as we got."

George tamped some Virginia burley into the bowl of his pipe and lit it. "What kind of hard time?"

The rebel private spit a stream of tobacco juice into the dying embers of the campfire around which the two men sat. "They liked to taunt us 'bout how they shelled us out of our tents and into the caves. Then after a spell, we'd holler back and ask them how they liked digging that canal by hand and how we had some latrines that needed digging. We would also called them out for being too scared to bring their basswood gunboats into range."

On the evening of April 4th, Brigadier General Walker assigned nearly half of the men from Baker's regiment to extended picket duty on the eastern side of the island with Eli as the officer in charge. A sudden thunderstorm descended from the north and drenched the pickets. Flashes of lightning began illuminating the entire area above the island. Suddenly, amid loud thunderclaps, the blast and roar of heavy cannon coming from the mainland shore could be heard. A Union gunboat, concealed in the dark waters of the storm-clouded night with silenced smoke-stacks, was trying to slip undetected past the mainland artillery batteries. But now the enemy vessel had been discovered and Confederate gunners quickly opened fire. With every flash of lightning, George and Eli could see the smoky discharge of Confederate cannon and hear the shriek of shells as the men at the batteries unleashed all of the fury they could muster. What effect the desperate nighttime barrage had on the exposed gunboat was not known at the time. All around George and Eli, men were shouting as they scrambled from their tents and ran to various locations, carrying their weapons and holding their caps to their heads against the wind and rain. The crack of musket fire could be heard coming from the shoreline batteries across the river, interrupted only by the cannon roar. Soon, musket fire from the eastern end of the island could be heard as rebel sentries and pickets began to fire reflexively at no visible target other than the darkness of the river. The noise of discharging musketry grew in intensity and became one constant cracking sound.

Once it was detected, the gunboat accelerated to full speed, making its way further down the river. As it approached a shoal near the island's northeastern edge, it came within range of an island battery of 32-pound and 64-pound pivot guns, considered the most lethal of the artillery on the island. Several infantry units, including Company B, had been hurriedly relocated there in order to reinforce units already supporting the battery.

There was a brief lull in the storm and the lightning stopped. The men were told to hold their fire. The only sounds were that of the wind and the surge of the fast-moving current. Within minutes, the men closest to the water's edge detected the splashing noise of a paddlewheel, above which could be heard from the same place a man excitedly shouting "Hard a-port!" The vessel barely missed sideswiping the island's point.

Realizing what was occurring, the gunnery commander of the easternmost island battery immediately cried out the order, "Elevate your guns!" The driving rain had forced the rebels to keep the muzzles lowered to stay dry. The gunners now worked feverishly to level the heavy weapons and direct them toward the gunboat, which had surprised them by appearing so close to the island's shore. The usually coolheaded artillerymen were unable to get their guns positioned fast enough to maximize their line of fire. They fired, but it wasn't the direct fire at close range that their captain had hoped and prayed for. The musket fire of infantrymen who were lined along the island shore fared no better. Their randomly fired shots were wasted on the gunboat, which had been lashed together with a barge filled with coal and hay in order to add to the already considerable protection that its iron plates afforded.

The Union gunboat steamed past the island batteries and down around the lower end, staying close to the island which tapered southward and disappeared into the water. The final land battery on the mainland shore opposite the island's lower end repeatedly fired its seven guns in the direction of the boat, but with no more lightning flashes illuminating the waters off the island, their efforts were also in vain.

The Confederates' last hope of stopping the enemy ironclad and averting the disastrous consequences of a Federal gunboat presence below as well as above the island fortress rested with the Columbiads and rifled 32-pounder mounted on the floating navy battery, positioned near the main channel just off the island's northwest bank. Although its guns were in working condition, the sailors who manned the battery were knee-deep in river water. The gunboat's splashing paddlewheel and its muffled steam emissions alerted the waiting Confederate gunners. As it approached in the darkened waters, the pale outline of the vessel was suddenly spotted by a rebel sailor perched as a lookout atop one of the floating battery's cannon. Momentary sparks flying from one of its twin stacks allowed the gunners at the water battery to swing their heavy weapons in the direction of the steam-driven craft, which was now moving under full steam. Half a dozen cannon shots were pounded off at the shadowy mass as it churned swiftly down river. One or two of the projectiles struck the moving vessel, but did no significant damage. Muskets were also fired at the passing gunboat, more out of frustration than any realistic expectation that they would halt its progress or kill any Yankee sailor aboard. As the ironclad swept further from the island, the reality of what had just happened began to sink in. The Federals had succeeded in getting one of their redoubtable gunboats past the Confederate defenses. The island stronghold and its formidable defenses had been breached. As if in a bad dream, beginning with a raging tempest and culminating in the swift torrent of a powerful river, the elements had conspired to keep the enemy vessel from the grasp of the rebel blockade. The tables had been turned.

ISLAND OF DESPAIR

The mood of the island defenders turned from frustration and anger to despair as they discussed their chances of escape and their odds of being captured by the Federals. At midnight, the rebel commander called off the high alert since it appeared that no other enemy gunboat, at least for the time being, would attempt to run the shore and island batteries. Physically and emotionally spent, most of the men returned to their camp. Some went to their tents, peeled off their wet clothing and tried to warm themselves in their bedrolls. Others, including George and his brothers, tried to dry themselves and their garments over campfires that were stoked. Salt pork and beans were quickly cooked and eaten by the men who had been on duty since the first artillery shot signaled the alarm.

The following morning General Mackall, along with Captain Humes, chief of the island's artillery, made the rounds to all the batteries, including the one floating. Mackall commended the officers and the enlisted men at each station for doing what they could under difficult conditions. He also sent a similar message to the upper river shore batteries and urged the defenders to remain vigilant. Mackall then called a council of his senior officers to discuss what their options were and what General Pope's next move might be.

The remainder of the day for the soldiers on Island No. 10 was uneventful. The men carried out their usual tasks, repairing the battlements eroded by bad weather and taking up their posts for sentry duty at the earthen mounds. It was different than before. Now there was a somberness about them as they went about their activities. There was none of the light-hearted banter that typically could be heard in off-duty hours. Instead, they kept themselves busy, doing their best to keep their thoughts focused on the present. Muskets were cleaned. Clothes were washed. Food was cooked. Letters were written. Bibles and other available reading materials were read, sometimes out loud for those who couldn't read. George's brother, Will, passed the time carving a pipe with his Bowie knife. A.J. watched some men play a game of cards.

That night, the talking was about the previous night's gunboat passing and what it meant. Having listened at Fort Donelson to soldiers' firsthand accounts of what had transpired previously at Fort Henry, George and Eli knew all too well what an effective weapon an ironclad gunboat could be. They chose not to share that knowledge with their comrades, though many of the island defenders had heard rumors about the Yankee's armored river fleet. There was also talk about how poorly the Confederates' five small wooden gunboats would fare against the ironclads when it came to a showdown. Most of the men thought the rebel fleet under Commodore George Hollins would be of no use against the Federal ironclads. Hollins' fleet had positioned itself safely downriver after the evacuation of the Confederate forts at New Madrid and the Federal occupation of that location.

Although well armed, the five vessels were not inclined to do more for Island No. 10, but seemed content to lie off shore at Tiptonville, on the Tennessee side of the river. There were reports of two additional rebel gunboats being completed in Memphis, and these were said to be bigger and faster than the five Hollins presently commanded. If these larger gunboats were added to Hollins' fleet, it might be possible to fend off the one ironclad that had by-passed the island's batteries. A flicker of hope fueled speculation that the rebels might have a chance at routing the Yankee land batteries located on the Missouri side both at Point Pleasant and seven miles south of there at Riddle's Point.

For the time being, however, the enemy artillery at these two locations kept Hollins' fleet fully occupied. The elusive Federal gunboat's inevitable arrival would pose a threat to any Confederate battery on the eastern side of the river below New Madrid. Without war vessels to contest the ironclad, the days would appear to be numbered for the five isolated Confederate batteries stretching from opposite the mouth of Bayou Saint John all the way down to just north of Tiptonville. If they were silenced, nothing would stand in the way of a river crossing by Pope's forces.

George awakened long before morning call on Sunday. It was April 6th, two days since the Federal gunboat had steamed past the island's artillery gauntlet. He threw some water onto his face and, with his fingers, combed his tousled hair, which now touched the back of his coat collar. Then he took a walk to the water's edge and scanned the river and landscape. His thoughts were of Ann Pritchard. He wondered how she was faring now that the Yankees controlled the area where she lived. He prayed that she was safe. George also thought of his parents back in Alabama. How were they managing with only one son to help with the springtime planting? George wanted the war to end, but he knew that would not happen anytime soon. He had long since lost his appetite for soldiering. He cast a worried look at his sleeping younger brother. Since the siege began at New Madrid, A.F. was looking increasingly pale and thin.

Walking back to camp, George saw a group of men standing by a small clump of trees with Bibles in hand. One soldier whom he recognized but didn't know by name was reading a testament passage and his deep, full voice could be heard at some distance.

"Though I walk through the valley of the shadow of death, I fear no evil for Thou art with me," bellowed the large man with a long, gray beard.

A young private raised his hand, "Reverend Sims, will you pray for me?"

The man stopped reading and looked at the young man who was little more than a boy. "I sure will, son. I'll pray for you and with you. Come on, men. Gather 'round young Tom as his brothers in Christ while I pray for him."

George listened for awhile to the prayers and singing before walking back to camp. He had to get ready for his duty shift near one of the island's batteries. Impending battle always brought both the fear of God and a desperate desire for His protection.

That evening George wrote a letter to Ann while he and his brothers listened to Jonah Tucker play his harmonica. Rendering one tune after another, Jonah finally exhausted his supply of melodies. At the urging of his listeners, he repeated his performance. The men were grateful. Any distraction was better than the reality that awaited them. Later that evening, the wind picked up. Dark clouds came over the area and, as it started to rain, the weary soldiers took to their tents.

At 2:00 a.m., Eli was jolted from his slumber by a blast of artillery. An emergency officers' briefing had lasted until midnight. As Eli sat on the edge of his cot, he tried to get his bearings. A young lieutenant stuck his head in Eli's tent and informed him that during an ensuing thunderstorm, another Federal gunboat had crept by the upper mainland batteries, managing to remain undetected until it was opposite the island's eastern battery. The stealth ironclad succeeded in not being hit by the ensuing artillery fire and minutes later had successfully evaded shots from the floating battery as it came round the island. This second armored vessel was now steaming toward New Madrid and its several large guns would be added to Pope's floating arsenal of weapons for use downriver against the Confederate batteries on the eastern shore. As far as Eli and George were concerned, time seemed to be running out.

General Mackall had five shore batteries in place on the eastern bank of the Mississippi River opposite to where Pope's army remained across the river. The Confederate land batteries extended from Water's Point one and a half miles across from Bayou Saint John in the north to near Tiptonville in the south, a distance of some eleven miles. The most important of these was located at Watson's Landing, where two 8-inch howitzers were mounted on a siege carriage within the one acre earthworks. The battery also included a 32-pounder. Mackal dispatched an infantry company from the Fortieth Tennessee to provide support.

Another battery was a mile and a half to the south, opposite Point Pleasant, Missouri, where part of General Plummer's division awaited transports and Pope's orders to cross the river and commence the long anticipated land assault. The opposing rebel battery, which included two 24-pound siege guns and two 10-pound Parrott guns, had done an admirable job of harassing Plummer's encampment for the better part of a week, sending random artillery fire across the river, both day and night.

At daybreak on the morning of April 6th, the first Federal gunboat that had successfully run Island No. 10's gauntlet, appeared before Watson's Battery and drew fire. The gunboat returned fire as it continued downriver. It was on a reconnaissance operation that took it to just north of Tiptonville. Pope's generals also wanted the rebel gunners to feel the ironclad's presence. Each shore battery greeted the Yankee craft with shot and shell, but to no effect. On each occasion, the boat's crew fired back, dropping shells into the white tents that were pitched behind the gun works. Near Tiptonville, two Confederate gunboats approached and fired a few shots at the Federal gunboat from long range, but there would be no battle on the river that day. Both sides withdrew, the Federal vessel turning upriver, and the Confederate gunboats steaming downriver to their starting point offshore from Tiptonville.

William Mackall had slept very little the night before. He knew he would have some tough decisions to make as he rose from his cot and stepped out of his tent before daybreak on that Sunday morning, April 6, 1862. Prior to replacing McCown at Island No. 10 on March 31st, he had served as an adjutant to Major General Albert Sidney Johnston, commander of the South's army in the west. Even before he arrived on the island fortress, he had been told that a successful defense of that strategic position would be very difficult and the best he could hope to accomplish was to delay the enemy's advance. That he had done. But the odds against him were mounting. Aside from the presence of a Union ironclad now on the river below Island No. 10, he faced yet another source of adversity. The island's supply line from below Tiptonville had been cut off, not by Union troops but by the rising river. Up until two days prior, he had had an uninterrupted railroad link with southwest Tennessee and Mississippi after passing a gap of only fifteen miles of land travel. The island defenders had been able to procure the provisions they needed. But the first days in April had seen heavy rain, which caused the Mississippi to flood the mainland east of the island and for miles south, making any attempt to move over land hazardous. The flooded landscape not only blocked the land route to the railway head, it also limited any possible withdrawal from the fortress by way of the Tiptonville road.

It was mid-afternoon when Mackall received word that an enemy gunboat had menaced the peninsula shore batteries at Watson's Landing and opposite Point Pleasant. He was convinced that an attempted landing by the enemy would be made the next morning. After conferring with his chief artillery commander for both island and mainland batteries, he ordered all but one of the remaining infantry regiments to immediately prepare to leave the island. They would march against the enemy in a daring counter offensive. The heavy artillery on the island and on the mainland shore opposite the island would hold their positions, but Captain Richard Stewart's light artillery and the entire Confederate infantry force under his command would attack the enemy at some undetermined point midway up the peninsula. The exception was Lieutenant Colonel Cook's Twelfth Arkansas, which would need to stay behind to guard the island. Mackall gave the order that they would be leaving at nightfall. He would not wait for Pope's army to cross the river before making his move. It would be better to fight each wave of the invaders as they landed on shore than wage an inland offensive against them after they had massed.

When the Federal gunboat returned to New Madrid from its downriver reconnaissance mission, everyone aboard knew that the encounter with the Confederate shore batteries would take place later that day or the next morning.

Shortly after daybreak on April 7th, the steam-driven ironclad set course for Watson's Landing. When the warcraft came within about a mile of the battery, the Confederate gunners opened fire. The gunboat slowed to half speed and made a gradual but deliberate move in the direction of the east shore installation. It steamed steadily toward the rebel position, the navy pilot carefully compensating for the swift current. When the gunboat drew to within three hundred yards of the battery, its guns—now trained on the target—began firing. The rebels replied striking the vessel and shattering two lifeboats. The firing from the ironclad became more rapid as if the crew were angered by their vessel having been hit. In addition, wave after wave of deadly volleys from the rifles of a group of army sharpshooters who were on board the ironclad targeted the island defenders. Nonetheless, Confederate gunners returned fire for about half an hour more until they could no longer withstand the Federal's heavy barrage. At that point, the young artillery captain in charge of the battery ordered his men to spike the heavy guns and prepare to immediately withdraw. He called for a volunteer to position himself behind a large cottonwood tree near the riverbank. The soldier was given two rifles. His task was to provide cover for his comrades as they hastily made their way through the woods behind their now silenced guns. The enemy would no doubt be sending a landing party from the gunboat and the retreating rebels needed time to put as much distance as possible between themselves and the approaching Yankees.

As blue-coated soldiers aboard the gunboat prepared to board two small boats that were to take them ashore, a shot coming from the bank rang out and struck one of the smokestacks. Other shots followed within short intervals of each other. The men on the boat were pinned down. An officer scanning the area with a spyglass finally spotted a lone Confederate soldier positioned behind the thick cottonwood set back from the bank of the river. From behind whatever cover they could find on the deck of the boat, the squad of sharpshooters unleashed a torrent of shots directed at the figure. It took nearly ten minutes, but the hailstorm of Yankee bullets finally convinced the lanky Southerner to make a break for the woods, running bent over from the waist. Although the tip of his nose had been shot off, he felt lucky to be alive.

The triumphant ironclad, along with the second gunboat that had passed the island fortress the night before, turned upriver and steamed in the direction of the next closest shore battery. This rebel installation's two guns offered little resistance as the rebel artillerymen quickly took to the flooded woods.

Only one shore battery, which consisted of an eight inch Columbiad, now remained on the peninsula. It, too, soon came under attack by Union gunboats. The Columbiad malfunctioned and blew up when the Southerners attempted to return fire.

With the upper peninsula batteries no longer a threat, a fleet of transport steamers and barges moved down the excavated channel and around the mouth of Bayou Saint John. At New Madrid, three thousand Union troops were loaded aboard. They had their orders. They would be transported three miles over river to Watson's Landing. There they would disembark, scramble up the river bank and move well away from the water's edge. The first wave of troops was to be followed by two others, until a total of 9,000 Yankee infantry would be positioned on the eastern shore. By nightfall, they would be well on their way along the inland road that led down the peninsula to Tiptonville. After taking Tiptonville, they would move directly against the lower or south end of the island fortress, while the Federal navy gunboats located upriver from the island attacked from the north.

THE GETAWAY

A light rain fell throughout the day as men from an Arkansas regiment mounted a 32 pound cannon on the north side of the island. From where they stood guard, George and Will watched as the gun was put in position.

Upon returning to their tents, they along with others in their company were told to roll up their gear and leave most of their personal items, taking only what could easily be carried. As George placed a packet of Ann Pritchard's letters inside the cover of a small Bible his mother had given him, he heard the talk among others in camp speculating that the Federals would be crossing the river from New Madrid sometime in the morning. Will and A.F. had listened to the same chatter. Tightening the cinch on his haversack, George slung it over his shoulder and exited the tent. Will and A.F. were waiting for him outside.

"George, it don't look none too good to me and Will. The boys in the company say them bluebellies will be on us hotter than a hornet's nest before nightfall." A.F. exclaimed, wide-eyed with concern.

George squeezed his younger brother's shoulder. "A.F., I reckon that's the reason we're breaking camp and moving out."

Will handed George a chunk of cornbread. "Here's your share of supper. Me and A.F. done ate ours."

While George took a bite of his cornbread, A.F. continued, "We shor'nuff could be dead, wounded or captured by this time tomorrow."

After taking a drink from his canteen, George wiped his mouth with the back of his sleeve and looked at his two brothers. "You could be right. Or you could be wrong. One thing's for sure. We won't be waitin' around for the

Yanks to get here. Besides, General Mackall might have a surprise or two up his sleeve. Only thing for us to do is to stick together and see what happens."

As the last of the departing troops from the island hurriedly moved to the sandy shore, a hard rain was ushered in by a cold wind coming from the west.

To the men of Company B's surprise, there were only two transports available to take them to the opposite shore. General Mackall had ordered all of the other transports to be cut loose and set adrift. The unoccupied vessels had scattered to various points as they drifted downriver. From the shoreline in the dim light of dusk, several of the abandoned transports could be seen aimlessly striking the shoals near the banks. The boats looked like ghost ships without sails, eerily moving silently downriver as if phantom pilots were guiding them. Apparently, Mackall's notion was that if he could not get the vessels safely downriver where they might be retrieved by the Confederate gunboat fleet, he would prefer to leave them to the river's many snares rather than fall into the hands of the enemy's navy. If he ordered them burned, it would be a signal to the Federal gunboat commanders upriver that he had rejected the option of a retreat by water to Fort Pillow or Memphis.

When the men boarded the small steamers that would make the short, choppy crossing to the mainland shore, many were heard bidding their former island domicile good riddance. They certainly would not regret leaving behind the damp, muddy campgrounds, nor would they miss the long hours of back breaking work fortifying the earthworks. Most of all, they would not be subjected to the unnerving bombardment of Federal gunboats.

Company B was the last one to complete the crossing. Despite the strong current and the closing darkness of the hour, neither of the two transport vessels or any of the men aboard were lost to the river.

When the last boatload landed, the men were assembled and readied for the march away from the river. Thirty-five hundred troops and one hundred and fifty horses began the trek over the narrow inland road of Madrid Bend. First, they headed southwest, proceeding at an agonizingly slow pace. It was challenging enough moving so many men, limbers, and horses in darkness, but it was even more difficult due to the rain-soaked condition of the ground over which they traveled. Storm clouds made it so dark at times they could barely see further than a few feet in front. The tired soldiers began to bump into those walking ahead of them.

By the time they arrived at the crossroads where the Tiptonville Road that they were on intersected with the road running from the upper peninsula to Reelfoot Lake below, the rain had begun to let up. General Mackall dismounted his horse and handed the reins to an aide. He stood alone, pondering the decision he had to make.

Mackall suspected that the enemy would cross the river and come on shore at Watson's Landing in the morning. Would he be able to get his force there in time? Would he have sufficient numbers and resources to repel the initial wave of invaders? Where were his reinforcements? He had sent out a courier with orders for Colonel Gantt's brigade, which had been camped just north of Tiptonville, to join him in an all out offensive. The additional infantry would bolster their number to 3,500, even though a number of the men were poorly armed. Still, they stood a chance.

With Gantt managing the enlarged infantry force and Stewart directing the light artillery, they just might be able to drive back Pope's amphibious assault before his troops could organize themselves for their inland march. They had to be stopped before they established a strong beachhead. If they did succeed in landing or if they landed four or five miles below Watson's Landing, what recourse would he have? Would his army be able to mount another offensive? Or should he abandon his planned offensive and attempt to save his infantry and light artillery by retreating south to Tiptonville or southeast to Reelfoot? The general massaged his forehead. He could feel another one of his throbbing headaches coming on. Too many questions and not enough answers.

A scouting party consisting of a junior officer and two enlisted men had just returned from assessing the condition of the road.

Eli wiped the dried mud from his face as he dismounted and saluted. General Mackall's attendant took the reins of Eli's sweat-drenched horse. Eli stood at attention.

"At ease, Lieutenant. Here, have a drink of this," Mackall said, handing Eli a canteen filled with rye whiskey. "This might help take away the damp chill. Now, tell me what condition the road is in."

"The road is passable, Sir—but just barely. Part of it is underwater, but I believe men and horses could move on it during daylight. I'm not sure about the artillery."

Mackall ran his hand through his hair. "That's better news than I expected—not what I hoped for, but a damn sight better than I expected. Some of the senior officers want to return to the island, Lieutenant. What do you think about that?"

Eli swallowed some of the whiskey. "Well, General, I'm only a junior officer, but I'd have to say that position would take us from having a chance—even if it's a long shot—to having no chance at all."

General Mackall smiled at Eli. "Lieutenant, it seems like I need to replace a few of my senior staff with some of my junior officers. I agree with your sentiment. A small chance is better than none. I've always been of the opinion that the best defensive strategy is a resolute offensive."

The long procession of men, horses and equipment turned and moved up onto the peninsula road in a northwest direction. The road seemed to get worse with each quarter mile they traveled. Men and horses slipped and struggled in the thick, oozing mud. The wheels of the artillery wagons became mired and each had to be pushed by five or six men. After traveling six miles at an agonizingly slow pace, the column came to a halt at a point where the road rose to a crest. General Mackall's scouts had found a reliable guide, a Negro field hand whose owner had leased the slave to work on Dan Watson's large plantation. He knew the way even at night. The guide informed the general that they needed to leave the road and head west over a cart path that cut through the woods and led to the river and boat landing which was their destination. In short order, they came to a clearing that marked the boundary of Watson's place. To Mackall's satisfaction, Colonel Baker and Major Causler confirmed the accuracy of the slave's directions based on their mid-March travels through the area. The darkness was beginning to lift in the pre-dawn sky.

After a brief rest break, Mackall ordered his weary troops again on the move. The front of the column turned onto the cart path and disappeared from the sight of those still on the peninsula road. Gantt's infantry brigade had not yet arrived and Mackall was beginning to wonder if they ever would. Meanwhile, word had been sent from Captain Jackson, who had been left in charge of the land forces along the Tennessee shore batteries opposite Island No. 10, that in addition to the two Federal ironclads, four or perhaps five transport steamers were now below the island. They had successfully traversed the canal that had been cut by Pope's engineers from the river to the bayou system just east of New Madrid.

Eli, the Spears brothers and their Company B companions were among the last of the troops to leave the road and take to the cart path. As with the other men on Mackall's all night march, they were too tired and cold to have gained any real rest at the crest of the road before turning onto the cart path. They were standing in shoes or boots that were wet and mud-covered. In the dim light, George looked around. They were in the midst of an impressive forest of ash, sycamore and cottonwood trees. He wished that he could linger there and take in the beauty of the place—maybe even gather his brothers and Eli and hide from what surely awaited them. Instead, he trudged on, part of the long column that was once again on the move, this time westward toward the river.

By daylight, the Confederate force arrived at the clearing that marked the rear portion of Dan Watson's sprawling plantation. General Mackall sent out a messenger to the lieutenant in charge of the shore battery near Watson's boat landing with news that he and his troops had arrived. Mackall ordered an extended defensive line formed facing the landing area, but well behind it. Captain Stewart interspersed his light artillery in front of the infantry positions. Pickets were sent north and south of the line as well as back toward the peninsula road. Then the waiting began.

John Pope had to be pleased when he met with his generals on the evening of April 6th. Since mid-February, he had devoted all of his waking hours to planning and executing the North's campaign to wrest control of the Mississippi River from the South at New Madrid and Island No. 10. The forty-year-old Union army commander of the military's District of the Mississippi knew that Mackall's situation was desperate. Federal gunboats controlled the river upstream from the island. Mackall's mainland shore batteries downriver from New Madrid were no match for the ironclads that had run the gauntlet of the island fortress' batteries. They would soon be silenced. His engineers had provided him with a sufficient number of transports and barges for crossing the Mississippi and landing his soldiers. With floating artillery in the form of the armored gunboats to provide cover for his troop landing, he could finally start his long-awaited attack aimed at the back door of the island fortress. Pope knew that the river's overflow had resulted in the island defenders being hemmed in. The Tiptonville road behind the fortress was their only way out.

On April 7th, in the pre-dawn darkness, two divisions of General Pope's army of almost 23,000 soldiers prepared to board light transport steamers that would take them across the river to the enemy-occupied shore. By mid-morning, the general received more good news. The two Federal gunboats operating out of New Madrid had succeeded in clearing the upper peninsula shore of the Confederate's heavy artillery. By 11:00 a.m. his long awaited offensive would begin. The initial wave would go ashore at Watson's Landing. Anticipating that Mackall might try to save his infantry and light artillery by retreating to Tiptonville, Pope ordered his troops to land and proceed to that location. He wouldn't have been as confident had he known that the bulk of Mackall's force was waiting at Watson's plantation to wage a counterattack against the first wave of Union troops to come ashore.

Meanwhile, General Mackall waited with his troops in position. At mid morning, loud blasts of cannon fire alerted them that the nearby shore battery's guns and those of at least one and perhaps two Federal gunboats were locked in battle. The rebel gunners fought the attackers for two hours in a fierce bombardment. Ninety minutes into the fighting, it was evident from the sounds of the explosions that the Federals were gaining the upper hand.

Mackall's fears were confirmed when a breathless artillery soldier, who had been dispatched from the earthwork after several of its cannon had been hit by enemy fire, informed the general and his command staff that the battery had finally been destroyed and abandoned as a result of the ironclads' guns and the rifle fire of sharpshooters.

It was becoming increasingly evident that reinforcements from Gantt's infantry regiments were not likely to be joining them. General Mackall would have to make do with what he had. To make matters worse, his thirty-five hundred troops were hungry and exhausted from lack of sleep. He ordered the men to rest and soon most of them were asleep in spite of a lightly falling rain.

As the hours passed, Mackall and his staff waited and watched. Scouting reports informed them that a contingent of enemy transports was seen steaming down river toward Watson's Landing. Under the protection of two ironclads, five transports were landing what appeared to be an entire division of Union infantry. An even greater number of Yankees was believed to be waiting at New Madrid for the boats to return in order to ferry them across.

Mackall held council with his regimental commanders and artillery officers. The council was unanimous in their belief that an assault against so great a number of the enemy would be senseless. Retreat was the only option. The enemy was minutes from landing and would soon be headed in their direction. There was no time to lose.

John Mackall reluctantly bowed to the wishes of his senior commanders and sent a messenger to Lieutenant Colonel Cook, who he had left in command at the island, as well as Captain Jackson, who was in charge of the mainland artillery on the shore opposite the island and what few soldiers still remained there. Cook and Jackson were instructed to hold the fortress as long as possible. When they could no longer maintain an adequate defense, they were to spike all the guns and escape with every last man by way of Reelfoot Lake. By 4:00 pm Cook had given the order to evacuate. With no artillery capable of being used against a land attack and with the threat of gunboats both upriver as well as downriver, he had little recourse.

The Confederate naval officer in charge of the island's floating battery had come under a surprise attack by an enemy cavalry unit that had approached from the direction opposite of where the battery's guns were pointed. He quickly gave the order to scuttle the craft. As soon as Lieutenant Averett had given the order to open the valves, he made his escape along with some of his crew of navy gunners. The others on board were either killed or captured.

Fearing the steamboat used to transport rebel troops across the river would fall into enemy hands, it too was ordered scuttled after transporting as many of the men as possible off the island.

At the same time, Captain Jackson acting on a scout's report that the enemy was less than an hour away, ordered the evacuation of the heavy artillery companies from the mainland batteries. Each captain was instructed to dispose of his guns and then lead his company to Reelfoot Lake, a mile to the south of Island No. 10. From there, they were to follow along the shore of the lake to Store's Ferry, some twenty miles through woods and swamps. From Store's Ferry, they would be able to cross the lake and proceed to Dyersburg.

The mass of infantry and light artillery that General Mackall had brought with him from Island No. 10, was making a hasty retreat down the interior peninsula road toward Tiptonville. It was now evident to every Confederate soldier at Madrid Bend that Mackall had conceded to the enemy Island No. 10 as well as the area extending all the way down to just north of Tiptonville. However, Tiptonville itself was still in Confederate hands. The Confederate fleet was there, as were McCown's transports, or so Mackall believed. In reality, two Federal gunboats had arrived and driven rebel gunboats and transports downriver to Fort Pillow. The general knew that Gantt, having failed to join him on the ill-fated offensive directed at Watson's Landing, was encamped down peninsula at a point several miles north of Tiptonville.

Colonel Gantt had a combined force of about twelve hundred infantry, light artillery and cavalry and was still in control of the road from the island fortress to the river town. There was yet a chance that Mackall could make it to Gantt's position, and from there save the combined force by a quick retreat. If they could get to Gantt's camp north of Tiptonville, there would be but one way open, a sluice just above the town which emptied into the river. From the sluice's banks, they might make their way to where they would board transports. The overflow covering the banks of the sluice might prevent the pursuing Federal force closing in on them from an inland direction. If the transports failed them, they might attempt a desperate dash over a narrow strip of higher ground to Reelfoot Lake where they would have to use rafts to cross to the other side. From there, they could march to the Memphis and Ohio Railroad and escape to the south. It was a long shot, but the alternatives were either to surrender or make a last ditch stand against an enemy that outnumbered them ten to one. General Mackall was compelled to choose the least objectionable option from a list of untenable options.

A damp, cool mist replaced the rain and engulfed the rebel encampment. Eli lit a cigar and offered one to George. "Try one of the general's cigars. I kept them dry."

George took the cigar from Eli and bit off the end before lighting it. "I'd rather have some hot food—or cold food for that matter."

Eli nodded in agreement. "It was generous of Mackall to share his cigars and whiskey after I made my report to him, but some hot vittles would have done better silencing the growl in my empty belly."

George pulled his coat collar tightly around his neck and exhaled a plume of smoke. "What we gonna do now, Eli, fight or run—or surrender?"

Eli paused several moments before responding. "I believe we will run for awhile—but in the end, my guess is what we will run out of is time."

George looked at Eli, but said nothing. The two friends smoked their cigars in silence, listening to the sounds of a tired and frustrated army.

14

BITTER SURRENDER

The men of Company B could hardly believe what they heard when the order went out to return along the road they had come the night before. The Yankees had made their landing and would soon be marching down the peninsula road. Word filtered down through the ranks that General Mackall was convinced that they must move or be captured. The weary Confederates turned back and followed the road over which they had just traversed. They walked in silence, abandoning equipment along the way. The sun had disappeared behind clouds and the cursed rain again began to fall, punishing the marchers all the more as they trudged along the muddy road. The exhausted procession of men moved slowly. Although there were many stragglers, none of the officers or sergeants seemed concerned enough to order them to keep pace. George was bone tired, but his brother, A.F., who had recovered from whatever had 'ailed him, seemed impervious to their dire circumstance.

"Hey George and Will, you reckon we gonna march straight back to Alabama? If we ain't gonna fight them Yanks, maybe we're done fightin' altogether. Maybe, they'll let us get on home. Maybe...."

"Shut up, A.F.," Will answered his younger brother. "Just shut your mouth and keep walking."

A.F. looked at his two brothers, his wishful thinking quickly evaporating. A hint of gloom covered his normally cheerful countenance.

The throng of weary and foot-sore marchers finally reached Gantt's encampment near the Tiptonville road above where the river town lie. Just as they were entering the camp, a brigade of Federal foot soldiers in clean blue uniforms and bearing repeating rifles unexpectedly appeared. They seemed as surprised as the rebels. Gunfire erupted and both sides withdrew in opposite directions.

Dusk began to fall and the rain eased as the last company involved in General Mackall's futile peninsula march made its way into camp. The members of Company B walked through the encampment and were welcomed by the men from Colonel Gantt's brigade who had occupied those grounds for three weeks, most of whom were volunteers from Arkansas. Mackall's soldiers broke the somber news that they were surrounded by several enemy brigades to the north and the south, high water on the east, and two union ironclads offshore to the west.

An advance Federal brigade had arrived earlier that afternoon and had taken up a position south of Tiptonville. Another had arrived some time later and positioned itself north of town. Five Confederate gunboats in the vicinity of Tiptonville had steamed upriver to fire on the Federal invaders. However, they hadn't reckoned on dealing with a contingent of the Union gunboat flotilla. After a brief exchange of cannon fire at long range with the rapidly closing union ironclads, the commander of the rebel fleet ordered his vessels to fall back and move down river.

Meanwhile, other Union troops fanned out along the lower- peninsula and met little or no resistance. Some took up positions along the Tiptonville road as well as along a line below the sluice that connected the river with Reelfoot Lake. The Federal line stretched from near the river eastward all the way to the lake.

Gantt's brigade had been preparing for the Union army's assault for some time. Although his primary task had been to defend Island No. 10 from a land invasion coming from the north, his immediate concern of late had been to keep the road open for Mackall's retreat down the peninsula which had arrived only minutes ahead of the enemy's advance brigade.

Gantt and Mackall immediately positioned light artillery below their combined forces near the sluice that connected the river with the Reelfoot Lake. These guns were now fixed on the enemy as they arrived and began to line the road. The rebel gunners opened fire and the Federals replied with their own artillery, including that of the two gunboats that now hugged the shore. While the artillery duel ensued, the Union general who had led the advance division dispatched a brigade along the riverfront and ordered his troops to move against the rebels. They quickly advanced through the town and spotted their adversaries a short distance away. The Confederate army at Madrid Bend was in imminent danger of being hemmed in. If they stayed where they were, they would be caught in a trap.

The rebels were prevented from moving northward along the river and they were also blocked from going south. The enemy's two gunboats waiting offshore at Tiptonville had moved up the river and taken a position opposite the small channel. When General Mackall and his command staff learned that the gunboats were there, they abandoned any thought of an escape in that direction.

As fortune would have it, the road coming from the island fortress divided close to Tiptonville. One branch followed the riverbank in front of the village. The other branch passed through the woods behind the village. At that point, the two roads again merged and followed the riverbank to where it intersected the sluice. In meeting up with Gantt's brigade, Mackall's army took the interior road, while the enemy's forward brigade had followed the road running along the bank of the river. Now, both roads were held by the enemy.

As the Confederates moved eastward, they came under artillery fire. The rebels quickly dropped behind the sluice banks and took cover in the woods where Mackall, Gantt and the other senior officers planned their next move. This delay allowed the second Union brigade that had pushed down the peninsula road to extend its troop line along the sluice to the lake and open fire with light artillery.

The rebel defenders, beset by bursting shells and flying fragments, were in desperate straits. Not only were they being pounded from two sides by enemy artillery, they were also exposed to long range cannon fire from the Federal gunboats. Even if they could weather the bombardment, they still faced the Union infantry which had virtually surrounded them. If Mackall's and Gantt's forces stood their ground and fought, they would be hopelessly outnumbered.

In a final desperate move, Mackall ordered a quick withdrawal to the east through woods and then swampland in hopes of reaching Reelfoot Lake. If they made it to the lake, his plan was to use small boats and rafts to cross the lake, and then board ferry flats to cross the Obion River. Once on the opposite side of the river, they would move eastward to Dyersburg.

Hindered by the growing darkness and increasingly swamp-like terrain, progress was slow. Finally, Mackall ordered his troops to halt and wait for daylight. They could go no further for the time being. They were too physically and mentally fatigued to do anything but rest. There, at the edge of an expansive cypress swamp, the Confederates spent their remaining hours of freedom.

The Federal brigade commanders anticipated Mackall's eastward retreat and countered by moving their troops closer to the fleeing rebels. When the Union brigades were close enough to realize that the rebels would not chance the swamp in darkness, they stopped their pursuit, opting to wait until daybreak when they would attack.

For the Confederate commander, John Mackall, the options were few. His choices came down to two—order his poorly armed and vastly out-numbered army to fight the enemy and then wade through swamp waters to Reelfoot Lake, or surrender to the enemy before it attacked at daybreak.

Mackall did not have the luxury of resting on his cot the night of April 7th, nor did he find time to eat. Instead, he called a council with his top officers to discuss the next move. Although much of the equipment was gone, they still had light artillery and considerable quantities of shot and shell. Could they hope for a miracle and fight off the tightening noose that Pope's army had fastened around the neck of the Confederate army at Madrid Bend?

John Mackall held out no hope of receiving any reinforcements from General Beauregard who was preoccupied with the aftermath of Shiloh. What had once been a formidable island fortress was now a trap. Federal gunboats were both upriver and downriver. Union troops had landed in waves and now numbered over 20,000. A substantial part of this force stood between his troops and the impeding swamps and high water that lay to the east. The Confederate general knew what he had to do. He would not needlessly sacrifice the lives of the men under his command, many of whom were in poor health due to prolonged exposure to the elements.

At 2:00 o'clock in the morning of April 8th, after consulting with his senior officers, John Mackall gave the order all knew was coming. Brigadier General Marsh Walker, the same officer with whom Eli had nearly come to blows, would be the one to deliver Mackall's decision. Walker mounted his horse and slowly rode out of camp, accompanied by two mounted aides. George and Eli watched as the three men crossed the perimeter guard and headed toward the campfires of the enemy entrenchment. One of the aides was bearing a white flag. The other carried a folder with a written communication from General Mackall tendering the unconditional surrender of his entire force. When the trio returned to report that the surrender had been accepted, Mackall sent out a second order, this one in the form of a general order to all officers and enlisted men under his immediate command to prepare for surrender. White flags were hoisted at various points along the camp's boundary to make sure there would be no mistaken firing on the defeated rebels. Many of the men, upon hearing of Mackall's decision, were determined not to be taken prisoner and made plans to risk the swamp waters in an attempt to make it to the lake.

Several hundred of them, leaving their muskets behind, waded into the dark waters of the cypress swamp. Some were from Colonel Henderson's Tennessee regiment and a few were fellow Alabamans from Company B. No one could say how many managed to elude their would-be captors. Undoubtedly, some drowned or were shot. Those who were caught attempting to escape, were brought back to where the others ended up being held. They looked half dead from exposure and extreme exhaustion. George was thankful that he and his brothers and Eli had not taken a chance on the black, infested waters of the swamp.

Before the break of day, after a fitful couple hours of sleep, the blurry-eyed Confederates of Company B shivered in the cold as they ate a distasteful breakfast of hardtack and bitter coffee. The mood among his companions was one of resignation that their ordeal was coming to an end. At the same time, they were disheartened by the prospects of becoming prisoners. Some spoke of being betrayed by their military commanders, Mackall and McCown, and of their contempt for the Confederate gunboat fleet commander, whom they regarded as a coward.

At 6:00 a.m., the Confederate troops under Mackall's command assembled as directed by their company sergeants and regimental officers. Those who still possessed blanket rolls, knapsacks, haversacks, army-issued muskets or their own squirrel rifles carried them along. Not knowing when or what their next meal in captivity would be, those who still possessed food stuffed what little they had into their pockets or into knapsacks. Upon the signal, they began to move forward in loose formation along the road to Tiptonville. Mackall and his command staff road on horseback. White flags were visible throughout the large column of men that tread the soggy ground. Here and there, considerable numbers of blue coats at various locations could be seen through the trees as the rebel soldiers slowly made their way. As they neared Tiptonville, rifle-bearing Union troops lined the road. By half past seven in the morning, the entire body had arrived at the outskirts of the village. A half hour later the formal surrender ceremony took place.

Federal regiments stood in tight formation positioning themselves in the shape of a three-sided enclosure near where the landing area and the woods met. A Union officer rode up to Mackall, who was still mounted on his horse, and spoke to the general. Mackall gave the order and began to lead his troops in "close-line formation" into the enclosure. They stood silently for a few seconds. Neither the Southerners nor the Northerners who stood on each side of the formation moved nor spoke. Acting in unison and as if on some silent command, the rebel soldiers held up their hands in a symbolic gesture that there would be no further resistance. Each regimental commander took his turn at ordering his troops to stack their firearms. Finally, Mackall surrendered his sword and the ceremony was over.

For the rest of the day, the rebel prisoners stood or sat in the enclosure. Throughout the afternoon, a cold wind blowing in from the river caused considerable discomfort. Men without coats wrapped themselves in dingy, worn cotton blankets. All the while, a large contingent of armed Federal soldiers stood guard around the perimeter of the human enclosure. No food or water was provided. Many of the men were sick and found no relief lying wrapped in their wet blankets on the damp ground. Later in the day, they were fed a supper of fatback pork, hardtack, cheese and coffee. For many, it had been their first food since breakfast. Some of the prisoners preferred their own rations to the pork, but drank the coffee and ate the hardtack. The senior officers among the Confederate prisoners were given the option of taking their supper with the Union commanders, and several accepted the invitation. General Mackall stayed behind with the others, but Gantt and Walker left to dine with the enemy.

While the sullen prisoners ate their provisions, the first of the transport steamers to move the captive rebel army to New Madrid arrived. Gantt's Arkansas units comprised the initial group to be loaded and sent up the river. About a quarter of the men had been transported by mid-evening, with the remainder to go the next day. This meant that over 3,000 Confederate and an even greater number of Union soldiers guarding them had to spend the night at the enclosure.

On that night, one of the severest rainstorms in years battered the area. Having no shelter to protect them from the driving rain and frigid cold, the exposed prisoners shivered through their first night spent in captivity. Rubber ponchos were lent by those who had them to the sick. George had kept his coat which he wore with a ragged woolen scarf stuffed around the collar. Most of the others in his company, including his two brothers, wrapped themselves in wet blankets and suffered through the stormy night.

W.A. "Doc" Martin, an army surgeon, was well liked by the men in the First Alabama, Tennessee, and Mississippi Regiment. He had tended to the sick throughout the night in a makeshift holding area, but without medicines, he could do little. The Union officers in charge of the prisoners ignored his pleas to move the very sick to tents. The other Confederate army surgeon who was also among the captured at Tiptonville was equally unsuccessful in his requests. Dr. Martin and the other doctor counted at least fifty seriously ill soldiers. Dysentery, measles, influenza, consumption and pneumonia kept the doctors and orderlies busy trying to make the afflicted soldiers as comfortable as possible. The mud and cold made their working conditions difficult. The lack of enough pits for latrines added to the prisoners' misery. The torrential rain quickly filled and overflowed those that had been dug, resulting in human excrement spilling out into the holding camp.

The sound of the incessant rain intermingled with the moans of the sick and suffering. W.A. Martin tried to adjust the wick on the lantern as he attempted to write a report on the condition of the sick and wounded prisoners under his care. An orderly stuck his head through the tent door. "Doc, there's a Lieutenant Forrest here to see you.

Removing his glasses, he motioned for Eli to come forward. "What ails you, Lieutenant?

Eli pulled the half-empty canteen of rye from his raincoat and offered it to the weary regimental surgeon. "I'm doing tolerably well, given the circumstances. I saw you working with some of the wounded in the rain and thought you might find some use for this."

Taking the whiskey from Eli's outstretched hand, Martin took a quick swig and set the canteen on his writing table. "Some of those poor boys will be lucky to make it through the night. Not enough shelter, not enough medicine or bandages....," the surgeon picked up the whiskey and took another drink. "Too late and too little, Lieutenant. Too late and too little."

Eli looked intently at Dr. Martin. "Looks like the fighting is over for us. I thought maybe I could be of some help to you."

Martin raised an eyebrow. "You're an officer, Forrest. I never heard of an officer volunteering to be an orderly. Lord knows, though, we could use the help. Do you know anything about medicine or tending the sick and wounded?"

"I apprenticed awhile with a doctor in Memphis after my father came home a cripple from the Mexican war."

"That so?" Martin replied. "Was he any good?"

"Yes Sir. He was the best doctor I've ever seen. He got my father back on his feet."

Rubbing the stubble on his chin, Martin continued. "How long did you work with him and what did that work entail?"

"Worked with Dr. Perkins for a little over a year, learning how to help my Ma take care of my father. He loaned me books from his medical library. I assisted him with some of his other cases—broken limbs, gun-shot wounds and such."

Martin folded his hands across his chest and peered intently at Eli. "But you didn't stick with it."

"No Sir, I didn't," Eli replied. My uncle Nathan paid for me to go to Virginia Military Institute to get an education."

"So did you? Did you get an education?"

Eli looked at the lantern's dancing flame. "More or less. Didn't graduate, but I did learn some things."

Martin stood and offered his hand to Eli. "Lieutenant, I would be much obliged for your help. You could be of great value to me and our other surgeon, Dr. Samuels, in helping these poor souls. Maybe, we could even teach you a thing or two. Another thing, most of the folks who know me, call me Doc Martin."

Shaking hands, the two men agreed that Eli would start the next day. As Eli exited the tent, Doc Martin called out to him, "Lieutenant Forrest…?"

"Yes Sir?" Eli replied.

"Thanks for the whiskey."

"How's that Yankee cheese?" Will queried Eli.

Eli tore off a chunk and offered it to Will who declined. "Not that bad considering the alternative. I suppose northern cows ain't all that different than their southern relatives."

George pulled his coat tighter around his neck. "Eli, I guess you were right. We finally ran out of time. I sure wish that sky would run out of rain."

Eli offered George a tin cup filled with coffee. "Here, drink this. It's not hot, but warm enough to do some good."

George took a sip and said to no one in particular, "I'd like someone to tell me what this sorry war has amounted to. All the politicians' promises and the generals' strategies winds up at the same place—a field full of dead and dying while the crop fields back home go untended. Doing your duty is one thing, but maybe the question ought to be asked whether or not the duty is worth doing?"

Eli looked up at the rain. "Well put, George. I expect all wars are sorry in their own way—especially for those of us on the losing end. If we have any duty left, it's the duty to survive and return home or what's left of it."

George handed the cup back to Eli. "I expect you're right. Surviving those Yankee prison camps will be a battle of a different kind—far from home and kin."

Eli drained the last of the coffee. "Yes sir—far from home and kin. Getting there is one thing, returning home is quite another."

George shut his eyes and wondered what Ann Pritchard was doing.

PRISONERS OF WAR

On April 9th, Corporal George Spears, weary and stiff-jointed from the damp cold, stood in a crowd with his two brothers and the rest of his company near the boat landing. A sense of gloom and foreboding settled in as they watched the transports steam into harbor. When the Yankees got off the boats and came onto the landing area to take custody of their charges, they found the rebel prisoners covered with grime and devoid of emotion. The mythical warriors from the South bore little resemblance to the image the Union troops had expected. The rebel yells had fallen silent. Only if one looked closely could the flicker of defiance still be detected in the eyes of the prisoners.

Very little was said among the prisoners as they kept in loose formation, waiting to board the vessels at the landing. The Union guards searched their knapsacks, haversacks, blanket rolls and pockets for hidden pistols and other weapons. Several Bowie knives were confiscated, but the captured soldiers were allowed to keep their small folding knives. When the Confederate officers protested giving up their weapons, they were told they could keep their swords and their side-arms, as long as they remained unloaded. Any food rations in the packs, along with whatever personal items the prisoners kept there, were left untouched. The captives were quickly loaded aboard the boats, where they found themselves pushed into whatever space remained unoccupied.

With over three hundred prisoners crowded onto the deck and lower area of the steamer, the men scarcely had room to bend over. George found himself on the upper deck near the rail, holding on with both hands to keep from being bumped overboard into the fast moving current. He preferred holding onto the rail rather being stuck in the middle of the crowded deck where a man could easily be trampled if he lost his balance and fell down. He was relieved to spot Will and A.F. several rows back to his left.

With the day's first load of rebel prisoners aboard, the transport steamer backed slowly from the landing at Tiptonville. With its large paddle wheel splashing and churning the murky water, the vessel gradually made its turn and began to move against the strong current, slowly making its way up the Mississippi River. The men remained silent for the most part during the short voyage upriver.

It was nearly noon when the steamer docked and the rebel prisoners were escorted off the transport at the New Madrid landing not far from the lower fort, which the Confederacy had known as Fort Thompson. The day was cloudy and damp, which complemented the gloom and despair of the demoralized Confederates as they were led through two lines of Yankee soldiers to the makeshift prisoner compound located behind the lower fort. They would remain in the compound until the evening of April 12th, when the last of the prisoners would leave New Madrid by steamboat for Northern prison camps. The men of Company B were forced to make camp in the open near the riverbank, exposed to weather's harshest elements. There would be no tents to protect them from the early April cold and rain. Wooden planks were provided for the prisoners to sleep on. Officers could choose to be taken to "prisoner quarters" within the lower fort where they would dine with Yankee officers of either junior or senior rank. Some did so, while others, including Eli, chose to remain in the compound where enlisted men and officers alike were given full rations, which consisted of salted pork, hardtack, something that resembled rice, and coffee to boil. Open fires were the only means of cooking and keeping warm. The prisoners had to rely on their own cooking utensils, but were allowed to collect firewood outside the compound in the company of armed guards who provided them with several worn and dull axes for chopping wood.

Eli, George and his brothers huddled around a small cook-fire.

"At least, the bluebellies gave us some vittles," Will said, fishing a sizzling piece of salt pork out of the small frying pan with his fingers.

"It's mostly fat," A.F. replied. "Ain't nothing like Mama's salt pork—thick and lean. Nobody can cook like Mama."

"Eat your supper before it gets cold," George instructed his younger brother. "Be glad you got something to put in your belly."

George rubbed his hands together over the fire. "How long you reckon we'll be here, Eli?"

Eli drank the last of his coffee and stood up. "Won't be long. Maybe, a few days. Doc Martin says we're headed to Illinois. Doc wants me to check on a couple of boys from Alabama. One's got pneumonia and the other one's got a leg wound. Looks like gangrene's setting in."

George stirred the campfire with a stick and looked up at Eli. "Why you doing it, Eli? Ain't like there's not enough suffering to get your fill of out here. Why you getting in the middle of it with Doc Martin?"

Eli looked down at his friend. "Can't say for sure. Guess it keeps me busy—maybe it's even about helping out Doc."

Eli cracked the hint of a smile. "Besides, Doc likes to take a nip every now and then and when he does, he saves a snort for me."

About 4,500 Confederate prisoners were brought to New Madrid from Tiptonville, Island No. 10, and the mainland shore areas across and above the island. The seriously ill and convalescent prisoners numbered over 350. There were no medicines for them nor access to a field hospital where the ailing men could be kept. Instead, they were kept on a small hospital boat or in a separate section of the compound without adequate protection from the cold and rain. They were tended to by a small number of army surgeons, including a few Union surgeons, who volunteered to work with the rebel prisoners. Prisoner orderlies assisted the hard-pressed surgeons in caring for the sick as best they could be under the difficult circumstances.

For two days, the prisoners at New Madrid spent their time standing, sitting or lying on the rough often wet ground. They talked about the prison camp at Chicago, where it was rumored the enlisted men would be sent. They hoped their confinement would last for only a short time until a prisoner exchange could be arranged. From his vantage point within the large open field that comprised the prison compound, George watched and studied the faces of his keepers. The perimeter of the closely-guarded compound consisted of Federal soldiers, mostly from Illinois and Iowa. As with their captives, the Union guards appeared to be farmers, although some were no doubt city dwellers. Most wore blue uniforms, but there were several different shades of blue. Their caps varied too. Each Yankee carried a muzzle-loading musket and acted as if under the slightest provocation, they wouldn't hesitate to use it. The guards seemed nervous and no doubt had orders to shoot to kill the rebel prisoners if any trouble erupted.

In the makeshift detention area, the guards and the guarded shared a common displeasure for the situation they found themselves in. The former were irritated at having drawn the undesirable duty of guarding rebels, while the latter were filled with the uncertainty and despair of demoralized men being held captive. The rain and cold fell on the guards and guarded alike, showing no distinction between the victors and the vanquished.

At night, throngs of men took turns standing near the flames in an attempt to get warm. Many had no coats or decent blankets to protect themselves from the elements. Firewood soon became scarce, and the wind and rain made it difficult to keep up the fires. The prisoners divided themselves into groups of one hundred for purposes of warming themselves or cooking over the camp-fires. Rations from their knapsacks and haversacks supplemented the substandard food their keepers provided. Cornmeal, rice and coffee were the mainstays, although some of the prisoners ate the suspect pork the Yankee quartermaster had supplied.

The temporary compound where the prisoners were confined provided no area for sewage sinks or drain pits. By the second day, the mud, filth and stench became unbearable. The health of many of the rebels, particularly those who had manned the island's partially submerged batteries knee-deep in river water, deteriorated under exposure to the elements, filthy conditions and an inadequate diet. The surgeons and orderlies did what they could, but the number of sick grew steadily. The most common symptoms were fever, heavy coughing and diarrhea. The worst among them were so sick and miserable, they weren't expected to survive.

On Friday afternoon, April 11th, Federal soldiers finally began the two day process of loading the prisoners of New Madrid aboard river steamboats that had been put into the service of the U.S. Navy. The sick and convalescent prisoners were taken first. The rickety steamer that served as a hospital boat had upwards of two hundred and fifty weak and exhausted men on board. Although they were literally piled and stacked in the cabin and staterooms, there was not enough space inside for all of them. Many of the sick had to remain on deck. In addition to the rebel surgeons and orderlies—including Eli,

George and his brothers—that accompanied the ill soldiers, crew members and Yankee guards added to the overloaded steamboat.

Eli leaned against the deck rail and lit the butt of a half-smoked cigar. "George, you, A.F. and Will might have fared better with the rest of Company B on another boat."

"Could be," George replied. "We talked about it and thought we might be more help on the hospital steamer."

"That's right," A.F. chimed in with a broad smile. "Will said we could help tend to them that need doctorin'. Ma and Pa would be proud of us for helping the sick."

Will looked at his younger brother and shook his head as he spat a stream of tobacco juice into the dark waters below.

"Besides," George added, lighting his briar, "I figured you might be in over your head volunteering for hospital duty."

"My guess is you figured right," Eli replied as he looked out into the cold mist.

One-by-one, the other transport steamers pulled into the large landing area located along the levee of the river town. As had happened with the hospital vessel, about three hundred men were loaded onto each of the steamboats that had been converted to prisoner transports. By early evening, when the transfer from land to river boats stopped for the day, half of the prisoners had been removed.

Steamer after steamer, including the hospital ship, slowly made their way up the swollen river. They were bound for Cairo, Illinois, district headquarters for the Union army and a transit center for prisoners of war being sent to camps in four adjoining states. The journey to Cairo was long and hard. A frigid wind blew along the river. The other Yankee steamers, laden down with prisoners, had men crammed in their grimy and poorly ventilated holds, which at least offered some shelter from the bone numbing cold on deck. The benefit of being sheltered from the chilling wind off the river was more than offset by the foul air in the squalid hold, smelling of unwashed men in filthy clothes. The close quarters soon reeked from the stench of buckets full of human waste.

Around mid-afternoon, the prisoners were given rations of salted pork fat and a ship biscuit to eat. Although there were no workable stoves to cook the pork, given their circumstances, there was little appetite anyway among the men. Many of those packed into the holds had become nauseated and could be heard retching and vomiting where they stood.

The prisoners who crowded onto the decks of the steamers suffered in a different way. Most were ill equipped for the biting wind. Some had coats and others wrapped themselves in blankets taken from knapsacks. Many had neither and shivered in their butternut colored pants and homespun shirts.

Even though there was little room aboard the hospital boat, the infirmed who became sickest with fever, uncontrolled shakes or severe coughing, were taken to the cabin and tended to by Eli and the other orderlies. The rebel soldiers remaining on the open deck who were able to eat, washed down the hardtack they consumed with rainwater.

Adding to the general misery of the captives being conveyed upriver was another horror. A number of the passing steamers were struck by sniper fire from unidentified shooters hidden along the riverbank. Several prisoners were hit and wounded by one such random sniper attack. Aside from this peril, there was also the danger of the older vessels' boilers suddenly exploding, sending a blast of scalding steam and boiling water over those crammed into the holds. Flames from a shattered boiler would quickly consume the worn wooden planks and creaking beams that comprised much of the dilapidated boats. George had heard tales of such river disasters when he was in Clarksville.

The Yankee soldiers who served as guards on the hospital boat's deck were from an Illinois regiment and none of them looked to be older than nineteen years of age. They were none too friendly and seemed inclined to use either end of their weapon if they felt provoked. Even though dressed in wool coats and caps and more accustomed to the climate, the guards also seemed to experience discomfort with the inclement weather. Discomfort was one thing and outright misery was another. It took nearly thirty hours for the churning paddlewheels to push the prison steamers against the strong current of the Mississippi before they reached their destination at the inlet on the river that served Cairo.

The process of unloading prisoners from the long convoy of steamers that had lined up to deposit their human cargo at the river port's large dock took nearly ten hours. Once on land, the rebel prisoners were led by their guards through town to an extensive military camp that had been refitted in army fashion to hold large numbers of prisoners of war. It was set on low ground and appeared to be a large stretch of mud interspersed with puddles of rainwater. Inside the stockade toward the rear of the encampment was a building with a porch over which was planted a pole with a wind-flapped Federal flag. The two-story wooden frame structure wore a sign over its entrance that read "headquarters." To its right stood a series of long, low buildings, neatly whitewashed and separated by alleys a few paces in width. To the left were stables, and then another small building, and finally a long commissary building. A hundred yards to the rear of the commissary was a hospital building, a large structure with wings extending at right angles.

Across the vast grounds of the camp was a secured enclosure consisting of a twelve-foot high wooden fence, topped by a walkway with narrow guard houses on its corners and sentinels pacing around it. Within the enclosure below, countless rows of tan-colored army tents were set up not more than three feet apart. These temporary shelters had been erected two months earlier in order to accommodate the thousands of Confederate prisoners captured by Grant in February at Fort Donelson. But they were left standing and now served as shelter for the rebels captured at Island No. 10 and east of Tiptonville.

For the next several days, the men of Company B and other prisoners stood around the grounds or rested in their tents, wiling away the time and wondering where they would be sent from Cairo.

Eli and George along with a dozen other rebel prisoners stood next to the stockade fence in hopes of blocking some of the chill blowing in from the west.

A burly, bearded sergeant from Tennessee gave voice to what everyone else was thinking. "I been hearin' rumors that we won't be here more'n a week or ten days."

A thin, balding corporal from Mississippi spoke up: "Word is they'll be sendin' most of us boys to camps in Ohio, Illinois, Indiana and Missouri."

"Maybe they'll send us back down south in one of them prisoner swaps," the sergeant replied as he turned toward Eli.

"What's yer take on it, Lieutenant? You reckon there's a chance we might end up back in Dixie?"

"Nothing I would like better," Eli replied, folding his arms. "Sadly, it's not likely to happen. Lincoln and his generals decided they got more folks than we do to carry the fight so why send us back home to fight another day. My guess is they aim to move us as far from the fighting as they can."

The sergeant stroked his beard. "A fella on the boat told me the Yankees took more'n 10,000 of our boys prisoner after Donelson fell."

"That sounds about right." Eli added as he watched the men grow silent, pondering their diminishing prospects.

On the morning of April 14th, it was announced that most of the Confederate officers were to be sent that day to Johnson's Island at Sandusky, Ohio. Beginning the following day, the remaining prisoners, amounting to approximately 4,300 enlisted men, would be incrementally processed for relocation to prison camps in Illinois and Ohio. They would be moved by rail. Company B learned that they were among 2,500 enlisted men to be sent to Camp Douglas in Chicago.

Approximately a thousand of these men would continue on to Camp Randall in Madison, Wisconsin. Prisoners in the camp hospital who were too sick to be moved immediately by rail would be placed on the steamboat *Evansville* and transported up the Mississippi River to a place called Prairie du Chien, Wisconsin. From there, they would be transported via railroad cars to Camp Randall prison camp.

Most of the men had turned in for the night, hoping to catch a few hours of anxious sleep before tomorrow's exodus began. George lit his pipe, casting a sideways glance at Eli who stared at the dying embers of the campfire. The two friends sat on a rough-hewn log bench, listening to the sounds of the night.

George pulled a letter and three cigars from his haversack and handed them to Eli.

"These three cigars cost me a good pocketknife so you best smoke them slow and easy."

Eli smiled as he placed two of the cigars in his coat pocket and looked at the letter in his hand.

George relit his pipe and exhaled a spiral of smoke into the night air. "That letter is for Mrs. Ann Pritchard in case a mishap befalls me before I reach Camp Randall."

Eli bit the end off a cigar and lit it with a stick from the remnants of the campfire. "The only thing that's likely to happen to you is that you and your brothers will get to our final destination a lot sooner than I will. A boatload of sick soldiers will take awhile to make its way to the cheerful Camp Randall."

George blew another plume of smoke. "I expect you are right about that, but just in case…."

"Here," Eli said, handing George a small jar, "Doc Martin passed a half pint jar of peach brandy on to me. If you don't like the taste of it, you can trade it to the Yankee guards for some tobacco."

"Let's have us a sip before we turn in," George replied as he unscrewed the cap.

Twenty minutes later, George turned up the jar and drank the last of the brandy. "It's agreeable enough. Reminds me of some sweet Georgia peaches I once had."

"Looks like you won't be trading that brandy for any tobacco," Eli laughed.

George looked at the empty jar. "Sure enough. I expect on this night I would rather drink it with you than trade it for anything a Yankee's got."

"I reckon so," Eli chuckled. "I reckon so."

The men sat in silence, each lost in his own thoughts.

Finally, Eli rose from the bench and placed a hand on George's shoulder. "George, you take care of yourself and those two brothers of yours. I'll look you up as soon as I get to Camp Randall."

George stood and extended his hand. "Good-byes seem to be getting harder for me the longer this war goes on."

Eli smiled. "Just remember, friend. Sometimes when you say good-bye, a hello isn't too far away."

The next morning, the business of moving thousands of men to the rail lines began. A long, winding procession of prisoners were led by hundreds of guards to one of Cairo's two train depots, where they were loaded onto passenger and freight cars belonging to the Illinois Central Railway. It was dusk before the first trainload of prisoners left Cairo bound north for Chicago.

The train ride to Chicago, some three hundred miles away, was a slow journey that took nearly twelve hours. Because of confusion over troop assignments, an inadequate number of Union soldiers were detailed to guard the prisoners. It was rumored that several men slipped away through a passenger car window shortly after the train had left Cairo.

The most fortunate prisoners rode in passenger cars, each of which contained a stove. The less fortunate ones, including George, his brothers and the others in Company B, made the trip in unheated freight cars. All were fed before they boarded, and those in the passenger cars were fed later on the train. The freight car passengers ate their breakfast outside when the train made a scheduled stop. All were given standard Union army rations of beef, beans, coffee, crackers or a biscuit. The train also made periodic stops to enable the prisoners to replenish their canteens with drinking water and to relieve themselves a few yards from the track. On one of the last stops, as dawn was breaking, George looked out over the rural landscape and was surprised at how flat it was. It was not at all like his familiar surroundings in Alabama. He wondered if he would ever see the forested hills and winding streams of southwest Alabama again. He longed to see his family. His thoughts then turned to Ann Pritchard. He removed her picture from his shirt and as he took in the memory of her gentle face, he felt a calm settle over him. George made a promise to himself that he would be with her again when this terrible war was finally over.

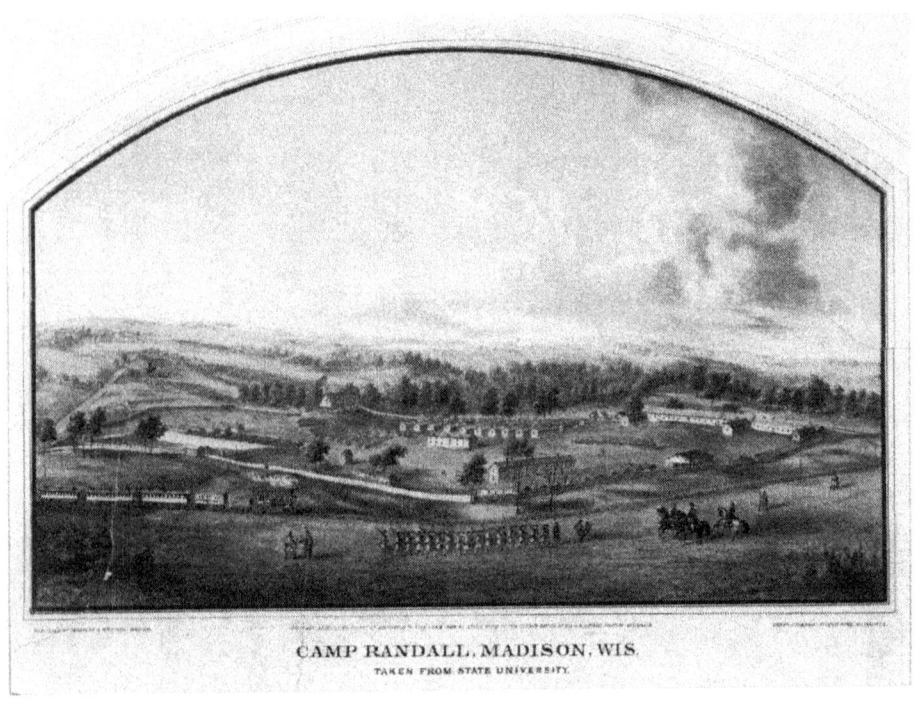

CAMP RANDALL, MADISON, WIS.
TAKEN FROM STATE UNIVERSITY.

CAMP RANDALL
MADISON, WISCONSIN
(Courtesy Wisconsin Historical Society)

CAMP RANDALL

Two hundred and fifty sick and disabled prisoners were unloaded from railway cars at the Madison depot. Surviving the journey aboard the transport steamer and train had been difficult. The few men who could stand milled about, talking among themselves. Others, too weak to stand, sat on the ground or lay on stretchers.

Civilian residents who had gathered to catch a glimpse of the second wave of "secesh prisoners," had expected to experience a similar back and forth they had enjoyed with the main body of prisoners who had arrived several weeks earlier—George and his brothers among them. Instead, the men and women of Madison stood in stunned silence as they observed the emaciated, pitiful men standing and laying before them.

"What a terrible sight to behold," gasped a well-dressed woman to her husband. "They look more like ghosts than men."

A newspaper reporter standing next to the couple placed his notepad and pencil in his coat pocket. "Ghosts, indeed. The prospects for these poor fellows are not promising. After all they have been through, I doubt even the most skillful care and treatment can save most of them."

Eli stood on the steps of the camp hospital. The new arrivals had been fed and made as comfortable as possible. Doc Martin had finagled a pass for Eli from the Union surgeon under the guise that he was to check on a sick prisoner in Barrack Number 8 which just happened to be where George and his brothers were housed.

Eli looked up at the night sky. "Camp Randall…Madison, Wisconsin… hellava place to be," he muttered to himself as he walked toward George's barracks.

On the train ride from the river town of Prairie du Chien to Madison, Doc Martin had garnered some details about the prison camp and the surrounding area from a friendly Union officer. Camp Randall apparently comprised an area of ten acres overlooking neatly fenced farms and groves of trees. To one side of the camp entrance where a small guardhouse stood was a stretch of neatly whitewashed barracks. To the left of these buildings was the horse stable and on the right of it stood the camp commissary. On a slight elevation where he stood was the camp hospital, a large, oblong-shaped structure with two wings at right angles extending from the main building. The Union surgeon's quarters was located next to the hospital. Further down from the hospital was a double row of barracks, fronted by a two-storied building that served as camp headquarters. Another structure toward the rear of the camp housed a sutler shop and the camp post office.

On Sundays, local residents liked to come to the camp following church services and mid-day family meals. Eli guessed that few, if any, of the locals had ever as much as set foot on Southern soil, let alone seen a rebel soldier in the flesh. More than likely, they were curious to find out if what they had read in newspapers or heard around town about Southern fighting men was true. Were they ignorant, wild backwoodsmen who could neither read nor write? Doc had also filled him in on the layout and construction of the camp.

Originally built as a military training facility, additional barracks had been constructed and fitted with cooking stoves since prisoners would be required to take their meals in the barracks. Each of the prisoner barracks was similar in construction. They were approximately eighty feet in length and twenty feet wide. Their roofing had tar paper covering it to keep out the rain. The outward appearance of the building was drab and dreary which matched the mood of the prisoners housed there.

The interior walls consisted of a solitary layer of one inch thick pine board. There was no ceiling other than a sloping roof where two skylights served the dual purpose of providing natural light and ventilation when propped open. A long table stretched down the middle of each barrack's interior to a kitchen, which was furnished with a large cook stove. Extending the entire length of each side of the building were three sets of triple-tier bunks. Straw ticks lay atop each berth which provided sleeping space for two men. Each barrack had two large wood burning box-stoves, one located midway and the other on the end opposite the kitchen. A single entrance door was located in the middle.

There was also a small, windowless guardhouse with double reinforced walls. It had formerly been used for the occasional unruly recruit but would now hold rebel prisoners charged with violating prison rules and discipline. As he entered the yard adjacent to Barrack Number 8, Eli heard A.F.'s voice.

"You bluebellies give me back my sweet potato!"

"Hold on there, Johnny Reb, this here sweet tater's contraband once you step out of your barrack," laughed a burly Yankee sergeant who along with a young recruit was making sport with A.F.

"Ain't no such rule," exclaimed a red-faced A.F. "That potato was given to me by my brother, Will."

The sergeant took a bite and handed it the recruit. "This tastes like a Northern tater to me—nice and juicy. If it was a Southern tater, it wouldn't be worth eating."

A.F. lunged for the sweet potato, catching the younger soldier by surprise and knocking him to the ground.

"Boy, you done got yourself in a heap o' trouble," shouted the older man as he cracked the butt of his rifle against A.F.'s head. Falling down, A.F. covered himself as best he could while the two guards kicked him. It was on the third kick that Eli intervened.

Reaching for a stout piece of firewood from a neatly stacked woodpile, Eli slammed the younger guard across the back of the head, sending him dazed and sprawling next to where A.F. lay. The bigger and stronger soldier pivoted toward Eli, his bayonet ready.

Grasping the firewood with both of his hands, in a single motion Eli blocked the bayonet thrust and rendered a sharp kick to the man's left knee, causing him to stumble backwards. From there, instinct took over as Eli rammed the firewood into the man's ample belly. The Yankee sergeant fell forward gasping for breath. The last thing Eli remembered was turning to see if A.F. was alright.

The smell of rose water on a spring day could only mean one thing—the war was over and he was on a picnic with a pretty Southern belle. Why then, did his head feel like it was full of cannon shot? Opening his eyes into a narrow slit, Eli realized a little bit of his dream was true. Standing over him was the prettiest woman he had ever seen. Maybe, he was addled from whatever had happened to him, but he had no doubt that the dark haired, blue-eyed nurse that was tending his wounds was a dream worth having.

Eli's parched lips formed a hoarse whisper as he looked up at the young woman. "You smell good."

Looking down at her battered charge with a look somewhere between amusement and professional disinterest, she replied. "Well, sir, you don't."

Eli tried to smile even though his whole face hurt for the effort as nurse Agatha Deveraux called for Doc Martin.

Doc Martin peered over the spectacles perched precariously on the bridge of his nose. "Eli, my boy, you were supposed to help me in the infirmary, not end up here as a patient."

"Sorry, Doc," Eli replied. "How's A.F.?"

"He's in the stockade for three days with a big knot on his head. Once you have recovered, your stay will be considerably longer. Lucky for you and the Spears boy, the Union officer, a Captain Chandler, who investigated the incident, seems to be a fair and decent man. He acknowledged the two Union guards played a role in the conflict which helped A.F. But you..."

"I didn't hurt 'em too bad, Doc. Look what they did to me? I don't even remember what happened."

"No doubt," Doc Martin continued, "Two other guards showed up and, between the four of them, they worked you over good. Might have been worse if the Yanks hadn't been faced down by a large group of your compatriots who heard the commotion going on outside the barrack. Anyway, the big one has a broken kneecap and bruised sternum and the younger one has a headache resulting from a mild concussion. "

Turning to the young nurse, Martin instructed her to go to the pharmacy and bring back fresh bandages and some liniment oil.

Eli took a sip of water from a tin cup the Doc offered him. "Tell me about her"

Doc Martin shook his head. "Aggie, the nurse?"

"That's right, Doc. Tell me about Aggie."

"Son, here you are, lying in a prison hospital beat to a pulp, facing a long stretch of solitary confinement and you want to know about Aggie Deveraux. You need to think about watching your back instead of watching her. You have made yourself a lot of enemies in this camp, especially the Yankee sergeant whose knee you permanently damaged. Besides, a blind man can tell that the men of the Nineteenth Wisconsin are for the most part, a poorly trained bunch of young farm boys and assorted misfits which makes them unpredictable."

Eli tried touching his swollen face. "No doubt you're right, Doc. But if I'm gonna do a long stretch in the lock-up, I'd like to have something to think about besides the cold and isolation."

The hint of a smile creased Doc's face. "I hadn't thought about it that way. What little I know about Miss Deveraux is that her father sent her and her mother and younger brother to live in Madison with her uncle, a successful farmer. They moved here a year ago before the war started while her father stayed behind with his trading business in New Orleans. Seems she was trained as a nurse in New Orleans…apparently against her father's wishes. Since the camp opened, she's served as a volunteer nurse."

"Thanks, Doc," Eli replied. "That will hold me for awhile… until I get to know her better. I can tell she has spunk…from the first minute I saw her I could tell that."

"You got about two weeks. When Captain Chandler hears that you have come to, he will come by and inform you how long the stay in solitary will be."

Aggie Deveraux arrived with the bandages and liniment oil.

With a slight twinkle in his eye, Doc Martin turned to her. "Nurse Deveraux will you be so kind as to change Lieutenant Forrest's bandages and dress his wounds while I attend to other patients."

"Eli, you ain't dead, are you?"

Eli opened his eyes in a squint to see A.F. standing over him next to George. "Not yet," he replied.

George looked intently at his friend. "The nurse said it would be alright to wake you."

"It's more than okay. I've been hoping they would let you pay me a visit."

A.F. touched Eli on the shoulder. "I sure do thank you for coming to my rescue. I never did get to eat that sweet potato—not even a bite."

"Sorry to hear that," Eli replied.

A.F. poured some water into a cup and offered it to Eli. "You want a sip of water? It might make you feel better."

Eli took a drink and thanked A.F.

George took off his hat and laid it on the cot. "The boys have been asking about you."

"Good to hear," Eli answered. "I've been wondering how the folks in Company B are doing. Seems I got waylaid on my way to visit them…What's your take on this place?"

George moved to the head of the cot. "So far, not too bad…could be worse. Don't think much of Lieutenant Colonel Whipple…too full of himself. Some of the boys make bird calls and refer to him as Colonel 'Whipple Will'."

Eli smiled at the thought of it.

"The townfolk are nice enough. Not like those Chicago people who were ready to lynch the whole lot of us when we come through. Met a fellow from Webster County in Kentucky who moved up here two years ago and bought a dry goods store. I asked him to mail a letter to Ann Pritchard and he obliged me. A Union major by the name of Bovay seems decent enough. Got us together to explain the camp rules. Told us about roll call, provisions, the latrines and such. Said any prisoner who crosses the line they call the 'dead zone' is subject to being shot on the spot. Breaches of camp rules and discipline can get you sent to the guardhouse. Heard you might be headed there when you heal up."

Eli rubbed the stubble on his chin. "You heard right."

"The major also told us how we can get to the camp sutler and post office. Seems we can mail letters home, but they'll read them first. I don't cotton much to anybody reading my letters to Ann Pritchard."

A young woman dressed in a nurse's uniform appeared. "You gentlemen need to leave shortly so that Lieutenant Forrest can have his bandages changed. I need to check on a patient down the hall. That should give you enough time to say your goodbyes." With that, Nurse Deveraux turned and walked away.

George raised an eyebrow and looked at Eli. "She seems a matter-of-fact kind of woman."

Eli watched Aggie Deveraux disappear down the hallway. "That, she is."

George grinned. "She brings a different look to your eye, Eli."

"A different look?"

"Yep. Kind of distant and all."

Eli folded his arms across his chest. "Astute observation, Corporal. Yet, I have only come to know Miss Deveraux for a short time."

George looked at Eli. "Time's got nothing to do with it. No way to know when it's coming, but when it does, the feeling becomes a part of you."

George stood and motioned to A.F. that it was time to leave. "Eli, it's good to see that you're mending."

Doc Martin placed two glasses on the table in front of him and poured them half-full of apple brandy. Handing one to Eli, he raised his glass. "Here's to your continued good health, given what you are about to endure."

Eli raised his glass in response as both men drank. Eli could feel the warmth of the brandy ease its way down his throat. "Good medicine, Doc."

"Compliments of Aggie's Uncle Hester," he replied as he refilled their glasses.

"I have to hand it to you, Lieutenant, You've made the most of the two past weeks. Once you got on your feet, you've been a big help which didn't go unnoticed by the Union surgeon in charge of this hospital. If you're fit after your three week stint in solitary, he's agreed to let you help me with the sick prisoners. I'll be able to pay you a visit once a week to check on your condition. I hear Spring's are cold and wet in these parts so you won't have an easy time of it."

Draining the last of his brandy, Doc Martin continued with a smile, "Although she's a mite hard to read, I've watched Aggie cast more than an occasional glance your way when you weren't looking. Matter of fact, I believe at this moment, she's folding bandages by herself in the examining room if you want to have a word with her before the captain and guards come for you."

Aggie was looking out the window, her arms down by her sides, when Eli entered the examination room. He stood beside her and looked out as well. "What do you see?" Eli asked.

Continuing to stare in silence at the prison grounds and the trees beyond, Aggie finally spoke. "I see a lot of needless suffering. Sick, dispirited Southerners wanting to live to see their homes and families and scared Northern farm boys, trying to cover their fear with their rifles and bayonets. What do you see, Lieutenant?"

"I see you," Eli replied, turning his face toward hers.

Aggie momentarily shifted her eyes in response as she continued looking out the window.

"Would you mind, Miss Deveraux, if I touched your hand?"

"Why, Lieutenant, would you want to touch my hand?"

"It would give me something to think about in the stockade—a good memory to hold onto in a bad place."

As Aggie and Eli returned to their private thoughts, she slowly moved the back of her left hand against the back on his right hand. Eli lightly wrapped his fingers around hers.

"Lieutenant Forrest, Captain Chandler is here," Doc Martin shouted from the next room.

As he turned to leave, Aggie touched his arm. "When you return, you may call me Aggie—like Doc Martin does."

Eli smiled at her. "And you can call me Eli."

PRISON LIFE

Twenty-one days of cold and damp were bad enough, but doing it alone made it seem like twenty-one years. Bread and water rations once a day were supplemented by the occasional piece of salt pork or beef that George and the men of Company B bribed the guards to give him. Unsteady and disoriented, Eli Forrest emerged from solitary on the 22nd day. After a physical examination by the Union surgeon and Doc Martin, he was allowed to bathe and then fed a hot, steaming bowl of porridge. Then he was put to bed on his old cot in Doc Martin's quarters. He slept for ten hours straight. The first words Eli heard were "You need a shave."

Still weak from three weeks of inactivity, he sat on the side of his cot while Aggie Deveraux shaved him and cut his hair. Aggie stood with her hands on her hips, admiring her handiwork.

"Lieutenant Forrest, when they brought you in, you were a dreadful sight. But I must say, you now look like you have returned to the land of the living."

"My name is Eli."

"I know…Eli." She said with a twinkle in her eyes.

Aggie spoke again, but this time in a tone hinting of bemusement. "Of course, your name is Eli in our private conversations. In public, around prying eyes, it is Lieutenant Forrest and my name in such instances is Nurse Deveraux."

Gathering her clippers and shaving razor, she looked at Eli and smiled. "Remember, in private, I'm Aggie and you are Eli. In public, I'm Nurse Deveraux and you are Lieutenant Forrest. Understood?"

Eli grinned. "Yes ma'am, Nurse Deveraux."

Within several days, Eli had rebounded well enough to return to his orderly duties. Doc Martin was glad to have him back. The sick prisoners were reluctant to come to the camp hospital and when they did, they didn't trust Union doctors or their staff to treat their ailments.

Rumors abounded, ranging from rebel prisoners dying from neglect to being poisoned by Yankee doctors. Other than Doc Martin, they requested Eli or Aggie with her Louisiana accent and Southern charm.

The clanging on the kettle signaled to the men of Company B that their evening meal was ready. While standing in line waiting for their portion, A.F. thrust a small bag of tobacco toward George. "Here you go, big brother. Some tobacco for your pipe."

"Thank you, A.F. You must have caught a work crew."

"I sure did," A.F. replied with a big grin. "We dug us some new latrines and hauled garbage. Will's crew chopped and stacked firewood. They paid us with tobacco."

George looked at the bag of tobacco he was holding. "A.F., this doesn't look like a full ration of tobacco. Do you reckon they might have short-changed you?"

"Naw," A.F. replied. "I gave the rest to Sergeant Susong 'cause he promised to bring me three sweet potatoes next week."

"Remember, what I told you about bartering with Yankees. Have you forgotten your trouble with O'Reilly and the days you spent in the guardhouse?"

A.F. looked at his older brother in earnest. "Sergeant Susong ain't nothing like that bully, O'Reilly. He's different. He promised me he'd bring those taters."

"We'll see little brother. We'll see."

Supper was good that evening. The company cook for that day had outdone himself. Plenty of beans, potatoes, a couple of onions, some salt pork and two rabbits Will's work crew had killed and dressed all came together in a fine stew. A generous ration of corn meal allowed each man to enjoy a slab of cornbread.

George liked to be alone after the evening meal. He lit his briar and walked the barrack's grounds. Jack Hutchins was carving another toy horse for his boys back home. Two of the older prisoners were playing dominoes on the steps of the barrack's entrance. Off to his right under a small scrub oak was the Reverend Bartley Sims. George remembered him from the prayer meetings he held on Island No. 10. Surrounded by a group of forlorn looking prisoners, Reverend Sims deep voice was rising in a crescendo.

"Come to me all you who are heavy laden. That's what the Master said. No matter the sorrow or suffering you have endured, if you will turn to Jesus, He will save you. He will give you the peace that passes understanding—now and forevermore! Come now, all you that don't know him while there is still time. Come and accept our Savior and be baptized into eternal life." A line of prisoners formed. While they were being baptized with water from a canteen, Reverend Sims led the men in song: "Amazing grace, how sweet the sound, that saved a wretch like me."

George walked over to a bench and sat down, leaning back against the outside wall of the barrack and thinking—thinking about the past and a possible future with Ann Pritchard. Memories of the terrible battle at Fort Donelson competed with memories of Desotoville, where he was raised. He imagined he and Ann walking past the weathered, two-story school building down the road to Bailey's store where he would buy each of them a sarsaparilla. Holding hands, they would continue past John Bryant's tavern, the blacksmith shop, cotton gin and grist mill. They would stop at the old Methodist church and sit on the stone bench next to the cemetery and look at the dogwood trees in full bloom.

"George, are you okay?"

George opened his eyes to see Eli standing in front of him.

"Here you go," Eli said, offering his friend a cup of coffee.

George held the steaming cup in both hands. "I guess my mind was doing a little wandering."

Eli smiled. "I have a good idea where it was wandering to."

George didn't take the bait. "It's good to see you back on your feet. With all that cold and rain, I wasn't sure how you would hold up with a 21 day stint in the guardhouse."

"Me neither," Eli replied as he sipped his coffee. Looks like the Yanks are treating the boys decent enough."

The two men walked over and stood next to the fire-pit which was located between Spears' barrack and the one nearest to it. George placed his tin cup on a large split log next to the fire-pit and rubbed his hands together over the open fire. "Provisions are okay. We get beef, some salt pork, beans and potatoes—also coffee. Plenty of firewood to cook with and keep the barrack as warm as possible although that ain't saying a lot…better than a tent, but not by much. Water's better too. Not like at Cairo."

Poking at the fire with a stick, George continued. "The boys don't like the way they treat our dead. They put 'em in a bag and throw them in a grave, then go get another one. I don't know how they do it around here, but where I come from, we like to give our dead a proper burial. 'Course a war's going on and from the look of things, regular ways of doing don't much seem to apply."

Eli drank the last of his coffee. "Our boys aren't used to the cold and damp of Wisconsin, not to mention the close quarters of the barracks. Whoever comes down with something seems to give it to everyone around them. We're seeing more and more folks brought to the hospital. By the way, I'm much obliged for the salt pork and beef you got the guard to slip me. Bread and water leaves a lot to be desired."

George smiled. "No thanks needed. The beef and pork cost Sergeant Kyte a pocket knife. He carved the initials 'J.D.' on the handle and told that Yankee farm-boy standing guard that the knife had at one time been the personal property of none other than President Jeff Davis."

"Well played," Eli replied with a chuckle.

George threw more wood into the fire-pit. "At first, I didn't take to the visitors from town coming on Sundays, gawking at us like we were some kind of misfits. But they turned out to be regular enough folks except that they all talk peculiar-like. We've told the fellows to mind their manners which isn't too hard to enforce with all the cakes and other vittles they bring us."

Eli nodded in agreement. "I hear they also donated clothes and reading material, including newspapers, magazines and books."

"That's right," George replied. "They even started a "prisoner postage fund". Because of it, I was able to mail more letters to Ann Pritchard and my folks. Strange thing, Eli, is that it ain't just the church folk helping us out— other groups too, like the Masons and even the Printers Guild. Makes a man kinda wonder what they're up to—why are they doing it?"

Eli watched a fight break out to his right between some prisoners from Alabama and Tennessee over a card game. "I don't know why, but it's a nice enough surprise after a bunch of bad ones. Did you know your brother Will's got a talent for drawing? Doc hung one of his pictures—a covey of quail taking flight—on his wall of the examination room."

George watched Sergeant Kyte break up the melee. "Will trades his draw-ings for tobacco and extra rations. His best drawings are of the boys around the barrack. Can't say as I much like them though. They make me homesick."

Eli pulled a half-smoked cigar from his coat pocket and lit it. Exhaling, he looked up at the gray afternoon sky. "Hard to believe a couple of years past, I thought we would have whipped the Yankees by Christmas. Seems like a lifetime ago."

George stared at the cook-fire. "I didn't much want to go fight, but when the second call for enlistment went out, me and a lot of other Alabama boys signed up. We didn't think we had much of a choice. It was our turn—the right thing to do. Mama cried her eyes out when the first of her boys marched off to war. I didn't understand her tears then, but I sure enough do now."

"Plenty of tears to go around, I expect," Eli added. "Seems like more pris-oners are getting sick and giving up hope."

George rubbed his hand through his hair. "So true. Not much to do but think about home and how far away you are from it. Horton and Yeager caught 'lung fever' and Lockridge has got the measles. Six others have bad cases of dysentery. The list grows longer each day."

Eli looked at George. "Why won't they come to the hospital? We have a civilian doctor from Madison that comes out to help out Doc Martin and the Union surgeon."

"Simple truth is they don't trust Yankee doctors and their hospitals," George replied with a shrug. "To them, it seems like the next stop for the ones who go to the hospital is a trip to the grave. They trust you and the Doc, but only in the barrack where their friends are there to keep watch."

Eli took one last puff from the stub of his cigar. "Even though they would receive better care in the hospital, I understand their sentiment. The local newspapers don't help ease their suspicions when they keep writing that we're all doing well—that we have adjusted to the cold and rain and are satisfied, if not pleased, with our accommodations. Too bad, it's not true."

George pulled the collar of his jacket more tightly around his neck. "May-be they're writing about another Camp Randall?"

Eli's face crinkled into a half-smile. "Maybe so."

"One other thing, Eli."

"What's that?"

"Watch your back. Word's out that the fat Yankee sergeant—I think O'Reilly's his name—is out to get you. He's already sent four of the boys in

Company B to the hospital. Around the barracks, O'Reilly and his goons are known as the 'blue bullies.'"

Eli put his hands in his pockets. "You mean the one who now walks with a limp and had a sore gut?"

"That's the one," George replied.

TROUBLE IN CAMP

While the end of April and the first part of May brought the promise of better weather, storm clouds of another kind were gathering over Camp Randall. The first signs of trouble came in late April when the local press was blocked from entering the camp.

Then on May 3rd, a story appeared in one of the daily newspapers that raised questions about the quality of the hospital care sick prisoners were receiving as well as the rising death toll.

As a result, the camp's prison hospital was put under the supervision of a local civilian physician. The order came through removing control from the Nineteenth Regiment's assistant surgeon and giving it to Dr. William Hobbins, a Madison civilian physician. It was a stinging rebuke to both the regiment and its medical corps.

The local press also underscored the increasing level of tension that existed in the prison camp between prisoners and their military guards. When three prisoners escaped in the early morning hours of April 29th, what little trust that existed between the keepers and the kept evaporated.

Doc Martin and Eli had finished checking on the sick in Prison Barrack Number 8 when George motioned for Eli to come over to where he and Will stood next to the cook-stove.

"Eli, have you or the Doc heard anything new on the escape? Word has been going around about an escape attempt by some fellows from the Fifty-fifth Tennessee Regiment. 'Course rumors are always plentiful around here. You can usually take your pick. I figure there must be something to this one 'cause the next thing we knew, we were all ordered to our barracks."

Eli waved to Doc Martin as he left the barrack.

"Captain Scherff filled Doc in out of concern that the trouble might escalate into more violence and more casualties. The story goes that three prisoners bribed a Yankee private by the name of Amos Carr to aid them with their escape plans. This fellow Carr was a guard at the prison hospital. Under the pretense of seeing some sick friends, the Tennessee boys escaped from a part of the hospital that runs up against the outside fence. Doc and I figure that Carr must have had them slip out a back window of the hospital. Once they made it to the wooden fence, it would have been easy enough to pry a board or two loose and squeeze through the opening without being detected by any of the perimeter guards. When they got to the other side of the fence, all they had to do was to crawl on their bellies a couple hundred yards until they were on the low side of where the ground rises up on the east border of the camp."

Will cut a plug of chewing tobacco and wedged it into his mouth. " I heard that the escapees high-tailed it into Madison and then split up, one heading southwest along the railroad line and the other two proceeding east of the city along the main road."

Eli nodded in agreement. "Doc and I heard the same. The one who headed out on his own hasn't been re-captured. Aggie thinks he might have jumped a freight train and rode it to Minnesota. The other two weren't so lucky. They were caught ten miles east of Madison with the help of some tracking hounds. Word is they stole a wagon, but didn't get far before the camp commander and the local law got them."

Will spat a stream of tobacco juice out of an open window. "O'Reilly and his blue bullies been bragging about parading the two Tennessee boys through the streets tied together like a couple of mules. When they brought 'em back to camp, we all gathered 'round and saw 'em on their way to the guardhouse. Them Yankee guards looked a might bit nervous—like we was all ready to start something. I expect if one of the boys had shouted "boo", they might have well opened fire."

"Will, that's more true than you might realize," George replied somberly. "Most of these guards are youngsters and poorly trained and with trash like O'Reilly egging them on, who knows what might happen."

Eli observed the guards standing watch outside the prison barracks' perimeter. Private Carr's been arrested and placed in irons. Both Carr and the escapees are under heavy guard."

"What did he get out of it?" Will asked.

" Some Confederate and Federal dollars were found in his trunk. Damned fool's looking at a court-martial—maybe even a death sentence." Eli replied.

Will looked off into the distance. "Ain't no doubt about it, things are getting worse. I ain't never seen it this bad."

"Me neither," George agreed. "Ann Pritchard's never seemed farther away. How about Miss Aggie—how is she holding up?"

Eli shrugged. "I have suggested she stay away until things blow over, but she'll have none of it. Even Doc can't seem to change her mind. She can be a bit stubborn when she takes to something."

"She'd have to be stubborn to take to you, Eli." Will said with a grin.

The three friends laughed at Will's remark in spite of themselves and their predicament.

Relations between the rebel captives and their military keepers continued to deteriorate into May. Although no other escape attempts were made, several shooting incidents involving guards and prisoners occurred during the first half of the month. On May 14th, a soldier on guard duty fired his musket point blank at a prisoner who had called the guard "a Bull Run son of a bitch." Fortunately for the prisoner, the weapon misfired. An account of the incident in the local press was an indication that the mood of some of the town-folk was shifting toward the negative.

Reverend Bartley Sims had just finished his Sunday sermon and George and Eli were sitting on a rough-hewn log bench taking advantage of warmer than usual May weather.

George lit his pipe. "Eli, why do you reckon prison brings out the worst in some men? Look over there at those Wisconsin soldiers who guard us. They're no different from the men of Company B. They speak the same language and worship the same God. I have seen enough meanness in here to last me a lifetime. Fights start for no good reason. Even the best guards like Sergeant Susong stand by and watch goons like O'Reilly hurt people just because they can. Susong did bring A.F. those sweet potatoes like he promised and he's shown kindness to others as well, but that doesn't let him off the hook for not stopping the harm that's in his power to prevent. I tell you, Eli, I have just about lost all faith in the goodness of my fellow man. If it isn't the Yankees with their foot on our necks, it's our own boys preying on the weak among their own kind."

Eli slipped a bottle out of his pocket and took a drink before handing it to George.

"Take a sip or two of Uncle Hester's apple brandy. It might lift your spirits. There's truth to what you say, my friend. The guards seem to have come to the point of shoot-first-and-ask-questions-later. Last night they just about shot one of their own. Dr. Hobbins failed to halt when crossing a line of sentries and the boys in blue thought he was a prisoner. It nearly cost him his life. We outnumber the guards seven to one so they're more than a little jittery. And they aren't the only ones out of control. We're losing control of our boys as well."

George looked back at the barrack solemnly. "You are right about that, Eli. Yesterday, I saw a Mississippi volunteer get killed by a Georgia boy over a piece of chicken. Private Kershaw took a club and beat the fellow from Mississippi to death over a chicken leg—a chicken leg! A man died over a piece of chicken. The guards just stood by and watched it all happen. We did as well…just watched it happen like we was made of stone. Stabbings, fighting, and thievery—there's plenty of trouble on both sides."

If the strained atmosphere that existed at the camp was due entirely to the shooting incidents, fights, and such, matters might have improved over time. But the mounting death toll of prisoners at the camp's hospital from the spread of disease fueled suspicion among the prisoner population that their sick comrades were not receiving proper medical care. The mood in camp continued on a downward spiral. In such a deteriorating atmosphere, new rumors took flight. Word spread that prisoners in the hospital were being prevented from receiving needed medicines. Another rumor involving a prisoner believed to have been shot by a camp guard turned out to be a beating incident. Acting Camp Commandant, Lieutenant Colonel Whipple, persisted in underestimating the volatility of conditions he was responsible for managing by describing the incident "tongue in cheek" as a case where "one prisoner had been shot with a club."

Not all the talk at the camp fed into prisoner fear and paranoia. At least on one occasion, a particular incident provided some comic relief to the captive community at the expense of those guarding them. It seems that an overanxious sentinel fired a shot at a stray dog during the soldier's night watch. He had mistaken the animal for a rebel prisoner in a restricted area. The shooting brought out the Nineteenth Wisconsin in full force scrambling to formation as they pulled up their trousers and clamored out of their quarters with muskets in hand. The rebels took great delight at the sight of their half-awake Yankee overseers standing outside in the dark, ready to defend themselves against a canine uprising. Will and some of the prisoners in the barrack began barking and howling like dogs which further infuriated the Yankees and added to the glee of the cheering rebels.

With the tight restrictions imposed on the prison camp following the escape in late April, the civilian presence at the camp all but disappeared. The sutler was one of the exceptions. He came to the camp regularly, but operated his business under the acting camp commander's watchful eye. Vendors delivering supplies to the military post were allowed into camp, but had to be accompanied by a guard. The only other civilian regulars at Camp Randall were Dr. Hobbins, the Madison physician who managed and worked in the prison hospital, and Nurse Deveraux.

Visitors to the camp could only be immediate relatives of sick prisoners confined to the camp's prison hospital. A few had come by train to visit ailing loved ones and could hardly be denied. But other would-be visitors were not allowed into camp because Lieutenant Colonel Whipple was convinced that civilian visitors somehow had a hand in assisting in the escape of the prisoners.

The adoption of the new visitation policy meant that the food, clothing, and reading materials which were being donated to the prisoners had all but stopped. Dr. Hobbins and Aggie brought what they could for the men in the prison hospital as well as for the sick men in the prisoner barracks. In addition to Aggie and Hobbins, several Protestant ministers were reluctantly permitted visits and they brought food baskets with them. The ministers, who could hardly be denied, were allowed in to conduct spiritual sessions with the prisoners and distribute the donated items to those attending these meetings. Reverend Sims, the rebel chaplain, encouraged prisoners to attend the sessions and the meetings grew larger with each service. Donated bibles were distributed and soon became the only source of new reading material received by prisoners other than the heavily censored incoming mail from relatives and friends. Any packages received from home were carefully inspected and if they included Southern newspapers, they were burned due to their "disloyal" content.

Rainy weather also limited the Confederate prisoners, keeping them mostly inside the barracks. The small pit fires that usually burned outside the barracks had become, for the most part, idle. The pits had been important places for passing the time with conversation. Low spirits now prevailed in every quarter of the camp. Complaints about poor rations, heavy-handed actions of certain guards like O'Reilly and his "blue bullies", and crowded conditions in poorly ventilated quarters increased daily. Petty quarrels among barrack dwellers became almost routine events. Between boredom and helplessness, despair grew like a silent cancer, especially for George and Will after A.F. took sick and had to go to the prison hospital.

When he took a turn for the worse, A.F. had asked to see his brothers and Eli. Doc Martin agreed to allow them a brief visit.

"Hey George and Will, Doc says I got me a bad case of consumption," A.F. exclaimed in a hoarse whisper. "You and Eli don't get too close. I don't want you to catch it."

Will's lower lip trembled and George struggled to find his voice. "Don't worry little brother, Doc and Nurse Aggie will take good care of you and we'll be close by."

A.F.'s face glistened with sweat from infection. "I know you will, George."

As Aggie placed another wet towel on his brow, he broke out in a big grin. "Know who I saw last night?"

"Who was that?" George replied in a strained voice.

"It was Ma. She had cooked all our favorites—fried rabbit, country ham and gravy, corn-on-the cob, biscuits, cane syrup and my special favorite, sweet taters. The table was set and there was plenty of sweet milk to drink. I ate and drank my fill 'til I was about to bust. All the while, Ma watched me and smiled. I tell you, it sure was good to be home."

Will patted his brother on the leg. "That sounds mighty good, A.F."

A.F. reached out and grabbed Will's hand. "Don't worry. Ma had a plate set for you and George. She said there would be plenty more for you."

A perplexed look came across his face when he looked at Eli. "Eli, I didn't see no plate set for you. I'll ask Ma about it tonight."

George gently wiped the sweat from his young brother's forehead. "I'm sure it will be fine, A.F. Ma will know what to do."

A.F. smiled. "Ma always knows what to do."

19

DARK DAYS

Sometimes, it's not clear what a person means to those who care for him until he's gone and his light is taken from the room. After A.F. died, George and Will were not the same. When they saw Eli, Aggie and Doc Martin approaching them, their hearts sank in their chests. Doc Martin sat down next to the two brothers. "A.F. has departed this life. I am truly sorry for your loss."

Outside the camp hospital a light rain was falling. Will, George and Eli stood together under an elm tree beginning to bud. Will looked at George and Eli with clinched fists. "I should have never let him join up. I blame myself for his dying in this miserable place." George put his hand on his brother's shoulder as tears welled up in his eyes. "You looked after A.F. as good as a brother could ask for. He's always been your shadow since he could walk. He wouldn't have had it any other way. You know that as well as I do."

Will rubbed his eyes. "Maybe so, but if he had a stayed home, we'd be looking forward to seeing him again with Ma and Pa, not lowering him in the ground in this God-forsaken place."

Later that afternoon Bartley Sims led a prayer service in memory of A.F., but his words brought little comfort to Will and George and the men of Company B.

Eli had tried to encourage his two friends. Although he didn't tell them, he felt as empty as they did—like a big weight had been placed on his chest. Later that afternoon, when all the patients had been tended to, Doc Martin had handed Eli a bottle of brandy and pointed him in the direction of the quarters they shared. Eli sat on his cot with his grief. He drank to remember and drank to forget.

Aggie stood quietly in the doorway and watched Eli pour another glass. "Don't you think maybe you have had enough?"

Looking up at Aggie, he drained the glass. "Maybe so, but I don't think there is enough brandy to wash away what I'm feeling. A.F. shouldn't have died—most of the boys who have died here should still be alive. What's going on is wrong—O'Reilly and others like him, tormenting those who can't defend themselves—crowded barracks and inadequate supplies of medicines—poor sanitation. And there's not a damned thing I can do about it."

Eli looked at the flickering flame from Doc's coal oil lamp. "I guess I never let myself get too attached to anyone before. It seemed easier that way. Somehow, George and I just fell in together—looked out for each other. I don't have a brother to lose like George and Will, but I guess George has been like a brother to me—maybe the only person in this war who cared if I lived or died."

Aggie bent over and lifted Eli's face toward hers. "There is someone else who cares."

Then she kissed him and pulled him to her. For the first time since his mother died, Eli Forrest felt that he was not alone.

It had been fifty-one days since sixteen year old Private Clarence Wicks left his family and the Green Lake County farm where he was born. When Major Smith, the army recruiter, came from Madison and gave a talk at the school house over at Seneca, Clarence and his older sister, Alice, were in attendance. Several of the young men from the area came to town to hear what Smith had to say about joining up, but only Clarence took the papers. His mother and sister could manage with the twenty acre farm as they had always done and could count on help from the Gardner family, whose farm adjoined theirs. At first, Sarah was opposed to her only son becoming a soldier, but eventually gave in.

Crop prices had fallen in 1861, it had been a hard winter and the Wicks family was in debt to the bank and other town creditors. They could use the one hundred dollar enlistment bonus and the thirteen dollar monthly wages that Clarence would be paid. Besides, Major Smith assured her that the war would not last long and her son would soon be back home, working on the farm. They could get by until then.

When he got off the train in Madison with his bag in hand, the conductor pointed the way to the army post west of the city. Clarence walked the short mile to the stockade exterior of Camp Randall. The young recruit soon found himself led to a barrack, where he was assigned a top bunk berth which he would be sharing with two other recently arrived recruits. His company was known as Company E and called itself the "Racine County Grays." Wicks was told his captain's name was Bennett. The first sergeant, who Wicks would meet within an hour of his arrival, was twenty-seven year-old Thomas Barns. It seemed that all the men took a liking to Sergeant Barns, who worked in a mill in Waterford before he enlisted in January of that year. The regimental officers were Colonel Sanders of Racine, Lieutenant Colonel Whipple of Eau Claire, and Major Bovay of Ripon.

Private Wicks had learned much about military life since arriving at Camp Randall, but nothing prepared him for the task of guarding the "seceshers." A thousand or more Confederates had been captured by General John Pope's Army of the Mississippi and sent to Madison for internment. It was no easy job guarding the rebels. Some were nice enough, but others like Sergeant O'Reilly said, "should be shot down like the dogs they are."

Wicks had received several weeks' worth of drill instruction from Sergeant Barns in addition to lessons on how to use the old style musket he had been assigned. Not knowing what to expect, he had been nervous at first. But after he got a feel for what the assignment entailed, he began to take a liking to the business of being a sentinel. Clarence liked the way the weight of the musket rested on his shoulder and the sense of power and authority he possessed. He began to look forward to guard duty even though the atmosphere in the camp had grown tense of late.

Sergeant Anderson had warned the men in the company to be alert for signs of trouble. Clarence had noted an unfamiliar and disturbing tone of defiance from many of the Southern captives. Since Lieutenant Colonel Whipple's order came clamping down on civilian visits and the prisoners' range of movement within the camp, the interaction between guards and prisoners had become increasingly contentious. In the wake of Private Carr's alleged perfidy in helping three rebel prisoners escape, most of the guards had become even more hardened toward the prisoners. Being young and new to the job, Clarence decided to follow their lead. He decided to go strictly by the book in all of his contacts with the seceshers. Besides, Sergeant O'Reilly had told him on more than one occasion, that if you gave them an inch, they would take a mile.

THE INCIDENT

At daybreak on May 16th, George rose from the bottom berth of the triple layer bunk that he and Will shared with five other men. Sleep had been hard to come by. He worried about what he would say in a letter to his parents about A.F.'s death. Will was emotionally exhausted and physically weak from a chronic intestinal disorder that continued to get worse by the day. George crawled over the sleeping figure below him and stepped into his well worn shoes. Walking to the nearest of the three wood-burning stoves that served the barrack, he set about starting a fire. Other silent figures, some wrapped in blankets, came and stood around the stove in the large, dimly lit room. All were trying their best to warm themselves while waiting patiently for the black coffee that was beginning to boil.

George saw that Will was awake and sitting on the edge of the berth with his worn coat draped over his shoulders. He sat motionless, staring straight ahead. The morning routine was interrupted when one of the guards appeared through the door as the bugle sounded and ordered the men in the barrack to prepare for morning roll call and prisoner count, a practice instituted since the escape. Each man was required to clearly and loudly call out his name irrespective of rank as a guard walked by and recorded the count. The men resented the practice and saw it as just another form of petty harassment.

After roll call was completed and the count of the prisoners cleared, the men shuffled back into the barrack to wait for breakfast. After they had eaten, George helped his brother to the camp hospital for some new medicine Doc Martin thought might help treat his ailment.

Eli brought George a fresh cup of coffee while Doc examined Will.

George looked at Eli, then at the floor. "Thanks, Eli, but I ain't much for coffee this morning."

The two friends sat in silence, one not knowing what to say and the other with nothing left to say. Finally, George raised his head and stared at Eli in desperation. "Eli, I'm suffocating in this place. I can't breathe anymore. Since A.F. died, I'm festering inside—eaten up with a kind of anger that's turning to hate. It's like a blindness where I can't see nothing else."

Eli looked at his friend with concern. "What about Ann—Ann Pritchard? She's something else—someone who can help you breathe again."

George thought about what Eli said, then turned away. "I'm not sure there's enough of me left to be any use to her."

Eli reached out and touched George's shoulder. "There's enough, George. Ann Pritchard can do for you what Aggie's done for me—help you learn to breathe again—give you some hope in the middle of the grief."

George looked at Eli. "Maybe you're right. I don't see it, but maybe…"

George reached into his coat pocket and took out a letter. Handing it to Eli, he tried to smile. "Just in case, I want you to give this to Ann Pritchard. I spent the better part of last week trying to get it right—letting her know how I feel about her—what her letters have meant to me… just in case."

"Somehow, things will work out," Eli began.

George waved him off. "Just in case, Eli. Just in case."

After supper, Will's bowels started acting up again. Doc Martin's medicine wasn't helping. Will left the barrack and walked quickly in the direction of the closest sinkhole. He had seen blood in his stool the day before and knew that meant being transferred to the hospital, a place he did not want to go. He was closing in on the nearest sinkhole located on the south end of the camp in the vicinity of Barrack Number 8. It had been freshly dug by a prisoner work crew, but was not quite finished. The sinkhole was located near a posted sentinel Will did not recognize. He hurried by the guard and arriving at the excavated drain receptacle, unbuttoned his pants, stripped them below his buttocks and squatted down.

Private Wicks saw the secesher come out of the barrack and hurry in his direction. The prisoner had a rolled newspaper in one hand and was heading toward where Wicks stood on his assigned beat, Sentinel Post No. 30. As the prisoner passed by him and quickly proceeded to his intended destination, Wicks saw him pull his pants down around his knees and crouch down.

"You're not allowed there. Move on!" Private Wicks shouted.

Will Spears ignored the guard's order and remained in a squatting position. He looked straight ahead in another direction. Wicks waited impatiently for the prisoner to respond to his order.

"That sink ain't to be used now. It ain't ready for use. Get up and go to one of the other sinks."

With his bowels in an uproar, Will ignored the guard.

"Are you deaf of hearing?…I'm not telling you again!," Wicks shouted, his voice slightly breaking. Again, there was no response from Will.

The young sentinel, perturbed at being ignored, picked up a small stone and threw it at the indisposed prisoner, hitting him on the side of his face. Ignoring Wicks' repeated orders to leave the partially dug latrine, even after he was struck by the stone, Will maintained his squatting position, staring straight ahead expressionless. He seemed devoid of any outward emotion. His demeanor was more oblivious than defiant.

A group of six or seven prisoners, George among them, were standing outside the barrack discussing the latest news on the exploits of "Stonewall" Jackson in Virginia's Shenandoah Valley. They stopped talking when they heard the shouting. All eyes turned toward what was happening between Will and the Yankee guard a short distance away. They heard the bluecoat shouting something at Will and watched as he picked up something off the ground and threw it at the indisposed man. At the sight of their indisposed comrade being struck in the face, a collective anger welled up to the surface and exploded. Here was one of their own being subjected to yet another dehumanizing experience, this time by no more than a whelp in a Yankee uniform.

As if upon a signal, the group began running in the direction of the newest object of their simmering enmity, yelling and cursing him as they ran. George was in the lead, shouting at the startled young sentinel, who turned and saw six rebels running toward him. He clutched his musket hard with both hands and instinctively raised it as the prisoners got closer. He felt his knees buckle and his hands shake as the angry mob drew closer. Clarence Wicks was more scared than he had ever been in his young life.

When George got within twenty-five feet of Wicks, he abruptly stopped. The others who were behind him also stopped.

Private Crosdel, a second guard from one of the two adjoining posts whose beat bordered on that of Wicks', observed what was happening. George glanced at his older brother crouching over the unfinished latrine. For a brief moment, time stood still and flashed back to when he and Will were boys collecting nuts and berries in the woods of West Alabama near their family farm. It was a typical spring day and they were walking through a patch of hickory and mimosa trees when George had to stop out of necessity. Will left him behind squatting amidst the beggar's-lice and told him to catch up or go back home. Another shout from the young sentry brought George back to the present and the knowledge that he was looking down the barrel of a loaded Yankee musket.

Later, there were a number of different accounts about what happened next. Whatever the version, the simple truth was that George Spears, a usually calm and deliberate man, snapped. He unleashed a volley of invectives and angry curses at the young guard who stood with his musket leveled squarely at George. Suddenly, George paused and stepped back a pace as his eyes met the cold, dull glaze of Clarence Wicks. The camp seemed oddly quiet. Everything seemed to stop. Then, as if in a dream, the loud report of the musket shattered the silence. George instantly felt a hard blow to his lower chest. The force knocked him backwards as he staggered to keep his balance. He looked puzzled, then angry.

"You damned son of a bitch. I will report you!" George exclaimed as he slumped to the ground.

Private Wicks looked bewildered. He had never shot a man before.

Private Crosdel hurried over from his post and stood next to Wicks. He held his musket at the ready against his shoulder and pointed it in the direction of the five rebel prisoners who were bent over their fallen comrade. Will pulled up his trousers and ran to where his brother lay. Tears streamed down his face as he frantically repeated George's name, pleading with God not to take his brother. One of the prisoners shouted for someone to get Doc Martin. The others shook their raised and clenched fists at the Yankee guards, calling them mongrel bastards and sons of bitches.

Within minutes, a dozen other guards arrived, led by Sergeant O'Reilly. The rebel prisoners were ordered back to the barrack while a grief-stricken Will was allowed to stay with his dead brother until the body was carried away. While waiting for the stretcher bearers, he overheard O'Reilly commending Wicks and Crosdel. "One less 'secesh' to guard. Well done, lads."

THE AFTERMATH

A military court of inquiry was convened at Camp Randall regarding the shooting death of Corporal George W. Spears, Company B, First Alabama, Tennessee and Mississippi Regiment, a prisoner of war, by Private Clarence Wicks, Company E, Nineteenth Regiment Wisconsin Volunteers, a sentinel on duty at Camp Randall. The military tribunal consisted of the regimental major and two company captains.

Wicks was the first witness to testify. He testified that he had orders to shoot rebels insulting him and that he shot the rebel prisoner after he had been insulted. Next to testify was Private Crosdel of Sentinel Post No. 31. Crosdel testified that Spears rushed toward Wicks with a stick or bone in his hand in an attempted assault. Neither Wicks nor any of the other soldiers who subsequently testified mentioned seeing Spears with a stick or a large bone in his hand prior to being shot. After Crosdel testified, eight other witnesses did so that afternoon. None of the prisoners were allowed to testify, even though Major Bovay, who was president of the tribunal, wanted the deceased's brother Will, to testify. He was outvoted by the two other members of the court.

From the beginning, Alvin Bovay took his role as military tribunal president seriously, as he had with other obligations in his life. He prided himself on being a man of conviction. Until now, he truly didn't know who or what to believe. He had begun with no preconceived notions about Wicks' culpability or anybody else's for that matter. He was not out to exonerate Wicks, nor was he determined to find fault with this farm boy. But now he felt compelled more than ever to get at the truth and find out what was behind the death of the rebel prisoner. Something rang true about Wicks' testimony.

By the same token, he had doubts about Crosdel's version of what transpired, specifically about the deceased having a stick or bone in his hand prior to being shot.

The testimony of the "officer of the guard" the morning of the shooting confirmed Bovay's intuitive reaction that Wicks was telling the truth about being under orders to shoot prisoners using insulting language.

Although Major Bovay was an ardent abolitionist and had no sympathy for those who fought to maintain the institution of slavery, he believed the law required that the Southerners held in captivity at Camp Randall be regarded as prisoners of war and not simply rebel insurgents. Bovay had held his military commission for less than four months, but had the trust of Colonel Sanders and was glad to see him finally return to camp and be in charge. The major disliked the heavy-handed Acting Camp Commandant, Lieutenant Colonel Whipple, whom he considered a braggart and intemperate both in his use of alcohol and his proclivity for profanity.

Bovay was deeply troubled by what he had heard from the witnesses who testified. The shooting of an unarmed prisoner in a military camp by an armed guard who testified he was under orders to shoot prisoners using insulting language could hardly be justified.

Bovay wanted to pursue the matter and find out where it would lead. He wanted to know who gave the orders and whether such orders were given with the knowledge and/or approval of Whipple in his role of acting regimental commander and as camp commandant. He suspected Whipple knew about the orders. If he didn't, he should have known. Bovay was troubled by the questionable legality of using deadly force against an unarmed prisoner whose only verifiable offense was calling a guard a son of a bitch. Had Private Wicks obeyed an unlawful order?

However, Bovay could only take the case to its logical next step if the other two panel members, Captains Chandler and Bates, went along with him. They refused to do so.

O'Reilly could hear Reverend Sims' camp church going full steam outside. Barrack Number 8 was empty. The Johnny Rebs were singing hymns and enjoying the baked goods provided from a rare visit by a Methodist ladies' church auxiliary from nearby Madison. Minutes earlier he had stopped beating a young, skinny Mississippi boy when the prisoner told him about the valuables Reverend Sims kept in a strong box under a loose floor board at the far end of the barrack. Sims called it his benevolence fund. O'Reilly snorted to himself. "Benevolence fund, my ass!"

O'Reilly propped his musket against the wall and commenced to checking the floorboards. Intent on finding the valuables, he began muttering under his breath as each board he pried loose yielded no treasure.

"Mr. O'Reilly, what brings you into our humble abode?"

Startled, O'Reilly looked up and saw Bartley Sims and four men standing before him.He thought about going for his musket, but as if on cue one of the men picked it up.

Reverend Sims was a tall, gaunt man with a long gray beard and piercing steel-blue eyes. "I ask you again Mr. O'Reilly. What are you doing in our barrack?"

Gathering himself up with all the bluster he could manage, he looked squarely at the reverend and said, "That would be Sergeant O'Reilly to the lot of you. And though it's none of your damn business, I have it on good authority that you are hiding contraband. I've a good mind to put the whole lot of you on report."

"Would that information have come from a young Mississippi 'lad' you were tormenting by the name of Perkins?" Reverend Sims replied.

O'Reilly could feel the hair stand up on the back of his neck. How could Sims know who had tipped him off? He was beginning to smell a set-up. "Tell you what, boys. I'm going to give you a pass this one time for disrespectin' a non-commissioned officer. Since it's Sunday, I'll let bygones be bygones."

The four men moved closer as Reverend Sims pulled a small, worn Bible from his breast pocket. "Tonight, Mr. O'Reilly, is the night your bygones have caught up to you."

The burly Union sergeant began to sweat. "Who the hell do you think you are? All I have to do is holler for help and there will be a dozen guards on top of you."

Sims looked at him as if talking to a child. "As you know, Mr. O'Reilly, I am Reverend Sims and these four men are what you might call deacons. Feel free to holler if you must. Maybe, you haven't noticed how loud and enthusiastic the ' lads' are singing outside tonight."

O'Reilly lunged for the door, trying to bull his way through the ring of four men. One man clubbed him across the shin while another cracked him across the shoulder blades. He went down in a heap. Two of the reverend's deacons picked up the winded sergeant and sat him on a bench.

Bartley Sims slowly stroked his beard. "Mr. O'Reilly you have caused a lot of harm and hurt in our camp. By your own hand or as a result of your evil intentions, you have caused the death of three innocent prisoners and serious injuries to countless others. The time has come for you to pay for your sins—to reap what you have sown."

"What do mean, 'pay for my sins'? You mean…you mean to kill me!"

Sims continued to stroke his beard. "Not by our direct hand, but the end result will be the same."

"You can't do that. You're a preacher. You're holding the Bible in your hand. You been telling folks to come to Jesus all over the camp."

"It's a shame, Mr. O'Reilly, that you didn't heed those words and take that message to heart. If you had, perhaps we wouldn't be having this conversation."

O'Reilly's face became flushed with fear. "You can't be causing my death. The Good Book speaks against it."

Reverend Sims brought the Bible to his chest. "Ah, Mr. O'Reilly, the part of the Good Book you are speaking of is the New Testament. Tonight, I'll be preaching from the Old. Tonight's not about the sweet mercy of Jesus. No, tonight's about justice and the terrible swift sword of the Lord."

O'Reilly's voice began to rise. "You'll never get away with it. You will all hang," he shouted before the swift stroke of a club brought him to his knees and silenced him. Sims instructed the four men to bind O'Reilly's hands behind his back and to stuff a cloth gag into his mouth. Wide-eyed with terror, he watched Reverend Sims and the four deacons gather in a circle and pray for the Lord's deliverance from the likes of Sergeant Gus O'Reilly.

Later that night, shots rang out. A terrible accident had occurred. For some unknown reason Sergeant O'Reilly wandered into the forbidden perimeter zone. He was ordered to halt and identify himself by two sentries. He didn't respond and continued to come forward in an erratic manner. Feeling threatened, the Union sentries shot and killed him. They told Sergeant Susong that they may have heard a muffled sound of some sort, but no clearly stated identification from the man in the dead zone.

Sergeant Susong, a quiet and unassuming man, was the same sergeant who had brought the three sweet potatoes to A.F. as promised—the same Union sergeant that was known to treat rebel prisoners with a modicum of respect—

the same one George had earlier accused of standing by and doing nothing while O'Reilly and his thugs beat and harassed the men of Company B. On that night, he instructed the two sentries to remain at their posts while he investigated the shooting victim which he concluded to be an unfortunate accident. In the darkness, no one observed the length of rope and cloth gag he stuffed in his breast pocket as walked back to his quarters.

The ultimate outcome of the proceedings and formal findings of the military court of inquiry into George Spears' death proved more problematic than that for the death of Sergeant Gus O'Reilly. The fallout from the Spears case did not go well for Lieutenant Colonel Whipple and Camp Randall. A scathing report was sent to Secretary of War, Edwin M. Stanton. The report was highly critical of the camp's management, including undisciplined and unreliable guards, misappropriation of heating fuel and straw for bedding which was allocated for prisoners, and theft of medicinal alcohol intended for sick and dying prisoners in the prison hospital. The report noted that the purveyor at Chicago had furnished 168 pint bottles to last six months but the supply had been used in five days, presumably by the Nineteenth's officers and enlisted men. In addition, the *Wisconsin Daily State Journal*, Madison's most influential newspaper, ran a story that soldiers from the camp on leave in the city had gotten drunk and worn out their welcome. A group of enlisted men, in the company of an officer from the regiment, had severely beaten a young male civilian who lived in town. This incident occurred not long after Spears was shot and killed by Wicks and on the day Whipple was replaced by Colonel Sanders as camp commandant. The following day, the *Wisconsin Weekly Argus* published an editorial highly critical of the way Camp Randall's command staff handled the Spears matter, questioning whether a mere insult justified shooting and killing a prisoner. The War Department had enough. It wasted no time in resolving the situation at Camp Randall. Six days later on Friday at approximately 11:00 a.m., all prisoners except the very sick were transported to another camp and Camp Randall's role as a prison for Confederate soldiers ended.

At 9:00 a.m. Doc Martin said his goodbyes to the civilian physician Bill Hobbins and to Aggie. Hobbins had brought in a bottle of Kentucky bourbon for the occasion.

Doc lifted his glass to Aggie, Eli and Hobbins in a toast. "Aggie, although I have grown quite fond of your Uncle Hester's apple brandy, I must confess that I still consider a fine Kentucky bourbon to be the nectar of the gods. Here's to departing friends."

William Hobbins followed with a toast of his own. "To you, Eli and Aggie, and especially to you, Dr. Martin—you may be a secessionist, but you are one fine physician—for your devotion and care of your fellow man under the most difficult of circumstances." By 10 a.m., the bottle was empty as the last toast was raised. Everyone had left the doctors' quarters except Eli and Aggie. Eli looked around the hospital room one last time. Taking Aggie's hands in his own, he kissed her lightly on the lips. "I can't ask you to wait for me. Who knows when this war will be over and how things will go for me and Doc Martin when we get to Camp Douglas in Chicago? Who knows what will happen?"

Aggie's eyes danced with a subtle look of defiance. "Eli Forrest you should know by now that I can answer for myself—even what you don't feel you can ask of me. If you think you can find your way back to Wisconsin, I will wait for you."

Eli smiled and pulled Aggie close to him. "Yes Nurse Deveraux, I believe I can."

Late that afternoon, 903 Confederate prisoners boarded 23 Chicago and Northwestern freight cars and were shipped to Chicago's Camp Douglas. Corporal George Spears and 132 rebel prisoners were not among the departing Southerners. They lie buried in specially marked graves in Madison's Forest Hill Cemetery.

THE ROAD HOME

The snow had quit falling and a sky full of stars glittered against the still, white landscape. Huddled around a small campfire under a lean-to fashioned from evergreen branches, Eli Forrest chewed on a piece of country ham, the last of the provisions Amos McCurdy had given him. Leaning back on his haversack, he pulled the wool blankets more tightly around him and thought about the last two months.

Will had died during the hellish August heat after their transfer to Camp Douglas. In September, Eli and the other rebel prisoners were shipped back to Vicksburg by transport steamer and released in one of the last prisoner swaps of the war. Doc Martin remained in Vicksburg to tend to some of the prisoners who were too sick to travel while Eli along with other fit rebels were reassigned to other Confederate units. The last fighting Eli saw was at the Battle of Atlanta where he was wounded by fragments from an exploding shell. A little more than a year later, the war was over. After recuperating from his wounds, Eli had obligations to keep before turning his face northward. First, he walked and hitched wagon rides to pay his respects to the Spears family in West Alabama, and then by rail he went to see Ann Pritchard in West Tennessee.

Staring at the crackling fire, Eli reflected on how his life had changed. He smiled when he remembered how uneasy George had been when they first met at Fort Donelson—two unlikely friends—he, an educated though disgraced officer and George, a small plantation owner's son from Alabama. Then came that terrible battle and escape from Fort Donelson, a bloody and cowardly affair, at least on the part of Generals Floyd and Pillow. He shook his head, trying to wipe away the memory of those wounded Yankees being caught in that grass fire. With permission from his Uncle Nathan, he left his uncle's cavalry headed for Nashville and made a wide circle around Fort Donelson, following what was likely George's route. He found his friend just in time to stop two Union scouts from doing him in. George was saved. Preacher and his son got their mule back as well. Eli turned and pulled a half-empty bottle of Tennessee sourmash whiskey from his haversack, compliments of Amos McCurdy. He had stopped by his place of business on the way from Ann Pritchard's, hoping to barter for some coffee and cornmeal and had been treated with great hospitality. Eli thought of the generous Humboldt merchant as he uncorked and drank the whiskey. McCurdy resupplied him with coffee, cornmeal, salt pork, tobacco and two bottles of sourmash whiskey. The pleasantness of that encounter was tempered with the weight of the sorrowful time he spent with the Spears family in Alabama and Ann Pritchard in Humboldt.

George's parents, Archibald and Elizabeth Spears, had been glad to see him and appreciated the few personal effects he was able to give them that belonged to their sons. Through the letters George had written to them, they had come to feel a genuine kinship with Eli and expressed such sentiment on several occasions during the three days he spent with them. Although he tried to spare them the worst details of the war and prison life, he could see the sadness growing in them as he recounted his experiences with George, Will, and A.F.

The only time either of them lost their composure was when he talked to them about A.F.'s final days and the dream he recounted with his brothers and Eli. After he had finished, Elizabeth Spears left the room. Eli and Archibald sat in silence, listening to her sobs in the adjoining bedroom. The Spears family had lost three of their four sons to a civil war that was anything but civil. Their youngest son, Andrew, had joined the Griffin Rifles of Choctaw County in 1864. Andrew Spears was recovering from wounds he had received in the battle at Bentonville and was to be paroled in early May of 1865. Andrew's return was the only thing left of the hope Archibald and Elizabeth anxiously clung to.

As he stared into the campfire, Eli felt a shiver as the wind picked up. He reached over to the small pile next to him and threw another piece of wood on the fire. Reaching into to his coat pocket, he pulled out the briar that had belonged to George. Archibald and Elizabeth had insisted he take the pipe as a remembrance of the friendship he shared with their son. He felt the rough texture of the well-worn pipe with his fingers as he tamped down the tobacco. Lighting it with a sliver of wood from the fire, he blew a spiral of smoke into the cold night air.

When he had arrived a week before in Humboldt, Ann Pritchard opened her door and didn't seem surprised to see him. Eli remembered her exact words: "I knew you would come." As he had done with George's parents, Eli spent the better part of a day telling her everything he could remember about George, including his dreams for a future that included the two of them. She would nod or comment when something he said corresponded with what George had written her. Only when Eli handed her the neatly tied packet of letters she had written George did the finality of it all touch her. Ann Pritchard bowed her head and wiped her eyes. They said their good-byes the next morning.

What a road he had traveled—surely not the one he would have chosen, but the one he was on nonetheless. Knocking the ashes out of his pipe, Eli looked up into the night sky and wondered where his road was about to take him. After more than three years, would Aggie still be waiting for him? He wasn't the same man. He had lost weight and his hair had prematurely turned gray, and there was a small ragged scar on his left check. Would she still be waiting? Falling off to sleep, Eli muttered to himself, "I will find out soon enough."

December 26, 1865, the day after Christmas, Aggie Deveraux looked out of the kitchen window at the last light of day and the falling snow. She and her Aunt Mary were making soup from the left-over turkey and preparing the rest of the evening meal while Uncle Hester fed the milk cows. Aggie's young cousin, Sam, stacked firewood on the hearth of the fireplace. Her Aunt turned to her. "You look a bit sad, Aggie. Thinking about your Eli?"

Aggie offered her Aunt a strained smile in response. "I know it sounds childish, but somehow I thought Eli would return to me by Christmas."

"Nothing wrong with being a little childish, my dear," Aunt Mary replied. "If we don't keep our dreams alive, where's a heart to go?"

Sam stuck his head through the kitchen door. "Aggie, there's someone at the door asking for you."

Aggie looked at her Aunt and tried to breathe.

Aunt Mary smoothed Aggie's hair and wiped a pinch of flour from her face. "I can't imagine who would call on you in such weather. Why don't you go see who it is?"

Eli was bone tired. He hadn't washed or shaved in several days. This wasn't how he had planned it, but it was what it was. He stood there with his cap in his hand, waiting to see if a promise that had been made would be kept.

He first saw Aggie enter the room. Then her face was next to his.

"I found my way back," he said.

"I waited," she replied as she kissed him. "Welcome home."

EPILOGUE

On June 1, 1864, the fighting in Virginia was fierce. During a charge across an open field at Turner's farm against an entrenched enemy position, a number of Union soldiers with the Thirty-sixth Wisconsin Volunteer Infantry were killed or wounded. Among the wounded taken to a Richmond prison hospital was Private Clarence Wicks.

After 45 days, Clarence knew his time was slipping away. He asked to see the prison chaplain. Chaplain Powell made his way through the poorly ventilated, overcrowded hospital. Although he had come to this place on many occasions, he never quite got used to it—the sounds of suffering and the smell of gangrenous flesh. The cries and pleas of the wounded and dying were accentuated by orders shouted from weary and exhausted surgeons.

Chaplain Powell pulled up a chair next to the cot where Private Wicks lay.

Clarence opened his eyes and looked at the chaplain. "You ever been to Wisconsin?"

"No, son, can't say as I have," the chaplain replied.

"It's nice there," Clarence coughed, turning his gaze to the ceiling. "My mother and my sister, Alice, live there. They're probably baking up an apple pie about now. There's plenty of lakes and streams with good fishing.....and the fields turn green in late spring. There's nothing like the smell of a fresh-turned field."

Chaplain Powell reached over and grasped Clarence's hand. "Sounds like a mighty nice place to be from."

Clarence looked earnestly at the chaplain. "I want you to know I ain't got no regrets about joining up and fightin' for the Union. I've known a lot of good men who wore the blue uniform."

"I expect you have," the chaplain replied, patting Clarence's hand.

"I do have one regret though that I need some praying over," Clarence said, his eyes clouding over.

Chaplain Powell leaned in closer. "What's that, son?"

"I shot a Johnny Reb by the name of George Spears when I was a guard at Camp Randall. He cussed me and I shot him."

Clarence closed his eyes. "I shouldn't a done that. I was scared, but I shouldn't of shot a man for something he said."

NOTES

Chapter One

A number of sources were instrumental in developing the historical background that follows, but most notably: Jack Hurst, *Men of Fire: Grant, Forrest, and the Campaign that Decided the Civil War*, (New York: Basic Books, 2007); Harry Hansen, *The Civil War: A History*, (New York: New American Library, 2001), and Benjamin Franklin Cooling, *Fort Henry and Donelson: The Key to the Confederate Heartland*, (Knoxville, TN: University of Tennessee Press, 1987).

Chapter Two

Cooling, Forts Henry and Donelson, 140-41; Hurst, *Men of Fire*, 222, 260-61; Lew Wallace, "The Capture of Fort Donelson," in Ned Bradford, ed., *Battles and Leaders of the Civil War*, (New York: Appleton-Century-Crofts, Inc., (1956), 407; Spencer C. Tucker, *Andrew Foote: Civil War Admiral on Western Waters*, (Annapolis, MD: Naval Institute Press, 2000), 152; Jay Wertz and Edwin C. Bearss, *Smithsonian's Great Battles of the Civil War*, (New York: Smithsonian Institution, William Morrow and Co. Inc., 1997), 540; Bruce Catton, *Terrible Swift Sword*, (Garden City, NY: Doubleday & Company, Inc., 1963), 111; E.B. Long and Barbara Long, *The Civil War Day by Day: An Almanac*, 1961-1865, (Garden City, NY: Doubleday & Company, Inc., 1971), 170.

Chapter Three

James D. Porter, "Tennessee" in Clement A. Evans, ed., *Confederate Military History*, Vol. III, (New York: Thomas Yoseloff, 1962), 23-24, 27; Wertz, *Smithsonian's Great Battles of the Civil War*, 540, 542; Hurst, *Men of Fire*, 275; Hansen, *The Civil War*, 114; Wallace, "The Capture of Fort Donelson," 71.

Chapters Four - Seven

Ann Harwell Gay, *Choctaw, Sumter, and Washington Counties' C.S.A. Companies*, Meridan, MS: Brown Printing Co., 2003.

Chapter Eight

Official Records of the Union and Confederate Armies (ORA), Ser. I., Vol. VIII, 125-27, 571; Alpheus Baker, "Dairy," March 2 & 4, 1962, (Montgomery, AL: Alabama Department of History and Archives); Larry J. Daniel and Lynn N. Bock, *Island No. 10: Struggle for the Mississippi Valley*, (Tuscaloosa, AL: University of Alabama Press, 1966), 57-58.

Chapter Nine

Baker Diary, March 13, 1862.

Chapter Ten

Baker Diary, March 14, 17 & 18, 1862; *Wisconsin Daily Patriot*, March 26, 1862; Daniel, *Island No. 10*, 122.

Chapter Eleven

Wisconsin Daily Patriot, March 26, 1862; Daniel, *Island No. 10*, 122; Porter, "Tennessee," 30; Alfred Roman, *The Military Operations of General Beauregard*, Vol. I, 358; *ORA*, Vol. III, 809; "Official Correspondence of Flag Officer Andrew H. Foote to Hon. Gideon Wells, Secretary of the Navy, "April 8, 1862, reprinted in the *Wisconsin Daily Patriot*, April 9, 1862; Wertz, *Smithsonian's Great Battles of the Civil War*, 546; *Wisconsin Daily State Journal*, April

10 & 16, 1862; Henry Walke, "The Western Flotilla at Fort Donelson, Island No. 10, Fort Pillow and Memphis" in Robert U. Johnson and Clarence C. Buel, eds., *Battles and Leaders of the Civil War*, Vol. I, (New York: Castle Books, 1887), 444-47.

Chapter Twelve

Tucker, *Andrew Foote*, 180; Daniel, *Island No. 10*, 12-13; *Official Records of the Union and Confederate Navies (ORN)*, Ser., Vol. XXII, 719; *Wisconsin Daily Patriot*, April 8, 1862.

Chapter Thirteen

Baker, "Island No. 10," *Southern Bivowac* (1882-83), 60-62; *ORA*, Ser. I, Vol. III, 133, 157-58.

Chapter Fourteen

ORA, Ser. I, Vol. VIII, 109-112; Baker "Island No. 10," 62; Daniel, *Island No. 10*, 137-38, 145; Junius Henri Browne, *Four Years in Secessia*, (Hartford, CT: O.D. Case, 1865, Reprinted Arno Press and *New York Times*, 1970), 130-31; *Wisconsin Daily Patriot*, May 6, 1862.

Chapter Fifteen

Daniel, *Island No. 10*, 159-60; George Levy, *To Die in Chicago: Confederate Prisoners at Camp Douglas, 1862-1865*, (Evanston, IL: Evanston Publishing Inc., 1994), 16-32.

Chapter Sixteen

Wisconsin Daily Patriot, April 25, 1862; S.D. Forbes, *Camp Randall and Environs*, (Madison, WI: Wisconsin State Historical Society, 1890); *Wisconsin Daily State Journal*, April 21, 1862.

Chapter Seventeen

Ann Harwell Gay, *Place Names in Choctaw County, Alabama* (Meridan, MS: Brown Printing Co., 1988, revised edition, 1998), 18.

Chapter Eighteen

Wisconsin Daily State Journal, May 3 & 15, 1962; *ORA*, Ser. II, Vol. III, 526; *Wisconsin Daily Patriot*, April 30, & May 15, 1862.

Chapter Nineteen

Wisconsin Daily Patriot, May 14, 1862; George J. Paddock, "Papers," May 15, 1862, (Madison, WI: Wisconsin State Historical Society); E.B. Quiner, "Papers," *Correspondence of Wisconsin Volunteers*, Vol. VI (Madison, WI: Wisconsin State Historical Society), 91.

Chapter Twenty

Wisconsin Daily State Journal, May 16, 1862; *Prairie Du Chen Courier*, May 29, 1862, citing *Wisconsin Daily Patriot*, undated; *ORA*, Ser. II, Vol. III, 581.

Chapter Twenty-one

ORA, Ser. II, Vol. III, "Proceedings of a Court of Inquiry Held at Camp Randall, May 16, 1862," 578-586; Carolyn Mattern, *Soldiers When They Go: The Story of Camp Randall, 1861-1865* (Madison, WI: Wisconsin State Historical Society, 1981), 57; *ORA*, Ser. II, Vol. III, 526, 542, 598, 678; *Wisconsin Daily State Journal*, May 19 & 24, 1862; *Wisconsin Weekly Argus*, May 20, 1862.

Epilogue

Frank L. Klement, *Wisconsin in the Civil War: The Home Front and the Battle Front, 1861-1865*, (Madison, WI: Wisconsin State Historical Society, 1997).

BIBLIOGRAPHY

PRIMARY SOURCES

Manuscript Materials

Alabama Department of Archives and History, Montgomery.

Fort Donelson National Battlefield Collection, Dover, Tennessee.

Marquette University Raynor Memorial Library Archives, Record Group C-1.7, Frank L.

Klement Papers Relating to The Civil War, Milwaukee.

Museum of the Confederacy, Richmond.

National Archives, Record Group 94, Card Entry No. 519a, Union Service Records for the Civil War, Washington, D.C.

National Archives, Record Group 109, Microfilm Publication, No. 598, Selected Records of the U.S. War Department Relating to Confederate Prisoners of War, Washington, D.C.

Southern Historical Society Papers, Virginia Historical Society Archives.

Tennessee State Library and Archives, Nashville.

Wisconsin State Historical Society Archives, Madison.

Government Publications

U.S. Department of the Navy. *Official Records of the Union and Confederate Navies in the War of the Rebellion*, Series I, Vol. XXII. Government Printing Office, Washington, D.C., 1908.

U.S. Department of the War. *The War of the Rebellion: A Compilation of the Official Records of the Union and Confederate Armies*, Series I, Vol. VIII, Series II, Vols. III & IV. Government Printing Office, Washington, D.C., 1898 and 1899.

State Publications

State of Wisconsin. Wisconsin State Historical Society. Annual Report of the Adjutant General's Office For the Year Ending December 31, 1865, Madison.

State of Wisconsin. Wisconsin State Historical Society. Miscellaneous Civil War Records, Adjutant General's Office, 1861-1865, Madison.

State of Wisconsin. Wisconsin State Historical Society. Report of the Adjutant General, 1864, Madison.

State of Wisconsin. Wisconsin State Historical Society. Wisconsin Volunteers: War of the Rebellion, 1861-1865. Adjutant General's Office, 1914. Madison.

Newspapers

Chicago Tribune
Harper's Weekly
Memphis Appeal
Milwaukee Journal Sentinel
Racine Weekly Advocate
Wisconsin Daily State Journal
Wisconsin Weekly Argus
Wisconsin Daily Patriot

Diaries, Correspondence and Personal Papers

Avery, William T. "Letters." Tennessee State Library and Archives, Nashville.

Baker, Alpheus. "Diary." Alabama Department of Archives and History, Montgomery.

_____. "Island No. 10" *Southern Bivowac_*(1882-1883).

Forbes, Seloftus D. *Camp Randall and Environs.* Wisconsin State Historical Society, Madison, 1890 (pamphlet collection).

Halleck, Henry W. *General's Papers and Books.* Special Civil War Collection. U.S. War Department, Adjutant General's Office, National Archives, Washington, D.C.

Hurn, Ethel Alice. *Wisconsin Women in the War Between the States,* "Original Papers, No. 6." May 1911. Wisconsin State Historical Society, Madison.

Lemke, Alan J. "The Noe Family's Involvement in the Civil War: A History of Wisconsin's 19th Volunteer Regiment with an Emphasis on its 'F' Company," Wisconsin State Historical Society, Madison.

Paddock, George J. and Edwin B. "Papers," 1861-1865. Wisconsin State Historical Society, Madison.

Quiner, Edwin Bentley. "Papers." *Correspondence of Wisconsin Volunteers*, 1861-65, Vol. 6, Wisconsin State Historical Society, Madison.

Read, C. W. "Reminiscences of the Confederate Navy" in J. William Jones, eds., *Southern Historical Society Papers*, Vol. I, No. 5, Richmond, VA: 1876. (Reprinted by Kraus Reprint Co., Millwood, N.Y., 1977).

Walke, Henry. "The Western Flotilla at Fort Donelson, Island No. 10, Fort Pillow and Memphis" in Robert U. Johnson and Clarence C. Buel, eds., *Battles and Leaders of the Civil War*. Four Volumes. New York: Castle Book, 1887.

Wallace, Lew. "The Capture of Fort Donelson" in Ned Bradford, ed., *Battles and Leaders of the Civil War*. New York: Appleton-Century-Crofts, Inc.,1956.

SECONDARY SOURCES

Barton, Michael and Larry M. Logue, eds., *The Civil War Soldier: A Historical Reader*, New York: New York University Press, 2002.

Barziza, Decimus, *The Adventures of a Prisoner of War, 1863-1864*, Austin: University of Texas press, 1964. (Edited by R. Henderson Shuffler).

Browne, Junius Henri, *Four Years of Secessia*, Hartford, CT: O. D. Case, 1865 Reprint, Arno Press, 1970.

Bryant, William O., *Cahaba Prison and the Sultana Disaster*, Tuscaloosa, AL: University of Alabama Press, 1990.

Catton, Bruce, *Terrible Swift Sword*, Garden City, New York: Doubleday & Company, Inc., 1963.

Connelly, Thomas L., *Civil War Tennessee: Battles and Leaders*, Knoxville: University of Tennessee Press, 1979.

Daniel, Larry J. and Lynn N. Bock, *Island No. 10: Struggle for the Mississippi Valley*, Tuscaloosa, AL: University of Alabama Press, 1996.

Evans, Clement A., ed., *Confederate Military History*, Vol. VIII, New York: Thomas Yoseloff 1962.

Gay, Ann Harwell, *Choctaw, Sumter and Washington Counties' C.S.A. Companies*, Meridian, MS: Brown Printing Co., 2003.

, *Place Names in Choctow County Alabama*, Meridian, MS: Brown Printing Co., 1988, revised edition 1998.

Gray, Michael P., *The Business of Captivity: Elmira and Its Civil War Prison*, Kent, Ohio: Kent State University Press, 2001.

Hansen, Harry, *The Civil War: A History*, New York: New American Library, 2001.

Hesseltine, William B., ed., *Civil War Prisons*, Kent, Ohio: Kent State University Press, 1962.

Horn, Stanley F., ed., *Tennessee's War, 1861-1865: Described by Participants*, Nashville: Tennessee Civil War Centennial Commission, 1965.

Hurst, Jack, *Men of Fire: Grant, Forrest, and the Campaign That Decided the Civil War*, New York: Basic Books, 2007.

Klement, Frank L., *Wisconsin in the Civil War: The Home Front and the Battle Front*, Madison, W.I.: Wisconsin State Historical Society of Wisconsin, 1997.

Levy, George, *To Die in Chicago: Confederate Prisoners at Camp Douglas*, 1862-1865, Evanston, I.L.: Evanston Publishing, Inc., 1994.

Long, E. B. and Barbara Long, *The Civil War Day by Day: An Almanac, 1861-1865*, Garden City, N.Y.: Doubleday, 1971.

Mattern, Carolyn J., *Soldiers When They Go: The Story of Camp Randall, 1861-1865*, Madison, W.I.: Wisconsin State Historical Society, 1981.

McMorries, Edward Y., *History of the First Regiment Alabama Volunteer Infantry, C.S.A.*, Montgomery, A.L.: Brown Printing Co., 1904.

Perry, James M., *Touched With Fire*, New York: Public Affairs, 2003.

Porter, James D., "Tennessee," in Clement A. Evan, ed., *Confederate Military History*, Vol. VIII, New York: Thomas Yoseloff, 1962.

Pratt, Fletcher, *Civil War in Pictures*, Garden City, N.Y.: Garden City Books, 1957.

Quiner, Edwin Bentley, *The Military History of Wisconsin*, Chicago: Clarke and Co. Publishers, 1866.

Stevenson, William G., *Thirteen Months in the Rebel Army*, New York: Barnes and Burr, 1864.

Temple, Brian, *The Union Prison at Fort Delaware: A Perfect Hell on Earth*, Jefferson, N.C.: McFarland & Co., Inc., 2003.

Tucker, Spencer C., *Andrew Foote: Civil War Admiral on Western Waters*, Annapolis, M.D.: Naval Institute Press, 2000.

U.S. Department of the Interior, National Park Service, "Fort Donelson National Battlefield," Washington, D.C.: Government Printing Office, 2005.

Wertz, Jay and Edwin C. Bearss, *Smithsonian's Great Battles and Battlefields of the Civil War*, New York: Smithsonian Institution, William Morrow and Co., Inc., 1997.

Zeitlin, Richard H., *All For the Union: Wisconsin and the Civil War*, Madison, W.I.: Wisconsin Veterans Museum, 1998.

ABOUT THE AUTHORS

Richard G. Zevitz

A former division director for the Sheriff's Department in San Francisco, Richard Zevitz also worked for a neighborhood legal aid society. He earned four degrees including a degree in history and economics, a Doctorate in Criminology from the University of California at Berkeley and a Juris Doctorate from the University of Nebraska. He is currently Associate Professor of Criminology and Law Studies at Marquette University. Richard has published more than two dozen journal articles, including an article on Confederate prisoners of war at Camp Randall Military Prison in Madison, Wisconsin.

Michael C. Braswell

A former prison psychologist and marriage and family therapist, Michael Braswell earned four degrees in counseling and psychology, including his PhD from the University of Southern Mississippi. He has taught ethics and human relations for more than 30 years and is currently, Professor Emeritus at East Tennessee State University. Michael's books include *Morality Stories, Justice, Crime and Ethics*, and the forthcoming *Interview with Joab*.